E.O. Chirovici was born in Transylvania to a Romanian-Hungarian-German family. He made his literary debut with a collection of short stories, and his first novel, *The Massacre*, sold over 100,000 copies in the Romanian language. He spent many years as a journalist, first running a prestigious newspaper, and later a major TV station. He has been writing full-time since 2013, and currently lives in Brussels.

THE BOOK OF MIRRORS

When big-shot literary agent Peter Katz receives an unfinished manuscript entitled *The Book of Mirrors*, he is intrigued. The author, Richard Flynn, is writing a memoir about his time at Princeton in the late 80s, documenting his relationship with the famous Professor Joseph Wieder. One night in 1987, Wieder was brutally murdered in his home, and the case was never solved. Peter is hell-bent on getting to the bottom of what happened, and is convinced the full manuscript will reveal who committed the violent crime. But other people's recollections are dangerous weapons to play with, and this might be one memory that is best kept buried . . .

E. O. CHIROVICI

THE BOOK OF MIRRORS

Complete and Unabridged

CHARNWOOD
Leicester

First published in Great Britain in 2017 by
Century
London

First Charnwood Edition
published 2017
by arrangement with
Century
Penguin Random House
London

The moral right of the author has been asserted

A catalogue record for this book is available
from the British Library.

ISBN 978–1–4448–3498–7

Published by
F. A. Thorpe (Publishing)
Anstey, Leicestershire

Set by Words & Graphics Ltd.
Anstey, Leicestershire
Printed and bound in Great Britain by
T. J. International Ltd., Padstow, Cornwall

This book is printed on acid-free paper

To my wife, Mihaela, who has never forgotten who we really are and where we came from.

Most people are other people.

Oscar Wilde

Part One

Peter Katz

Memories are like bullets. Some whiz by and only spook you. Others tear you open and leave you in pieces.

Richard Kadrey, *Kill the Dead*

I received the submission in January, when everybody at the agency was still trying to recover from the post-festive-season hangovers.

The message had deftly missed my junk folder, turning up in my inbox, where it formed part of a queue with a few dozen others. I cast a glance at the query and found it intriguing, so I printed it off along with the attached pages from the partial manuscript and put them in my desk drawer. Busy completing a deal, I forgot about them until nearly the end of the month. It was on the weekend extended by Martin Luther King Day that I rediscovered the papers, lying in a pile of submissions I was planning on reading during the holiday.

The query letter was signed 'Richard Flynn' and went like this:

Dear Peter,

My name is Richard Flynn and twenty-seven years ago I majored in English at Princeton. I dreamed of becoming a writer, published a few short stories in magazines, and even wrote a three hundred paged novel, which I abandoned after it was rejected by a number of publishers (and which I myself now find mediocre and dull). After that, I got a job at a small advertising agency in New Jersey and I've remained in the industry to this day. At first I fooled myself into believing that advertising could be likened to literature and that one day I'd go back to being a writer. Obviously nothing of the sort happened. I think that for most people growing up means, unfortunately, gaining the ability to lock their dreams in a box and throw it in the East River. I was no exception to the rule, it would seem.

But a few months ago I discovered something important, which brought back to my memory a series of tragic events that took place in the fall and winter of 1987, my last year at Princeton. You probably know how it is: you think you've forgotten something — an event, a person, a situation — and then all of a sudden you realise that the memory has been languishing in some secret room in your mind and that it's always been there, as if it happened only yesterday. It's like opening an old closet, full of junk, and all you have to do is move one box for it all to come crashing down on you.

That thing was like a detonator. An hour after I found out the news, I was still thinking about its significance. I sat down at my desk and, overwhelmed by memories, I wrote. By the time I stopped it was long after midnight and I'd written more than five thousand words. It was as if I'd suddenly rediscovered who I was, after completely forgetting myself. When I went to the bathroom to brush my teeth, it seemed to me as if a different person was looking at me from the mirror.

For the first time in many years I fell asleep without taking a pill first, and the next day, after telling the people at the agency that I'd be off sick for the next two weeks, I continued to write.

The details of those months in '87 came back to my mind with such force and clarity that they quickly grew more vivid and powerful than anything else in my present life. It was as if I'd woken up from a deep sleep, during which my mind had silently been preparing itself for the moment when I'd begin to write about the events whose protagonists were Laura Baines, Professor Joseph Wieder and me.

Of course, given its tragic outcome, the story had found its way into the newspapers at the time, at least in part. I myself got harassed by police detectives and reporters for quite a while. That was one of the factors that led me to leave Princeton and pursue my MA at Cornell, living for two long and dusty years in Ithaca. But nobody ever found out the truth about the whole story, one that changed my life forever.

As I said, I chanced upon the truth three months ago, and I realised that I had to share it with others, even though the anger and frustration that I felt, and still feel, were overwhelming. But sometimes hatred and pain can be a fuel just as strong as love. The result of that intention is the manuscript I

5

recently completed, after an effort that left me physically and mentally exhausted. I attach a sample, in accordance with the instructions I found on your website. The manuscript is complete and ready for submission. If you'd be interested in reading the whole thing, I'll send it to you immediately. The working title I've chosen is *The Book of Mirrors*.

I'll stop here, because my laptop says that I've already exceeded the 500-word limit for a query. Anyhow, there's not much else to say about me. I was born and raised in Brooklyn, I've never been married, nor had children, partly, I believe, because I've never truly forgotten Laura. I have a brother, Eddie, who lives in Philadelphia and whom I see very rarely. My career in advertising has been uneventful, with neither outstanding achievements nor unpleasant incident — a dazzling grey life, hidden among the shadows of Babel. Today, I'm a senior copywriter at a middling agency based in Manhattan, quite close to Chelsea, where I've lived for more than two decades. I don't drive a Porsche and I don't book five-star hotels, but nor do I have to worry about what the next day will bring, at least not when it comes to money.

Thank you for your time and please let me know whether you'd like to read the full manuscript. You'll find my address and phone number below.

Yours sincerely,
Richard Flynn

There followed an address near Penn Station. I knew the area well, because I'd lived there myself for a while.

The query was rather unusual.

I'd read hundreds, if not thousands of queries during my five years as an agent for Bronson & Matters. The agency, where I'd started as a junior assistant, had always had an open submissions policy. Most of the query letters were awkward, lifeless, lacking that certain something that suggests that the potential author is talking to you personally and not just any of the hundreds of agents whose names and addresses you can find on Literary Market Place. Some of them were too long and full of pointless details. But Richard Flynn's letter didn't fall into either of those categories. It was concise, well written, and above all it gave off human warmth. He didn't say that he'd only contacted me, but I was almost certain, without being able to say why, that this was the case. For some reason he hadn't seen fit to declare in that short missive, he'd chosen me.

I was hoping to love the manuscript as much as I loved the submission letter, and to be able to give a positive answer to the man who'd sent it, a man towards whom I already felt, in some almost unexplainable way, a secret sympathy.

I set aside the other manuscripts I'd been planning to take a look at, made some coffee, settled down on the couch in the living room and began to read the excerpt.

1

For most Americans, 1987 was the year when the stock market rose sky-high only to come crashing back down, the Iran-Contra affair continued to rock Ronald Reagan's chair in the White House, and *The Bold and the Beautiful* began to invade our homes. For me, it was the year when I fell in love and found out that the devil exists.

I'd been a student at Princeton for a little over three years and I was living in an ugly old building on Bayard Lane, between the art museum and the theological seminary library. It had a living room and an open kitchen on the ground floor, and upstairs there were two double bedrooms, each with an adjoining bathroom. It was only a ten-minute walk from McCosh Hall, where I attended most of my English courses.

One October afternoon, when I got back home and entered the kitchen, I was surprised to find there a tall, slim young woman with long blonde hair parted in the middle. She gave me a friendly glance from behind thick-framed spectacles, which lent her a simultaneously stern and sexy air. She was trying to squirt mustard from a tube, without realising that you first have to peel off the tinfoil seal. I unscrewed the cap, took off the seal and gave the tube back to her. She thanked me, spreading the yellow paste over the jumbo hot dog she'd just boiled.

9

'Hey, thanks,' she said, in an accent she'd brought with her from the Midwest and which she seemed disinclined to shed merely to keep in step with fashion. 'Want some?'

'No, I'm fine, thanks. By the way, I'm Richard Flynn. Are you the new tenant?'

She nodded. She'd taken a hungry bite of the hot dog and now she tried to swallow it quickly before replying.

'Laura Baines. Pleased to meet you. Did the person who lived here before me have a pet skunk or something? The stench up there's enough to make your nose hairs drop out. I'll have to repaint it anyway. And is there something wrong with the boiler? I had to wait half an hour for the water to heat up.'

'A heavy smoker,' I explained. 'I mean the dude, not the boiler, and not just cigarettes, if you get my meaning. But other than that, he's a nice guy. He decided overnight to take a sabbatical, so he's gone back home. He was lucky the landlady didn't make him pay the rent for the rest of the year. As for the boiler, three different plumbers have come over to fix it. No luck, but I still live in hope.'

'Bon voyage,' Laura said between bites, addressing the erstwhile tenant. Then she pointed at the microwave oven on the worktop. 'I'm making some Jolly Time, and then I'm going to watch some TV — they're showing Jessica live on CNN.'

'Who's Jessica?' I asked.

The microwave pinged to let us know the popcorn was ready to be poured into the large glass bowl Laura had extracted from the depths of the cupboard above the sink.

'Jessica McClure is a little girl' — *l'il gal* — 'who fell down a well in Texas,' she explained. 'CNN is broadcasting the rescue operation live. How come you never heard about it? Everybody's talking about it.'

She put the popcorn in the bowl and signalled for me to follow her into the den.

We sat down on the couch and she turned on the TV set. For a while, neither of us said anything as we watched events unfold on the screen. It was a mild, warm October, almost entirely lacking the usual rain, and calm twilight was creeping along the sliding glass doors. Beyond lay the park that surrounded Trinity Church, dark and mysterious.

Laura finished eating her hot dog, then took a handful of popcorn from the bowl. She seemed to have completely forgotten about me. On the TV screen, an engineer was explaining to a reporter how work was progressing on a parallel well shaft, designed to allow the rescuers to gain access to the child trapped underground. Laura kicked off her slippers and curled her feet under herself on the couch. I noticed that her toenails were painted with purple varnish.

'What are you studying?' I asked her finally.

'I'm getting my master's degree in psychology,' she said without taking her eyes from the screen. 'It's my second. I've already got one in math from the University of Chicago. Born and raised in Evanston, Illinois. Ever been there? Where folks chew Red Man and burn crosses?'

I realised she must be two or three years older than me, and that daunted me a little. When you're that age, a three-year difference seems like a lot.

'I thought that's Mississippi,' I said. 'No, never been to Illinois. I was born and raised in Brooklyn. I've only ever been to the Midwest once, one summer, when I was fifteen, I guess, and my dad and I went fishing in the Ozarks, Missouri. We also visited St Louis, if I remember rightly. Psychology, after math?'

'Well, I was reckoned to be a kind of genius at school,' she said. 'In high school, I won all kinds of international math competitions, and at twenty-one I'd already finished a master's degree, getting ready to do my PhD. But I turned down all the scholarships and came here to do psychology. My MS helped me get onto a research programme.'

'Okay, but you still haven't answered my question.'

'Have a little patience.'

She brushed the popcorn crumbs off her T-shirt.

I remember it well. She was wearing a pair of stone-washed jeans, of the kind with several zippers, which were coming into fashion at the time, and a white T-shirt.

She went to the fridge to fetch a Coke, asking me if I wanted one. She opened the cans, stuck a straw in each, and returned to the couch, handing one to me.

'The summer after I graduated, I fell in love with a boy' — she pronounced it *buoy* — 'from

12

Evanston. He was home for the holidays. He was doing a master's degree in electronics at MIT, something to do with computers. A handsome and apparently smart guy, named John R. Findley. He was two years older than me, and we'd known each other vaguely in high school. But a month later he was stolen from me by Julia Craig, one of the dumbest creatures I've ever met, a kind of hominid who'd learned to articulate around a dozen words, to wax her legs, and how to use a knife and fork. I realised that I was good at equations and integrals, but I didn't have the faintest clue about how people think in general, and men in particular. I understood that if I wasn't careful, I'd end up spending my life surrounded by cats, guinea pigs and parrots. So that's why I came here, the following fall. Mom was worried and tried to change my mind, but she already knew me well enough to understand that it'd have been easier to teach me how to fly on a broomstick. I'm now in my last year and I've never regretted my decision.'

'I'm in my final year too. Have you learned what you set out to?' I asked. 'I mean, about the way men think?'

For the first time she looked me straight in the eye.

'Not sure, but I think I've made progress. John broke up with Godzilla after just a few weeks. I didn't answer his calls after that, even though he's been trying to get in touch with me for months. Maybe I'm just picky, you know.'

She finished off her Coke and put the empty can on the table.

We continued to watch the rescue of the *li'l gal* from Texas on TV, and chatted almost until midnight, drinking coffee and going outside into the garden from time to time to smoke the Marlboros she'd fetched from her room. At one point I helped her carry inside the rest of her stuff from the trunk of her old Hyundai, which was parked in the garage.

Laura was nice, she had a sense of humour, and I realised that she was very well read. Like any new adult, I was a seething mass of hormones. At the time, I didn't have a girlfriend and I was desperate to have sex, but I remember clearly that in the beginning I never thought about the possibility of getting in bed with her. I was sure she must have a boyfriend, although we never talked about it. But I was disturbed in a pleasant sort of way at the prospect of sharing a house with a woman, which was something I'd never done up until then. It was as if, all of a sudden, I was going to have access to mysteries that had previously been forbidden.

★   ★   ★

The reality was that I didn't like it at college and I could hardly wait to complete my final year and get out of there.

I'd been born and raised in Brooklyn, in Williamsburg, near Grand Street, where homes were a lot cheaper than they are nowadays. Mom taught history at the Boys and Girls High School in Bed-Stuy, and dad was a medical assistant at Kings County Hospital. I wasn't working class,

14

in other words, but I felt as if I were, given the blue-collar neighbourhood where I lived.

I grew up without any major material troubles, but at the same time my folks couldn't afford a large number of things we'd have liked to have. Brooklynites were interesting to me, and I felt like a fish in water among that Babel of different races and customs. The seventies were hard times for the city of New York, and I remember that a lot of folks were dirt poor and violence was widespread.

When I arrived at Princeton I joined a few academic societies, became a member of one of those famous eating clubs on the Street, and hung out with the amateur actors from the Triangle Club.

In front of a literary circle with an exotic name, I read a number of the short stories I'd written towards the end of high school. The group was run by a vaguely famous author, who taught as a visiting professor, and its members vied with one another in torturing the English language to produce meaningless poems. When they realised that my stories were 'classic' in style and that I was finding inspiration in the novels of Hemingway and Steinbeck, they started viewing me as a freak. In any event, a year later I was spending my free time in the library or at home.

Most of the students were from the East Coast middle class, which had had a big fright in the sixties, when their whole world had seemed to fall apart, and which had educated its scions in such a way as to prevent the madness from ever being repeated. The sixties had had music, marches, the summer of love, experimentation with drugs, Woodstock and contraceptives. The seventies saw the end of the Vietnam nightmare and the introduction of disco, flared pants and racial emancipation. So I had the feeling that there was nothing epic about the eighties, and that our generation had missed the train. Mr Ronald Reagan, like a cunning old shaman, had summoned up the spirits of the fifties to addle the nation's brains. Money was demolishing the altars of every other god one by one, preparing to perform its victory dance, while chubby angels with Stetsons perched on their blonde curls chanted hymns to free enterprise. *Go, Ronnie, go!*

I found the other students to be snobbish conformists, despite the rebellious poses they struck, no doubt in the belief that this was demanded of Ivy Leaguers as a kind of vague memory of previous decades. Traditions were a big thing at Princeton but to me they were nothing but playacting — time had emptied them of all meaning.

I regarded most of the professors as mediocrities clinging to a fancy job. The students who played at being Marxists and revolutionaries on their rich parents' money never tired of reading doorstops like *Das Kapital*, while those who thought of themselves as conservatives behaved as if they were the direct descendants of that pilgrim on the *Mayflower* who, perched on top of the mast and shading his eyes against the sun, had shouted: *Land!* To the former, I was a petit bourgeois whose class was to be despised and whose values were to be trampled underfoot;

to the latter, I was just a white trash kid from Brooklyn, who'd somehow managed to infiltrate their wonderful campus with some dubious and undoubtedly damnable aims. To me, Princeton seemed as if it was overrun with hoity-toity robots speaking with a Boston accent.

But it's possible that all these things existed only in my mind. After I'd decided to become a writer towards the end of high school, I'd gradually built for myself a gloomy and sceptical vision of the world, with the inestimable assistance of Messrs Cormac McCarthy, Philip Roth and Don DeLillo. I'd been convinced that a real writer had to be sad and lonely, while receiving fat royalty cheques and spending holidays in expensive European resorts. I told myself that if the devil hadn't reduced him to sitting broken and weary on the dung heap, then Job would never have made a name for himself, and mankind would have been deprived of a literary masterpiece.

I tried to avoid spending any longer than necessary on campus, so on weekends I usually went back to New York. I'd roam the second-hand bookshops of the Upper East Side, watch plays at obscure theatres in Chelsea, and go to concerts by Bill Frisell, Cecil Taylor and Sonic Youth at the Knitting Factory, which had just opened on Houston Street. I used to go to the cafes on Myrtle Avenue, or cross the bridge to the Lower East Side and have dinner with my parents and younger brother Eddie, who was still in high school, in one of those family-run restaurants where everybody knows each other's name.

I passed my exams without effort, nestling in the comfort zone of B grades, so that I wouldn't come up against any hassle and have time to write. I wrote dozens of short stories and started a novel, which didn't make it past a few chapters. I used an old Remington typewriter, which Dad had found in the attic of a house, repaired, and given to me as a present when I'd left for college. After rereading my texts and correcting them time and again, they mostly ended up in the trash can. Every time I discovered a new author, I'd imitate him without knowing it, like a chimp overwhelmed with admiration at the sight of a woman in red.

For one reason or another I didn't enjoy doing drugs. I'd smoked weed for the first time at fourteen, during a class trip to the Botanical Garden. A boy named Martin had brought two joints, which five or six of us had passed around in a hidden spot, with the feeling that the murky waters of criminality were dragging us into their depths for good. In high school I'd smoked again a few times, and also got drunk on cheap beer at a couple of parties in shady apartments on Driggs Avenue. But I hadn't found any pleasure in getting high or drunk, to my folks' relief. In those days, if you were inclined to stray from the straight and narrow, you were more likely to end up stabbed to death or killed by an overdose than find a decent job. I studied hard at school, got top marks and received offers from both Cornell and Princeton, accepting the second, considered more progressive at the time.

Television had not yet become an endless parade of shows in which various losers are forced to sing, to be insulted by vulgar hosts or to climb into swimming pools full of snakes. American TV shows hadn't transformed into a tale told by an idiot, full of sound and laughter, signifying nothing. But nor did I find anything of interest in the hypo-critical political debates of those days, or in the off-colour jokes and B-movies about plastic-looking teenagers. The few decent producers and journalists from the sixties and seventies who were still in charge at the TV studios seemed awkward and as uneasy as dinosaurs spotting the meteorite that heralded the end of their age.

But as I was to discover, Laura liked to get a nightly fix of junk television, claiming that it was the only way her brain could achieve a kind of stasis, allowing it to classify, systematise and store all the stuff it had accumulated during the day. So, in the fall of the year of Our Lord 1987 I watched more TV than ever before, finding a kind of masochistic pleasure in sitting slumped on the couch beside her, commenting on every talk show, news story and weekly drama, like the two cavilling old-timers on the balcony in The Muppet Show.

She didn't tell me about Professor Joseph Wieder straight away. It wasn't until Halloween that she mentioned that she knew him. He was one of the most important figures teaching at Princeton in those years, regarded as a kind of

Prometheus who'd descended among mere mortals to share the secret of fire. We were watching *Larry King Live*, on which Wieder had been invited to talk about drug addiction — three young men had died of overdoses the day before, in a cabin near Eugene, Oregon. Apparently Laura and the professor were 'good friends', she told me. I must already have been in love with her by then, even if I didn't know it at the time.

2

The weeks that followed were probably the happiest of my entire life.

The majority of the psychology courses were held in Green Hall, which was just a few minutes' walk from McCosh and Dickinson, where I attended English classes, so we were almost always together. We'd go to the Firestone Library, walk past the Princeton stadium on our way home, stop off at the Art Museum and one of the cafes around it, or take the train to New York City, where we watched movies like *Dirty Dancing*, *Spaceball* and *The Untouchables*.

Laura had lots of friends, most of them fellow psychology students. She introduced me to some of them, but she preferred to spend her time with me. As far as music went, we didn't have the same tastes. She liked the latest sounds, which in those days meant Lionel Richie, George Michael or Fleetwood Mac, but she stalwartly listened along when I played my alternative rock and jazz cassettes and CDs.

Sometimes we'd sit up talking until early in the morning, doped up on nicotine and caffeine, and then groggily go to lectures after just two or three hours' sleep. Although she had a car, she rarely used it and we both preferred to walk or cycle. On those evenings when she didn't feel like watching TV, Laura used to conjure up the spirit that lurked in an NES console, so we'd shoot ducks or play at being Bubbles the fish in *Clu Clu Land*.

One day, after we'd been playing games like that for a couple of hours, she said to me, 'Richard — ' she never shortened my name to Richie or Dick — 'did you know that we, by which I mean our *brains*, can't tell the difference between fiction and reality most of the time? That's why we're able to cry at one movie and laugh at another, even though we *know* that what we're seeing is just acting and that the story was dreamed up by a writer. Without this 'defect' of ours, we'd be nothing more than R.O.B.s.'

R.O.B. meant Robotic Operating Buddy, a gadget invented for lonely teens by the Japanese. Laura dreamed of buying such a device, calling it Armand and teaching it to bring her coffee in bed and to buy her flowers when she was feeling blue. What she didn't know was that I'd happily have done all these things and many others for her without any training.

★　★　★

You don't know what pain is until you get a cut deep enough to make you realise that previous wounds have been only scratches. In early spring, my problems with adapting to life at Princeton had been compounded by a tragic event — I lost Dad.

A heart attack had killed him almost instantly, while he was at work. Not even the swift intervention of his colleagues had been able save him, and he'd been declared dead less than an

22

hour after he'd collapsed in the corridor of the surgery section on the third floor of the hospital. My brother had given me the news over the phone, while Mom took care of the formalities.

I'd jumped on the first train and gone to the apartment. When I'd arrived, our home had already been already full of relatives and neighbours and family friends. Dad was buried at Evergreen and before long, at the beginning of summer, Mom had decided to move to Philadelphia, taking Eddie with her. She had a younger sister there, called Cornelia. It'd come as a terrible shock to realise in the following weeks that everything which had linked me to my childhood was going to vanish, and that I'd never again enter the two-bed apartment where I'd spent my entire life up till then.

I'd always suspected that Mom hated Brooklyn, and that the only reason she'd stayed there had been because of Dad. She was a bookish and melancholic person, thanks to her upbringing, her father being a Lutheran pastor of German origin by the name of Reinhardt Knopf. I had vague memories of visiting him just once a year, on his birthday. He'd been a tall and stern man who'd lived in Queens, in a spotlessly clean house, which had a small backyard. Even the little patch of lawn there had given you the impression that each blade of grass had been carefully combed. His wife had died during childbirth, when my aunt was born, and he'd never remarried, raising his daughters single-handedly.

He'd died of lung cancer when I was ten, but,

23

from time to time, while Grandpa was still alive, Mom had used to demand that we move to Queens — *a clean, decent place*, as she called it — saying that she wanted to be closer to her father. In the end, however, she'd given up, understanding that it was a lost cause: Michael Flynn, my dad, had been stubborn, Irish, born and raised in Brooklyn, and he'd had no intention of moving anywhere else.

So my departure to Princeton for the start of my new year at college had coincided with Mom and my brother moving to Philly. When I'd first met Laura, it was only just beginning to dawn on me that I'd never be able to go back to Brooklyn except as a guest. I felt as if I'd been plundered of all that I'd had. The belongings that I didn't take with me to Princeton had ended up in a two-room apartment on Jefferson Avenue in Philly, near Central Station. I'd visited my mother and brother soon after they'd moved, realising straight away that the place would never be *home* for me. What was more, the family income had shrunk. My grades weren't good enough to obtain a scholarship, so I had to look for a part-time job to pay my way until graduation.

Dad had passed away suddenly, so it was hard to get used to the fact that he was gone, and a lot of the time I thought of him as if he were still with us. Sometimes the departed are stronger than when they were here. Their memory — or what we think we remember about them — forces us to try to please them in a way that they'd never have persuaded us to do when they

24

were alive. Dad's death made me feel more responsible and less inclined to float above things. The living are constantly making mistakes, but the dead are quickly wrapped in an aura of infallibility by those they've left behind.

So my new friendship with Laura was blossoming at a time in my life when I felt lonelier than ever before, and that's why her presence became even more important to me.

★ ★ ★

It was two weeks before Thanksgiving, and the weather was starting to turn gloomy, when Laura suggested that she introduce me to Professor Joseph Wieder. She was working under his supervision on a research project that she was going to write up for her graduate thesis.

Laura specialised in cognitive psychology, which was something of a pioneering field in those days, when the term 'artificial intelligence' had come to be on everyone's lips after computers had made their triumphal entry into our homes and lives. Many people were convinced that within a decade we'd be having conversations with our toasters and asking a washing machine for advice concerning our careers.

She often told me about her work, but I didn't understand it much, and with an egotism characteristic of all young males I didn't make an effort to figure it out. What I retained was that Professor Wieder — who'd also studied in Europe and had a PhD in psychiatry from Cambridge — was approaching the end of a monumental research project, which Laura said would be a real game changer when it came to understanding the way the human mind works and the connection between mental stimulus and reaction. From what Laura said, I understood that it had something to do with memory and the way recollections are formed. Laura claimed that her knowledge of math had been a real gold mine for Wieder, because the exact sciences had always been his Achilles heel, and his research involved the use of mathematical formulae to quantify variables.

The evening I met Wieder for the first time was to be memorable for me, but for a different reason than the one I might have expected.

One Saturday afternoon in mid-November, we let our pockets bleed and bought a bottle of Côtes du Rhône Rouge, which the clerk at the delicatessen had recommended to us, and we set off for the professor's house. He lived in West Windsor, so Laura decided that we should travel by car.

About twenty minutes later we parked in front of a Queen Anne-style house, near a small lake that gleamed mysteriously in the light of dusk; the property was surrounded by a low stone wall. The gate was open and we set off down a gravelled path, which cut across a well-tended lawn, bordered by rose and blackberry bushes. On the left there was a huge oak and its leafless crown spread above the tiled roof of the building.

Laura rang the bell and a tall, well-built man opened the door. He was almost completely bald and had a grey beard that reached down to his chest. He was wearing jeans, trainers and a green Timberland T-shirt with the sleeves rolled up. He looked like a football coach, rather than a famous college professor who was about to throw the scientific world into turmoil with an earth-shattering revelation, and he had that self-confident air that people have when everything's going their way.

He gave me a firm handshake and then kissed Laura on both cheeks.

'Delighted to meet you, Richard,' he said in an unexpectedly youthful voice. 'Laura has told me a lot about you. Usually,' he went on as we entered a high-ceilinged hall, the walls of which were adorned with paintings, and hung our coats on the rack, 'she's sarcastic and catty about all people that cross her path. But she's had nothing but good things to say about you. I was very curious to make your acquaintance. Please follow me, guys.'

We entered a huge split-level living room. In one corner there was a cooking area with a massive worktop in the middle and all kinds of brass pots and pans hanging above it. An old desk with bronze hinges, with a leather-upholstered chair, stood against the west wall, its top scattered with pieces of paper, books and pencils.

A pleasant scent of food was drifting in the air, mingling with the smell of tobacco. We sat down on a couch covered in canvas adorned with oriental motifs and he fixed us each a gin and tonic, declaring that he'd save the wine we'd brought for dinner.

The interior of the house intimidated me slightly. It was stuffed with artworks — bronzes, paintings and antiques — like a museum. Over the polished floors hand-woven rugs were spread here and there. It was the first time I'd ever entered a home like that.

He made himself a Scotch and soda and sat down on the armchair in front of us, lighting a cigarette.

'Richard, I bought this house four years ago, and I worked on it for two years to get it to look the way it does now. The lake was nothing but a stinking, mosquito-ridden swamp. But I think it was worth it, even if it's a bit isolated. From what I've been told by a guy who knows about such things, its value has almost doubled in the meantime.'

'It's really great,' I assured him.

'Later, I'll show you the library upstairs. That's my pride and joy; all the rest are just trifles. I hope you'll come again. I sometimes hold parties on Saturdays. Nothing sophisticated, just a few friends and colleagues. And on the last Friday evening of the month, I play poker with some pals. We play just for change, don't worry.'

The conversation unfolded smoothly and half an hour later, when we sat down at the table to eat (he'd made spaghetti Bolognese from a recipe from a colleague in Italy), it already felt as though we'd known each other for quite some time, and my initial feelings of embarrassment had completely vanished.

Laura was almost absent from the conversation as she acted as hostess. She served the food, and at the end of the meal she cleared away the plates and cutlery, putting them in the dishwasher. She didn't call Wieder 'Professor' or 'sir' or 'Mr Wieder', but simply 'Joe'. She seemed at home, and it was obvious that she'd played this role before, while the professor perorated on various topics, chain-smoking and accompanying his words with sweeping gestures of his hands.

At one point I wondered how close they really were, but then I told myself that it wasn't any of my business, as at the time I didn't suspect they could be more than just good friends.

Wieder praised the wine we'd brought and went into a long divagation about French vineyards, explaining to me the different rules for serving wine according to the grape variety. Somehow he managed to do so without making himself look like a snob. Then he told me that he'd lived in Paris for a couple of years when he was young. He'd earned a master's degree in psychiatry at the Sorbonne, and then gone to England, where he took his PhD and published his first book.

After a while he got up and from somewhere in the depths of the house grabbed another bottle of French wine, which we drank. Laura was still on her first glass — she'd explained to the professor that she had to drive back home. She seemed delighted that we were getting along so well, watching us like a babysitter happy that the kids she was looking after weren't breaking their toys and fighting with each other.

As I remember, the conversation with him was rather chaotic. He talked a lot, jumping from one subject to another with the ease of a conjurer. He had an opinion about everything, from the Giants' last season to nineteenth-century Russian literature. True, I was astonished by his knowledge, and it was obvious that he'd read a lot and that age had dulled none of his intellectual curiosity. (For someone barely out of his teens, a grown-up in his late fifties was already old.) But at the same time, he gave the impression of being a conscientious missionary who saw it as his task to patiently educate the savages, on whose mental capacities he didn't set much store. He'd engage in Socratic questioning and then give the answers himself, before I could open my mouth to say anything, and then he'd provide counter-arguments, only to demolish these too a few minutes later.

In fact, as I remember it, the conversation was nothing but a long monologue. After a couple of hours I was convinced that he might just go on talking even after we left.

During the evening the phone, which he kept in the hall, rang a number of times and he answered it, apologising to us and quickly ending the conversations. At one point, however, he had a long talk, speaking in a low voice so that he wouldn't be overheard from the living room. I couldn't make out what he was saying, but his voice betrayed annoyance.

He came back looking upset.

'These guys are out of their minds,' he said to Laura angrily. 'How can you ask a scientist like me to do something like that? You give them an inch and they take a mile. It was the dumbest thing I ever did in my life, getting mixed up with these morons.'

Laura made no reply and vanished somewhere in the house. I wondered who he was talking about, but he went out and brought in another bottle of wine. After we drank it, he seemed to forget about the unpleasant call and jokingly stated that real men drink whisky. He went off again and brought back a bottle of Lagavulin and a bowl of ice. The bottle was already half empty when he changed his mind. He said that vodka was the best booze for celebrating the beginning of a beautiful friendship.

I realised how drunk I was when I got up to go to the bathroom — I'd been heroically holding myself up until then. My legs wouldn't obey me and I almost fell headlong onto the floor. I wasn't a teetotaller, but I'd never had so much to drink. Wieder watched me closely, as if I were an amusing puppy.

In the bathroom I looked in the mirror above the sink and saw two familiar faces staring back at me, which caused me to burst out laughing. In the hall I remembered that I hadn't washed my hands, so I went back. The water was too hot and I scalded myself.

Laura came back, gave us a long hard stare, and then made us both a cup of coffee. I tried to figure out whether the professor was also drunk, but he looked sober to me, as if I'd been drinking on my own. I felt as though I was the victim of some practical joke, noticing that I was having trouble articulating words. I'd had too many cigarettes and my chest ached. Grey clouds of smoke were wafting through the room like ghosts, even though both windows were wide open.

We continued to chew the fat for another hour or so, without drinking anything except coffee and water, then Laura signalled to me that it was time to leave. Wieder walked with us to the car, bid us farewell and told me that he sincerely hoped I'd come again.

As Laura drove down Colonial Avenue, which was almost deserted at that hour, I said to her, 'Nice guy, isn't he? I've never met a man who could hold his booze so well. Geez! Do you have any idea how much we drank?'

'Maybe he took something beforehand. I mean a pill or something. He doesn't usually drink that much. And you're not a psychologist, so you didn't realise that he was pumping you for information about yourself, without giving anything away about himself.'

'He told me lots of stuff about himself,' I said, contradicting her and trying to figure out whether we should stop the car so that I could throw up behind some tree at the side of the road. My head was spinning and I must have smelled as if I'd just taken a bath in booze.

'He didn't tell you anything,' she said curtly, 'apart from stuff that's common knowledge, which you could have found out from the dust jackets of any of his books. But you, on the other hand, told him that you're afraid of snakes, and that at the age of four and a half you almost got raped by a crazy neighbour, whom your dad then almost beat to death. Those are significant things

32

to say about yourself.'

'Told him that? I can't remember — '

'His favourite game is to rummage around in other people's minds, like he'd explore a house. With him it's more than just a professional habit. It's almost a pathological curiosity, which he rarely manages to keep in check. That's why he agreed to supervise that programme, the one that — '

She stopped mid-sentence, as if grasping all of a sudden that she was about to say too much.

I didn't ask her what she'd been going to say. I opened the window and felt my head start to clear. A pale half-moon was hanging in the sky.

That night we became lovers.

It happened in a simple way, without prior, hypocritical discussions of the 'I don't want to ruin our friendship' variety. After she parked the car in the garage, we stood for a few minutes in the backyard, which was bathed in the yellowish glow of the street light, and we shared a cigarette, saying nothing. We went inside and when I tried to turn the light on in the den she stopped me, took me by the hand and led me to her bedroom.

★   ★   ★

The next day was a Sunday. We stayed in the house all day, making love and discovering each other. I remember that we barely spoke. In the late afternoon we went to the Peacock Inn where we ate, then we walked in the Community Park North for a while, until it got dark. I'd told her about my intention to find a job and when I brought it up again, she asked me straight away whether I'd be tempted to work with Wieder. He was looking for somebody to arrange the books in the library he'd mentioned, but hadn't got around to showing me the night before. I was surprised.

'Do you think he'll agree?'

'I've already talked to him about it. That's why he wanted to meet you. But like typical men, you didn't get around to discussing it. I think he liked you, so there won't be any difficulty.'

I asked myself whether I liked him.

'In that case, it's fine by me.'

She leaned towards me and kissed me. Beneath her left clavicle, above her breast, she had a brown mole the size of a quarter. I studied her in detail that day, as if I wanted to be sure that I'd never forget any part of her body. Her ankles were unusually slender, and her toes very long — she called them her 'basketball team'. I discovered each mark and blemish on her skin that still showed traces of her summer tan.

In those days, fast love had already become as common as fast food and I was no exception to the rule. I'd lost my virginity at fifteen, in a bed above which hung a big Michael Jackson poster. The bed had belonged to a girl called Joelle, who'd been two years older than me and lived on Fulton Street. In the years that followed, I'd had many partners and two or three times I'd even thought I was in love.

But on that evening I knew that I'd been mistaken. Maybe in some cases what I'd felt had been an attraction, passion or attachment. But with Laura it was completely different, all those things and something more: the strong desire to be with her every minute and every second. Perhaps I dimly sensed that our period together was to be short-lived, so I was in a hurry to gather enough memories of her to see me through the rest of my life.

3

I started working on Wieder's library the very next weekend, visiting him on my own, taking the bus from Trinity Station. He and I drank a beer together on a bench by the lake and he explained to me how he wanted his few thousand books to be organised.

The professor had bought a new computer which he'd set up in a room upstairs. The chamber had no windows and the walls were covered with long wooden shelves. He wanted me to put together a codified record, so that a search engine would be able to indicate the location of each book. That meant typing in the data — titles, authors, publishers, Library of Congress numbers and so on — and arranging the books by categories. We both made a rough calculation and reached the conclusion that the whole business would take up my every weekend for the next six months, unless I was able to spend a couple of additional days working on it each week. I'd started writing up my final research thesis but I still hoped that I could find an odd afternoon during the week to allow me to finish the library record Wieder had hired me for.

He proposed to pay me weekly. The sum was more than generous and he gave me a cheque for the first three weeks in advance. I noticed that when Laura wasn't there he was less voluble and spoke more to the point.

He told me he was going to work out in the basement, where he had a small gym, and he left me to my own devices in the library.

I spent two or three hours familiarising myself with the computer and the software, during which time Wieder didn't return. When I finally left the library I found him in the kitchen, making sandwiches. We ate together, talking about politics. Somewhat surprisingly for me, he was very conservative in his opinions and regarded 'liberals' as being as dangerous as commies. He thought that Reagan was doing the best thing by shaking his fist in Moscow's face, whereas his predecessor, Jimmy Carter, had done nothing but kiss the Russians' butts.

We were smoking in the living room, and the coffee machine was grumbling in the kitchen, when he asked me, 'Are you and Laura just pals?'

His question took me by surprise and I found formulating an answer very awkward. I was on the verge of telling him that the relationship between Laura and me was none of his business. But I knew that Laura valued her friendship with him a great deal, so I tried to stay cool.

'Just buddies,' I lied. 'She happened to move into the same house as me and we became friends, although we don't have much in common.'

'Do you have a girlfriend?'

'It just so happens that I'm single at the moment.'

'Well then? She's beautiful, intelligent and attractive in every way. You spend a lot of time together, from what she's told me.'

'I don't know what to say — sometimes it happens, sometimes it doesn't.'

He fetched the cups of coffee and handed me one, then lit another cigarette and gazed at me in a grave, searching sort of way.

'Has she told you anything about me?'

I felt the conversation was becoming more and more uncomfortable.

'She holds you in great esteem and she's happy around you. I gather that you're both working on a special project, which will profoundly change the way we understand the human mind, something connected with memory. That's all.'

'Did she tell you any details about what exactly the project is about?' he asked quickly.

'No. Unfortunately I'm in a completely different field, and Laura has given up trying to initiate me into the mysteries of psychology,' I said, making an effort to seem relaxed. 'The idea of combing people's minds doesn't turn me on. No offence.'

'But you want to be a writer, don't you?' he said, annoyed. 'How are you going to develop your characters if you haven't got a clue about the way people think?'

'That's like saying you have to be a geologist to be able to enjoy rock climbing,' I said. 'Joe, I think you've got me wrong.' He had insisted that I call him by his first name, although I found it awkward to do so. 'Sometimes I sit in a cafe just so I can watch people, study their gestures and expressions. Sometimes I try to imagine what's going on behind those gestures and expressions.

But that's what they *want* to reveal, whether consciously or not, and — '

He didn't let me finish my sentence. 'So you think I'm some kind of voyeur, peeping through a keyhole? Not a bit. People often need to be helped to understand themselves better, so you have to know how to give them that helping hand, without which their personalities would start to disintegrate. In any event, the aim is completely different. You realise that such a research subject — or maybe you don't realise, but you'll have to take my word for it — needs to be approached with the greatest discretion, up until the moment when I make the results public. I've already signed a contract with a publisher, but not our university press, so there've been rumblings on the board. I don't think I need to tell you about envy in the academic world. You've been a student long enough to see how it works. And there's also another reason why a lot of discretion is required for the time being, but I can't reveal it to you. How are things going in the library?'

It was in keeping with his style to change the subject abruptly, as if he were always trying to catch me out. I told him that I'd familiarised myself with the computer and the software, and that everything seemed to be all right.

A quarter of an hour later, just as I was about to leave, he stopped me at the front door and told me there was something else we needed to talk about.

'After you visited me last week, did anybody approach you and try to question you about what I'm working on? A colleague? A friend? Maybe even a stranger?'

'No, especially given that I haven't told anybody but Laura that I came here.'

'That's great, then. Don't tell anybody in future, either. The business with the library is just between us. By the way, why didn't Laura come today?'

'She's in New York, with a friend of hers. She promised to go with her to a show, and they're staying with the friend's parents overnight. They're coming back tomorrow morning.'

He stared at me for a few long moments.

'Excellent. I'm curious as to what she thought of the show. What's her friend's name?'

'Dharma, if I'm not mistaken.'

'Names like Daisy and Nancy just didn't cut it for those hippies twenty years ago, did they? Bye now, Richard. I'll see you after Thanksgiving. I'd have invited you here to celebrate with me, but I'm going to Chicago tomorrow and I won't be back until Friday. Laura has a spare set of keys you can use. You know what you have to do, and if you have time you can come while I'm away. Take care.'

★ ★ ★

Instead of heading directly for the bus stop, I wandered the streets around his house, smoking and thinking about our conversation.

So, Laura had a spare set of keys to Wieder's house. That seemed strange to me, because I hadn't been aware up until then that they were

40

that close. If I understood correctly, Wieder had insinuated that Laura had lied to me when she'd said she was going to the theatre with her friend. And he'd been very circumspect when it came to questioning me about the nature of the relationship between the two of us.

I arrived back home in a bad mood, putting the cheque in a drawer of the wardrobe in my room with the unpleasant feeling that it was payment for some fishy transaction I didn't understand. For the first time since I'd met Laura, I was going to be spending Saturday evening on my own and the house seemed dark and hostile.

I took a shower, ordered a pizza and watched an episode of *Married with Children*, finding nothing amusing about the exploits of the Bundy family. I could sense Laura's smell, as if she were sitting next to me on the couch. It'd only been a few weeks since I'd first met her, but I had the impression that we'd known each other for years — she was already part of my life.

I listened to a B. B. King cassette, leafed through a Norman Mailer novel and thought about her and Professor Wieder.

He'd treated me nicely and offered me a job, for which I ought to have been grateful. He was a leading figure in the academic world, so I was lucky he took any notice of me at all, even if it was at the suggestion of his protégée. Yet despite appearances, I sensed something dark and strange in his behaviour, something I couldn't yet put a name to, but it was there, lurking hidden beneath his amiability and near-constant stream of words.

And worst of all, I'd already begun to wonder

41

whether Laura was telling me the truth. I dreamed up all kinds of scenarios by which I might check the veracity of what she'd told me, but by then it was too late to take the train to New York. And besides, I'd have felt ridiculous spying on her from afar, like in a bad B-movie.

With these thoughts popping up in my mind, I fell asleep on the couch then woke up in the middle of the night and went to bed upstairs. I dreamed I was beside a huge lake and its shore was covered in reeds. I looked into the dark water, and all of a sudden I had a strong feeling of danger. I glimpsed the scaly, muddy form of a huge gator which was stalking me through the vegetation. But when the reptile opened its eyes and stared at me, I saw that they were the same watery blue as Professor Wieder's.

* * *

Laura came back the next afternoon. I'd spent the entire day wandering around campus with two acquaintances, and at lunch I went over to their house, on Nassau Street, to eat pizza and listen to music. When I heard her car pull up, I was making myself a cup of coffee.

She looked tired and had dark circles under her eyes. She kissed me in a way that seemed quite reserved, and then shot off upstairs to her room to change and take a shower. While I waited for her, I poured two cups and stretched out on the couch. When she came downstairs, she thanked me for the coffee, grabbed the remote control and started channel hopping. She didn't look as though she was in the mood to talk, so I left her alone. At one point she suggested we go outside for a smoke.

'The show was stupid,' she told me, taking a hungry drag on her cigarette. 'Dharma's parents nagged us the whole evening. And there was an accident up ahead in the tunnel on my way back, so I had to wait, stuck in traffic for half an hour. That crappy car of mine has started making a weird noise. I think I ought to get somebody to look at it.'

It was drizzling outside and the droplets of water in her hair glinted like diamonds.

'What was the name of the show?' I asked. 'If anybody asks me, I'll help them save thirty bucks.'

'*Starlight Express*,' she answered quickly. 'It's had good reviews, but I just wasn't in the right mood.'

She knew I'd gone to meet Wieder, so she asked me how it went and whether we'd come to an agreement about the library. I told her that he'd given me a cheque, which I was going to use to pay the rent, and that I'd already put in a few hours' work.

After we went back inside and sat down on the couch, she asked, 'Something's wrong, Richard. Do you want to talk about it?'

I decided it was pointless trying to conceal it, so I said, 'Wieder asked me questions about our relationship. And — '

'What kind of questions?'

'Strange questions . . . He also asked me whether anybody had approached me about him

43

and was asking what you told me about the research the two of you are doing.'

'Aha.'

I waited for her to continue, but she didn't.

'What's more, he insinuated that you might have been lying to me and that you went to New York for some other reason.'

For a few moments she said nothing, and then she asked me, 'And you believe him?'

I shrugged. 'I don't know what to think any more. I don't know whether I have the right to question you about what you do or don't do. You're not my property and I don't think I'm a suspicious guy.'

She was holding the cup between her palms as if it were a bird she was about to release.

'All right, so do you want us to clear things up?'

'Sure.'

She put the cup on the table and turned off the TV. We'd agreed not to smoke inside the house, but she lit a cigarette. I regarded it as an exceptional circumstance, so the rules were momentarily suspended.

'Right, let's take things one at a time. When I moved here, it never even crossed my mind to embark on a relationship, either with you or with anybody else. At the end of my first year, I started seeing a guy majoring in economics. We spent the summer apart; each of us went home. We picked up our relationship again in the fall, and for a while everything seemed good. I was in love with him, or so I thought, even if I was aware that the feeling wasn't mutual — he was flighty, without making any emotional commitment. I suspected he was seeing other girls, so I was angry at myself for tolerating it.

'It was during that time that I started working for Wieder. At first I was just a volunteer, the same as some twenty or thirty other students, but soon after, we started to discuss his work and I think he liked me. I got involved at a higher level. I became a kind of assistant to him, if you like. The boyfriend I've been telling you about became jealous. He started to follow me and question me about my relationship with Wieder. The dean received an anonymous letter accusing me and the professor of being lovers.'

'What was the guy's name?'

'Are you sure you want to know?'

'Yes, I'm sure.'

'His name's Timothy Sanders. He's still here, taking a master's course. Remember when we were at Robert's Bar, on Lincoln, right after we first met?'

'I remember.'

'He was there with a girl.'

'All right, go on.'

'After that letter to the dean, Wieder got mad. I was very eager to continue working with him, as I was already involved in his research programme. It was my chance to make a career for myself in the field. I wasn't going to let Timothy ruin that chance.

'I confessed to Wieder that I'd certain suspicions as to the sender of that letter. He made me promise to end my relationship with Timothy, which I'd been intending to do anyway.

45

Timothy and I talked, and I told him that I didn't want us to go on seeing each other. Ironically, it was only then that he seemed to genuinely fall in love with me. He followed me wherever I went, and sent me letters with long sob stories, warning me that he was seriously thinking about ending his life and that I'd have to live with the guilt. He sent me flowers at home and at school, and begged me to meet him at least for a few minutes. I kept my resolve and refused to talk to him. Wieder asked me once or twice whether the guy was still a part of my life and he seemed to be satisfied when I told him that I'd broken up with Timothy for good and that whatever happened, I'd no intention of changing my mind.

'Then Timothy adopted a different tactic and started making veiled threats and dirty insinuations. He seemed completely obsessed. Once, I saw him hanging around outside Wieder's house, sitting in his car, which was parked under the street lighting pole on the corner. He's the reason I moved out of my old place and came here.

'He vanished for a while and I saw him again, as I told you, that evening at Robert's. After that, he came up to me on campus and I made the mistake of agreeing to have a cup of coffee with him. I was sure that he's okay with the fact that it's all over, given that he stopped harassing me.'

'Excuse me for interrupting,' I said, 'but why didn't you call the cops?'

'I didn't want trouble. Timothy wasn't violent. He never once tried to hit me, so I didn't feel like I was in any physical danger. And I doubt that the cops would have been very interested in some lovesick guy pining for a grad student, as long as he hadn't broken the law. But after that coffee together, he started all over again. He told me that he was sure I still loved him and that I didn't want to accept the idea, but sooner or later I'd realise it. That he'd been so upset when we broke up that he'd been going to therapy sessions in New York. I was worried he might come here and cause a scene, and that you'd get angry.

'In short, I agreed to go with him to one of his therapy sessions, to demonstrate to the psychologist that I was a flesh-and-blood person and not some figment of his imagination, some kind of invented girlfriend, as he suspected the psychologist had begun to believe. That's why I went to New York. He'd already found out my new address. After the visit to the psychologist, I met Dharma and spent the night at her parents', like I told you. And that's all. Timothy promised never to try to find me again.'

'Why didn't you tell me the truth? Wouldn't it have been easier?'

'Because I'd have had to tell you everything I've just told you, and I didn't want to. That guy is nothing but a shadow from my past and that's where I want him to stay, with the other shadows. Richard, we all have things we'd rather forget about and there's nothing we can do about it. And things from the past shouldn't be displayed in public for all to see, because sometimes their meaning is too complicated and sometimes it's too painful. More often than not, it's best just to keep them hidden.'

'And that was all? You went to the session, talked to the shrink, and then you each went your separate ways?'

She looked at me in amazement.

'Yes, I told you, that was all.'

'And what did the doctor say?'

'He was convinced that Timothy had been making up the whole story about our relationship. That this ex-girlfriend was a kind of projection he'd created for himself and that it probably didn't have any connection with a real person named Laura. It all had something to do with him being brought up by a stepmother who didn't love him and he couldn't bear the idea of being rejected. But why are you interested in all this crap?'

It was getting dark but neither of us got up to turn on the light. We were sitting in the shadows, like in a Rembrandt canvas entitled *Laura Begging for Richard's Forgiveness*.

I wanted her — I couldn't wait to take her clothes off and feel her body next to mine — but at the same time I felt as if I'd been lied to and betrayed. I was at a dead end and I didn't know how to move forward.

'Did Wieder know about all this?' I asked. 'Did he know the real reason you were going to New York?'

She told me he did.

'And why did he feel the need to alert me to it?'

'Because that's just what he does,' she snapped

angrily. 'Because he probably doesn't like that we're in a relationship. He might be jealous and he couldn't resist lighting a fuse, because that's what he knows how to do best — to manipulate, to play with other people's minds. I warned you that you don't know what he's really like.'

'But you described him as a genius, a sort of demigod, and told me you're good friends. Now — '

'Well, it seems that sometimes even a genius can be a real jerk.'

I knew I was taking an enormous risk by asking the question, but I went ahead regardless. 'Laura, have you ever had a relationship with Wieder?'

'No.'

I was grateful that she gave me a straight answer, without any hypocritical indignation or the (almost) inevitable *how could you even think such a thing?*

But all the same, a few moments later she added, 'I'm sorry such a thing crossed your mind, Richard. But given the circumstances, I understand.'

'I was a little surprised to find out you have a set of keys to his house. Wieder told me.'

'If you'd asked me, I'd have told you too. It's no secret. He's all alone, doesn't have a partner. A woman comes every Friday to do the cleaning, and a former patient of his, who lives nearby, comes whenever he needs a handyman. He gave me a set of keys just in case. I've never used them so much as once, believe me. I've never been there when he wasn't at home.'

Her face was barely visible in the gloom of the living room, and I wondered who Laura Baines really was, the Laura Baines I'd met just a few weeks before and about whom I ultimately knew nothing. Then I answered my own question: she was the woman I was in love with, and that was all that was really important.

★   ★   ★

That evening, after we'd agreed never to talk about the incident again — I was young enough to make promises impossible to keep — Laura told me about the experiments Wieder was doing. Not even she knew all the details.

The professor's connections with the authorities had begun about seven years previously, when he'd first been called as an expert witness in a murder case. The accused's attorney had insisted that his client couldn't stand trial by reason of insanity. In such cases, explained Laura, a team of three experts is assembled and together they draw up a report on the mental state of the accused, and then the court decides whether the case for the defence is justified or not. If the experts confirm that the accused is suffering from a mental illness that renders him incapable of understanding the nature of the charges against him, then he's committed to a forensic mental hospital. Later, at the request of the lawyer, the patient can be moved to a regular psychiatric hospital or even released, if the judge rules in his favour.

Wieder, who'd been teaching at Cornell at the

time, had argued that a certain John Tiburon, aged forty-eight, accused of murdering a neighbour, was faking amnesia, although the other two experts had believed that he was psychotic, suffering from paranoid schizophrenia, and that his alleged memory loss was real.

In the end, it'd been proven that Wieder was right. The investigators had discovered a journal that Tiburon had been keeping, in which he described his deeds in great detail. The neighbour hadn't been his only victim. Moreover, he'd been collecting information on the symptoms of various psychoses that might constitute grounds for acquittal. In other words, he'd made sure that in the event that he was caught, he'd be able to play-act convincingly enough to persuade the experts that he was mentally ill.

After that case, Wieder had continued to be called upon as an advisor, and he'd become increasingly interested in studying memory and analysing repressed memories, which were all the rage after the publication of *Michelle Remembers*, a book written by a psychiatrist and a supposed victim of satanic ritual abuse in childhood. Wieder had examined hundreds of such cases, even using hypnosis to further his research. He'd visited prisons and forensic mental hospitals to speak to dangerous criminals and studied countless cases of amnesia.

Finally, he'd reached the conclusion that certain cases of repressed memories, especially when the subjects have suffered serious psychological trauma, occur when a kind of autoimmune system kicks in — the subject quite simply erases the traumatic memories or sanitises them to make them bearable, the same way a white blood cell attacks a virus that has invaded a body. So our brains are endowed with a recycle bin.

But if such processes occurred spontaneously, might their mechanism be deciphered to allow it to be triggered and managed by a therapist? Because spontaneous triggering of the mechanism more often than not caused irreversible damage, and benign memories could be erased along with the traumatic ones, a patient's attempt to evade the trauma would result in a new trauma that in some cases was greater than the original one. It'd be like solving the problem of an ugly scar or burn by cutting the whole arm off.

Wieder had continued his research, meanwhile moving to Princeton.

It was there that he'd been approached by the representatives of an agency, as he'd mysteriously put it in a conversation with Laura, to become the supervisor of a programme developed by that institution. Laura didn't know anything more than that, but she suspected the project involved erasing or 'tidying up' traumatic memories suffered by soldiers and secret agents. Wieder was reluctant to talk about it. Things hadn't been going smoothly and the relationship between them and the professor had grown tense.

What she was telling me sent chills down my spine. It seemed strange to me to discover that what I believed to be indubitable pieces of reality might have been in fact just results of my subjective perspective about a thing or a situation As she said, our memories were nothing but a kind of film reel that a skilled image editor could splice at will, or a kind of gelatine that could be moulded into any shape.

I told her it was difficult for me to agree with such a theory, but she contradicted me. 'Haven't you ever had the impression that you already experienced something, that you were in a particular place, and then find out that you'd never been there, but had just heard stories about it, when you were a child, for example? Your memory merely erased the recollection of your being told the story and replaced it with an event.'

I remembered that for a long time I'd thought I'd watched the 1970 Super Bowl on TV, that I'd seen the Kansas City Chiefs beat the Minnesota Vikings. But really, I was only four back then and had thought I'd seen it — just because I'd heard Dad telling stories about that game so many times.

'See? And a typical example is how hard it is for investigators to manage eyewitness statements. Most of the time they offer information that contradicts each other, even down to details that ought to be obvious: the colour of the car that was involved in a hit-and-run accident, for example. Some say it was red, others are ready to swear under oath that it was blue, and in the end it turns out to have been yellow. Our memory isn't a video camera that records everything that passes in front of the lens, Richard, but more like a screenwriter and director all rolled into one, who make up their own movies from snatches of reality.'

★ ★ ★

I don't know why, but I paid more attention than usual to what she said that evening. In the end, I couldn't care less about what Wieder was up to. But I did wonder whether she'd been telling the truth about Timothy Sanders.

Laura had been right about the power of names, and that is why I can remember his almost thirty years later. I also wondered again that evening whether her relationship with the professor was strictly professional. Sexual harassment had become a fashionable subject in the eighties, and universities weren't immune to scandals. A mere accusation was sometimes enough to destroy a career, or at least cast suspicion. So I found it hard to believe that a figure of Wieder's standing would be capable of risking everything for the sake of a sordid affair with a student, no matter how attracted to her he might be.

That night we both slept on the couch in the living room, and long after she'd fallen asleep I stayed awake, looking at her bared body, her long legs, the curve of her thighs, her straight shoulders. She was sleeping like a baby, with her fists clenched. I decided to believe her: sometimes we purely and simply need to believe that an elephant might be pulled out of a top hat.

4

We spent Thanksgiving together the following Thursday. We bought a cooked turkey from a small family restaurant on Irving Street and invited a couple of fellow students over, friends of Laura. My brother Eddie was ill — he had a cold and my mother had quite a scare when she found him one morning in the throes of a high fever — and I spoke to them on the phone for over an hour, giving them the news that I'd found a part-time job. Neither Laura nor I mentioned Timothy Sanders or Wieder. We stayed up until almost the next morning, having fun, and then we went to New York, where we spent the weekend at a small B&B in Brooklyn Heights.

In the week that followed I went to Wieder's house twice, using the keys he'd left Laura, while he was at the university.

I liked that quiet, spacious place, which was almost magical to somebody like me who'd spent his entire life in dark, noisy hovels. The silence inside the house seemed almost unnatural and the windows in the living room had a view over the lake. I could stand there for hours, looking at the outlines of the willows leaning over the water, like a pointillist painting.

I made a discreet survey of my surroundings.

Downstairs there was a living room, a kitchen, a bathroom and a larder. Upstairs there was the library, two bedrooms, another bathroom and a dressing room large enough to be used as an additional bedroom when needed. In the basement there was a small wine cellar and a gym, with weights scattered on the floor. From the ceiling hung a red Everlast heavy bag, and a pair of boxing gloves dangled from a nail in the wall. The gym reeked of sweat and male deodorant.

I've always been a bookish guy, so organising Wieder's library was more of a privilege than a job. The shelves were full of rare editions and titles I'd never even heard of. About half of them were medical, psychological and psychiatric textbooks, but the rest were literature, art and history. I worked out my time in such a way that half would remain for reading, as I doubted the professor would be willing to lend me any of his more precious volumes.

I was there for the second time that week, having a short lunch break. Eating a sandwich I'd brought with me and gazing at the lake through the window, I realised that the house had a strange effect on me, just like its owner. It both attracted and repelled me at the same time.

It attracted me because it was the kind of house I'd have liked to live in if I were a successful writer and if that success put a pot of gold in my pocket. As my time at Princeton drew to a close, and as I began to think seriously about what I'd do next, I was increasingly worried that things might not work out the way I wanted. The handful of short stories I'd sent to literary magazines up to then had received rejections, though some of them were accompanied by a few words of encouragement from the editors. I was working on a novel, but it wasn't at all clear to me whether it was really worth persevering with it.

The alternative would be a dull life as an impoverished, misanthropic English teacher in some small town, surrounded by mocking teens. I'd have ended up wearing tweed jackets with leather patches on the elbows, carrying a never-to-be-finished book project in a briefcase, like a millstone around my neck.

That house was a universally acknowledged symbol of success, and for a couple of minutes I imagined it was mine and that I lived there with the woman I loved, who was my wife by now. I was taking a break from writing my next bestseller, waiting calm and relaxed for Laura to arrive so that we could go out and spend the evening at the Tavern on the Green or the Four Seasons, where we'd be recognised and watched with curiosity and admiration.

But the image quickly began to dissolve, as if in contact with a destructive chemical substance, when I remembered the fact that the home belonged to a man I didn't fully trust. Although I was inclined to believe that Laura had been telling me the truth and their relationship was strictly professional, whenever I was in that house I couldn't stop my imagination from running wild. It was as if I could see them coupling right there on the living room couch, or going upstairs to the bedroom, already naked and gambolling together even before they hit the sheets. I imagined all the perverse games Laura submitted to in order to excite the old man, crawling under his desk with a kinky grin on her face, while he unbuttoned his pants and made lewd suggestions.

Even when he wasn't there, Wieder was able to mark his territory, as if every object was part of his personal shrine.

★ ★ ★

That morning I'd agreed to meet Laura by the Battle Monument in the park at 3 p.m., so that we could then catch the train to New York. At 2 p.m. I locked the door to the library and went downstairs to get ready to leave. I almost fainted when I saw a tall guy sitting in the middle of the living room. He was holding an object which in the next instant I identified as a hammer.

It wasn't a dangerous neighbourhood, but in those years the newspapers were always full of stories about burglaries, and even murders.

The guy, who wore a parka, a cotton sweatshirt and a pair of jeans, stopped and gazed at me. My throat had gone dry and when I tried to speak, I barely recognised my voice. 'Who the hell are you, man?'

He stayed frozen for a few moments, as if he didn't know what to say. He had a large, round, unnaturally pale face, dishevelled hair and a few days' stubble on his cheeks.

'I'm Derek,' he said finally, as if I ought to have heard of him. 'Joe — I mean Professor Wieder — asked me to repair that pelmet.'

He pointed his hammer at one of the windows and I noticed a toolbox on the floor.

'How did you get in?' I asked.

'I've got keys,' he said, pointing at the coffee table by the couch, on which there lay the items in question. 'You're the library guy, right?'

I gathered that he was that ex-patient Laura had mentioned who looked after repairs at Wieder's house.

I was in a hurry, so I didn't hang around to ask him any more questions, and nor did I call Wieder to check out Derek's claims. When I met Laura around an hour later, I told her about the encounter that had almost given me a heart attack.

'The guy's name is Derek Simmons,' she told me. 'He's been with the professor for a few years. In effect, it's Wieder who takes care of him.'

On our way to Princeton Junction, where we were going to take the train to New York, Laura told me Derek's story.

★ ★ ★

Four years previously, he'd been accused of murdering his wife. They'd lived in Princeton, had been married for five years and had no children. Derek had worked as a maintenance man, and his wife, Anne, had been a waitress at a coffee shop on Nassau Street. As neighbours and friends of the family were later to declare, they'd never argued and they'd seemed to have a happy marriage.

Early one morning, Derek had called for an

ambulance from home, telling the operator that his wife was in a serious condition. The paramedics had found her in the hall, lying lifeless in a pool of blood, having been stabbed repeatedly in the neck and chest. An assistant medical examiner had declared her deceased at the scene and crime scene investigators had been called.

Derek's version of the tragedy had been as follows:

He'd got back home at around 7 p.m., after doing some shopping at a store near where they lived. He'd eaten, watched TV and then gone to bed, knowing that Anne would be working the evening shift and wouldn't get back until late.

He'd woken up at 6 a.m. as usual, and seen that his wife wasn't in bed next to him. Coming out of the bedroom, he'd found her lying in the hall, covered in blood. He didn't know whether she was alive or dead, so he'd called an ambulance.

Initially, the investigators had thought that it was possible that the man was telling the truth. The door had been unlocked and there was no sign of a break-in, so probably somebody had followed her, attacking her as she was entering the apartment. Maybe then the perpetrator had realised that there was somebody else in the home and fled without stealing anything. (The victim's handbag, still containing approximately forty dollars in cash, had been found next to her body.) The coroner had determined that she'd died at around 3 a.m. There was no motive for Simmons to have murdered his wife and he'd seemed devastated by her loss. He hadn't had any debts, hadn't been having an affair, and minded his own business at work. He was generally seen as hard-working and quiet.

Laura knew all the details from Wieder, who'd been one of the three experts brought in to assess Derek's mental condition after he'd been accused of his wife's murder; his attorney had been demanding he be declared not guilty by reason of insanity. For one reason or another, Wieder had accorded the case the utmost importance.

The detectives had subsequently discovered a number of things that cast Derek in a very bad light.

First, Anne Simmons had started having an affair a few months before she was murdered. The identity of her lover was never discovered — or at least it was never made public — but it seemed that the relationship had been serious, and that the two had been planning to marry, after Anne filed for a divorce. On the evening of the murder, Anne had finished her shift and locked up the cafe at around 10 p.m. The lovers had then gone to a cheap one-bed apartment on the same street as the cafe, rented by Anne two months previously, where they'd stayed until around midnight, after which she'd taken a cab home. According to the driver and the information recorded on the meter, Anne Simmons had been dropped off in front of her building at 1.12 a.m.

Derek had claimed he'd had no idea his wife was having an affair, but the investigators had thought this was highly unlikely. So, now they'd had motive — jealousy — and the murder could easily have been a crime of passion.

Second, the woman had wounds on her arms, called 'defensive wounds' by the investigators. In other words, she'd lifted her arms trying to defend herself against the perpetrator, who had most probably used a big knife. Even if Derek had been asleep upstairs while his wife was fighting for her life, it was unlikely for him not to have heard anything. Anne would almost certainly have screamed for help. (Two neighbours later claimed to have heard her screaming, but had failed to call the police as the screams had stopped before they'd had a chance to fully wake up.)

Third, a friend of the victim had confirmed that a knife was missing from the Simmonses' kitchen, a knife she remembered, because just a few weeks earlier she'd helped Anne prepare the food for a birthday party. When asked about the knife in question, whose description pointed to its being the murder weapon, Derek could only shrug. Yes, such a knife had existed, but he hadn't known what'd happened to it, because his wife had looked after the kitchen.

Finally, detectives had also discovered that many years previously, Derek, a teenager at the time, had suffered a severe nervous breakdown. He'd been admitted to Marlboro Psychiatric Hospital and kept there for two months, missing his final year of high school. He'd been diagnosed as a schizophrenic, and had been on medication ever since his release. Although he'd been a very good student up until then, he'd later given up on the idea of going to college and had qualified as an electrician instead, getting a low-level job at Siemens.

The detectives had consequently built a damning theory and concluded that the timeline had been as follows:

Anne had arrived home at 1.12 a.m., and an argument had broken out. Her husband had accused her of having an affair, and she'd probably informed him of her intention to seek a divorce. Two hours later, Derek had taken a knife from the kitchen and killed her. He'd then disposed of the murder weapon, and he called for an ambulance, as if he'd just discovered his wife's body. He may have been having a mental breakdown or a schizophrenic episode, but only the doctors could come to a conclusion about that.

After Simmons was arrested on a murder charge, his attorney had latched on to the mental breakdown theory and asked for his client to be declared not guilty by reason of insanity. Meanwhile, the accused had stubbornly continued to claim he was innocent, refusing any kind of deal.

After examining him a number of times, Joseph Wieder had reached the conclusion that Derek Simmons was suffering from a rare form of dissociative disorder and had been wrongly diagnosed with schizophrenia as a young man. The psychosis in question involved the periodic occurrence of so-called fugue states, during which the patient lost all self-awareness, memories and sense of identity. In extreme cases, such persons might go missing from home and be found years later in another city or state, living under a completely new identity, without remembering anything about their old life. Some returned to their old identities, but completely forgot about the other ones they'd constructed in the meantime; others remained completely captive to their new life.

If Wieder's diagnosis was correct, it was possible that Simmons mightn't have remembered anything about what he'd done that night, when, because of stress and the modified consciousness induced by the sudden transition from sleep to waking, he'd reacted as if he were a completely different person.

Wieder's report had convinced the court, and the judge had ruled that Simmons was to be committed to Trenton Psychiatric Hospital, alongside other potentially dangerous mental patients. With the agreement of the institution and the patient's lawyer, Wieder had continued to give Simmons therapy, using hypnosis and a revolutionary treatment involving a mixture of anticonvulsant drugs.

Unfortunately, after a few months in the hospital, Simmons had been attacked by another patient and suffered a serious head wound, which had substantially worsened his condition. Derek Simmons had completely lost his memory and never recovered it. His brain was able to form and store new memories, but the old ones proved impossible to recover. Laura explained to me that this kind of trauma was called retrograde amnesia.

A year later, at Wieder's insistence, Derek had

been transferred to Marlboro Psychiatric Hospital, where the regime was less strict. There the professor had helped him reconstruct his personality. In fact, Laura said, that was only half true: the patient became Derek Simmons once more only in the sense that he had the same name and physical appearance. He knew how to write, but he had no idea where he'd learned to do so, given that he had no memories of ever going to school. He was still able to do the work of an electrician but, again, he had no idea where he'd learned his trade. All his memories up until the moment he'd been attacked in the hospital were locked away somewhere in the synapses of his brain.

In the spring of 1985, a judge had approved his lawyer's request to discharge Simmons from the mental hospital, given the complexity of the case and the patient's complete lack of any violent tendencies. But, Laura said, it'd been clear that Derek Simmons wouldn't be able to fend for himself. He'd had no prospects of employment, and sooner or later he'd have ended up in a mental institution. He was an only child, and his mother had died of cancer when he was a toddler. His father, to whom Derek hadn't been very close, had moved out of town after the tragedy, leaving no forwarding address, and had seemed uninterested in his son's fate.

So Wieder had rented a small one-bed apartment for him not far from his own home, and paid him a monthly wage to keep up his house. Derek lived alone, his neighbours viewing him as a freak. Now and then he'd lock himself

up and wouldn't emerge for days or weeks.
During these periods it was Wieder who brought
him food and made sure he took his medication.

★ ★ ★

Derek Simmons's story touched me, as did
Wieder's attitude towards him. It was with
Wieder's help that the guy, murderer or not, was
able to live a decent life. And he was free, even if
his freedom was restricted by his illness. Without
Wieder, he'd have ended up in an asylum, an
unwanted wreck, surrounded by brutal guards
and dangerous patients. Laura told me that she'd
visited the hospital in Trenton with the professor
a few times to do fieldwork; she thought that a
mental hospital was maybe the most sinister
place on the face of the earth.

The following week, when the first snows
began to fall, I'd visited Wieder's house three
times and each time found Derek there, doing
some minor repairs. We chatted and smoked
together, looking at the lake, which seemed
crushed beneath the weight of the gloomy sky. If
I hadn't known about his condition, I'd have
thought he was a normal person, albeit shy,
reclusive and not very clever. In any event, he
seemed gentle and incapable of doing anybody
any harm. He spoke of Wieder with veneration
and understood how much he owed the
professor. He told me that he'd recently adopted
a puppy from a shelter. He called him Jack and
took him for a walk in the nearby park every
evening.

I mention Derek and his story here because he was to play an important role in the tragedy that followed.

5

It was early in December when I received one of the most important pieces of news in my life up to then.

One of the librarians at the Firestone, a friend of mine by the name of Lisa Wheeler, told me that an editor from *Signature*, a New York literary magazine, would be giving a lecture at Nassau Hall. The magazine, which is now defunct, was quite well regarded at the time, despite having a limited circulation. Knowing that I wanted to get published, Lisa got me an invitation and advised me to speak to the editor after the lecture, asking him to read my stories. I wasn't shy, but nor was I pushy, so over the following three days I was in a ferment as to what to do. In the end, mostly at Laura's insistence, I chose three short stories, put them in an envelope along with a résumé, and turned up at the lecture with the package tucked under my arm.

★   ★   ★

I arrived too early, so I waited in front of the building, smoking a cigarette. Outside the auditorium the air was leaden grey and filled with the cries of the crows that nested in the nearby trees.

It'd been snowing again, and the two bronze

68

tigers that guarded the hall's entrance looked like marzipan figurines on some huge cake, dusted with powdered sugar. A slim man, wearing one of those corduroy jackets with leather patches on the elbows and a matching tie, walked up to me and asked me for a light. He rolled his own cigarettes and smoked them in a long bone or ivory holder, which he clasped between his thumb and forefinger like an Edwardian dandy.

We started talking and he asked me what I thought of the subject matter of the lecture. I confessed that I didn't really know what it was about, but that I was hoping to give some of my short stories to the speaker, who was an editor at *Signature* magazine.

'Splendid,' he said, exhaling a cloud of bluish smoke into the air. He had a slender pencil moustache, ragtime-style. 'And what are your stories about?'

I shrugged. 'Difficult to say — I'd rather they were read than talk about them.'

'Do you know that William Faulkner said the same thing? That a good book can only be read, not talked about. Very well, let me have them. I'll wager they are in that envelope.'

I was left gaping in astonishment.

'John M. Hartley,' the man said, moving the cigarette holder to his left hand and stretching out his right.

I shook his hand, with a feeling that I'd got off to a bad start. He noticed my embarrassment and gave me a smile of encouragement, revealing two rows of tobacco-yellowed teeth. I handed him the envelope containing my stories and résumé. He took it and thrust it into the battered leather briefcase that was leaning against the metal stem of the ashtray between us. We finished our cigarettes and walked into the auditorium without saying another word.

At the end of the lecture, after all the questions from the audience had been answered, he discreetly beckoned me over and when I went up to him, handed me a business card and told me to get in touch a week later.

I told Laura about what had happened.

'It's a sign,' she said, triumphant and highly convinced of it.

She was sitting naked, perched on the makeshift desk I'd put together in one corner of the living room. She was waving her legs back and forth to dry the freshly painted varnish on her toes, and at the same time was wiping the lenses of her glasses with a piece of leather.

'This is what happens when something is written in the stars,' she went on. 'Everything comes together and flows in a natural sort of way, like a good piece of prose. Welcome to the writer's world, Mr Richard Flynn, sir.'

'Let's just wait and see what happens,' I said sceptically. 'I wonder whether I made a good choice with the stories, and whether he'll even bother to look at them. Maybe they're in the trash already.'

She was short-sighted and when she wasn't wearing her glasses had to screw up her eyes to be able to see, which made her look angry. She cast me such a glance, with her eyebrows bunched up, and stuck her tongue out at me.

'Don't be such a dogged pessimist! Pessimists get on my nerves, especially when they're young. Whenever I tried anything new when I was a child, my dad could never shut up about how many insurmountable difficulties stood between me and my dream. I think that's why I gave up painting when I was fifteen, even though my teacher said I was very talented. When I went to my first international math competition, which was held in France, he warned me that the jury would be biased in favour of the French entrants, so I shouldn't get my hopes up.'

'And was he right? Were they biased in favour of the cheese-eaters?'

'Not one bit. I won first place, and a kid from Maryland came in second.'

She put the piece of leather on the desk, placed her glasses on her nose and drew her knees up to her chest, clasping them with her arms, as if all of a sudden she was cold.

'I have a feeling that it's going to turn out all right, Richard. You were born to be a writer, I know it and you know it too. But nothing comes to you on a silver platter. After my dad died, when I was sixteen, I looked at all the stuff he'd kept under lock and key in the drawers of his desk, the desk I'd always wanted to rummage through. Among his papers, I found a small black-and-white picture of a girl about my age, with her hair swept back under an Alice band. She wasn't very pretty — she had a common look — but she had nice eyes. I showed the picture to my mom and she curtly told me that she'd been my dad's girlfriend in high school.

71

For some reason he'd kept the picture all those years. You know what I mean? It was like he hadn't had the courage to stay with that girl, God knows why, and he'd accumulated so much unhappiness inside him that he spread it all around him, like a cuttlefish squirting ink to hide itself. Now, drop those trousers, Cap'n. Can't you see there's a naked lady waiting for you?'

★ ★ ★

Laura proved to be right.

A week later we were eating a pizza in an Italian restaurant on Nassau Street when I suddenly got it in my head to call the *Signature* office there and then. I went to the phone booth by the door to the restroom, put a couple of quarters in the slot and dialled the number on the business card I'd been carrying around since the lecture. A young lady answered and I asked for Mr Hartley, telling her who I was. A few seconds later I heard the editor's voice at the other end of the line.

I reminded him who I was and he got straight to the point. 'Good news, Richard. I'm putting you in the next issue, which is out in January. It will be a strong issue. After the holidays, we always have an increase in readers. I haven't changed so much as a comma.'

I was overwhelmed.

'Which story did you choose?'

'They're short, so I decided to publish all three. I'm giving you five pages. By the way, we'll need a photo of you, black-and-white, portrait format. We also need a brief bio.'

'It sounds incredible . . . ' I said, and then stammered my thanks.

'You've written some very good stories, and it's natural that they should be read. I'd like us to meet after the holidays, so that we can get to know each other better. If you keep it up, you've got a good future ahead of you, Richard. Happy holidays. I'm glad to have been able to give you some good news.'

I wished him happy holidays and hung up.

'You're radiant,' Laura said when I sat back down at our table. 'Good news?'

'They're going to publish all three in January,' I said. 'All three, can you imagine! In *Signature*!'

We didn't celebrate with champagne. We didn't even go to a fancy restaurant. We spent the evening at home, just the two of us, making plans for the future. It felt as if the stars were close enough for us to reach out and touch them. Words like '*Signature* magazine', 'three short stories', 'black-and-white photo' and 'published writer' whirled around my head like a merry-go-round, forming an invisible halo of glory and immortality.

Today, I realise that I was overwhelmed by the sudden change that had occurred in my life at that moment, and that I was exaggerating its importance in every respect — *Signature* was hardly the *New Yorker*, and its authors were paid in free copies rather than cheques. What I didn't register at the time was that something about Laura had also changed in the previous few days. Looking back on it, she seemed distant, she was always preoccupied with something, and she started speaking to me less and less. Two or three times I caught her talking on the phone in a hushed voice, and each time she hung up as soon as she noticed I was in the room.

I continued to go to Wieder's house almost every day, working for three or four hours each time in the library, which was slowly beginning to take on an organised shape, and I spent my evenings with Laura, giving up every other activity. But most of the time she brought her work home, and sat hunched up on the floor, surrounded by books, piles of paper and pens, like a shaman officiating some secret ritual. If I remember correctly, we no longer even made love. Although I got up early in the mornings, most of the time I'd find that she'd already left without waking me.

★   ★   ★

And then one day I came upon the manuscript in Wieder's library.

At the bottom of the shelves opposite the door there was a small cupboard, which I hadn't been curious enough to open up until then. I was looking for some writing paper, wanting to make a diagram of the final arrangement for the shelves by the door, which was where I'd begun my work, so rather than go back downstairs to fetch some from the professor's desk I decided to look in the cupboard. I opened it and found a ream of paper, a couple of old magazines, bunches of pencils, ballpoint pens and markers.

As I was pulling the paper from the cupboard I dropped it and the sheets scattered all over the floor. Kneeling down to pick them up, I noticed that the point of one of the pencils in the cupboard seemed to be wedged in the wall, poking inside the place where two of the sides ought to have joined together. I leaned forward to get a better look, moved the other objects out of the way and discovered that the left side of the cupboard had a false wall, which opened to reveal a space the size of a phonebook. And in that niche I found a sheaf of papers inside a cardboard file.

I pulled it out and saw that there was no inscription on the cover that might identify the manuscript. Leafing through it, I observed it was a work of psychiatry or psychology, but there was no page giving the title or author.

The pages seemed to have been written by at least two different hands. Some were typewritten, others were covered in very small handwriting, in black ink, and others still were in a different hand, with large scrawling letters that leaned to the left and were written in blue ballpoint pen. Both the typewritten and handwritten pages were covered in corrections and, in places, additions of one or two paragraphs had been attached to the pages with clear adhesive tape.

I wondered whether it might be a draft (or one of the drafts) of Professor Wieder's famous book that Laura had told me about, or whether it was the manuscript of some older, already published work.

I quickly read the first couple of pages, which abounded in scientific terms unfamiliar to me, and then I put the manuscript back, taking care to arrange the objects more or less the way I'd found them. I didn't want Wieder to notice that I'd discovered his secret hiding place or that I'd been rummaging through his house.

★　★　★

One afternoon I lost track of the time and when I went downstairs I bumped into the professor, who was talking to Derek. Derek left and Wieder invited me to stay for dinner. He was tired and looked gloomy and preoccupied. In passing, he congratulated me about my stories being accepted for publication, which he'd probably found out from Laura, but he didn't ask me for more details, which I would have been very happy to offer. It'd started to snow heavily and I thought to myself that it'd be better if I left, as the roads might get blocked, but I was unable to refuse his invitation.

'Why don't you tell Laura to come over?' he suggested. 'Come on, I insist. If I'd known you were here, I'd have invited her myself. We were working together today.'

While he was looking for some steaks in the fridge, I went into the hall and called home. Laura answered almost immediately and I told her that I was at Wieder's and that he'd invited us both for dinner.

'Did he suggest that you call me?' she asked in a quarrelsome tone of voice. 'Where is he now?'

'He's in the kitchen. Why?'

'I don't feel well, Richard. The weather's bad and I'd advise you to come home as quickly as possible.'

I didn't insist. I told her that I'd get back as quickly as I could before hanging up.

Wieder gave me a quizzical look when I returned to the den. He'd taken off his jacket and was wearing a white apron; on the chest was embroidered in red: 'I Don't Know What I'm Doing'. He looked to me as if he'd lost weight and the circles under his eyes were darker than ever. Bathed in the harsh neon light from the kitchen, his face looked ten years older, and the confident demeanour he'd had on the evening we'd met seemed to have given way to an almost hunted appearance.

'Well, what did she say?'

'She said she doesn't feel like going out in this weather. And — '

He interrupted me with a gesture. 'She could at least have come up with a better excuse.'

He picked up one of the steaks and tossed it back in the fridge, slamming the door.

'Women can say that they are *indisposed*, can't they, without going into details? It's one of their major advantages in life. Go down into the cellar, will you, and pick out a bottle of red wine, please. We're about to have a sad, lonely bachelor dinner. Neither of us is a football fan, but we could watch a game afterwards, have a beer, belch, do whatever contented men are supposed to do.'

When I came back from the cellar with the

wine, the steaks were sizzling in a big frying pan, and he was making some instant mashed potato. One of the windows was wide open and the wind was blowing large snowflakes inside, which melted instantly in the warm air. I opened the bottle of wine and poured it into a paunchy carafe, following his instructions.

'No offence, but if I'd asked Laura to come over a year ago, she'd have been here like a shot, even if it were raining brimstone outside,' he said, after taking a large gulp of whisky. 'Listen to an old man's advice, Richard. When a woman senses that you've got something for her, then she'll start testing her power and try to dominate you.'

'What do you mean by 'something'?' I asked.

He didn't answer, but merely gave me a long look.

We ate in silence. He'd cooked the steaks in a rush and they were almost raw, and the mashed potato was full of lumps. He finished off almost the whole bottle of wine himself, and when we moved on to coffee, he poured a big shot of bourbon in his and drank it. Outside, the storm had turned into a blizzard, which writhed against the windows.

After dinner he put the plates in the dishwasher and lit a cigar, which he took from a wooden box. I declined his offer and lit a Marlboro. For a while he smoked absently, seeming to forget that I was there. I was getting ready to thank him for dinner and tell him I was leaving when he started to speak.

'What is your earliest memory, Richard?

Chronologically, I mean. Usually a person's memories start from the age of two and a half or three years old.'

The neon light in the kitchen was on, but the living room was in semi-darkness. As he spoke he waved his hands and the incandescent tip of the cigar traced complicated patterns in the gloom. His long beard gave him the look of a biblical prophet, drained of visions, trying to hear the voice from heaven one more time. On the ring finger of his right hand he wore a red gemstone, which glinted mysteriously when he puffed on his cigar. The table between us, covered with a large white cloth, looked like the surface of a deep, cold lake, separating us more starkly than a wall.

I'd never thought about my first recollection 'in chronological order', as he'd put it. But after only a few moments the memory he referred to began to take shape in my mind and I shared it with him.

'I was in Philly, at Aunt Cornelia's house. You're right: I must have been three years old, or it was a month or so before my third birthday, at the beginning of the summer of 1969. I was on a balcony, which seemed very big to me, trying to pull a wooden slat off a green cupboard. I wore shorts and white sandals. Then my mom came and took me away from there. I don't remember the journey by train or car, and I don't remember the inside of my aunt's house or what she and her husband looked like then. I just remember that slat, the cupboard, and the balcony, which had butter-coloured floor tiles, and also a strong smell of cooking, which must have been coming from the kitchen, somewhere near the balcony.'

'So you were around three when Armstrong walked on the moon,' he said. 'Did you have a TV in your house at the time? It happened during the summer you're talking about.'

'Sure. It was a small colour TV, on a stand in the living room, by the window. Later we got a bigger one, a Sony.'

'Your parents more than likely watched the moon landing, one of the most important moments in history since the beginning of the world. Do you remember anything about that?'

'I know they watched the coverage because they talked about it for years afterwards. That day, Dad had been to the dentist's, and Mom made him chamomile tea to gargle with. He somehow managed to scald his mouth with the tea. I heard the story dozens of times. But I don't remember Neil Armstrong saying his famous words, or seeing him bouncing around like a big white doll on the moon's surface. I saw that scene later, of course.'

'See? For you, at that age, the landing didn't mean anything at all. A little piece of wood was more important to you, for whatever reason. But what if you'd found out that you never went to Philly, and that it was all an image cooked up by your own mind, rather than a real memory?'

'I've had these kinds of conversations with Laura. Maybe some memories are relative, maybe our memories gloss over things or even alter them, but I think that they're only relative up to a point.'

'They aren't relative up to a point,' he told me. 'Let me give you an example. When you were little, did you ever get lost in a mall when your parents were shopping?'

'I don't remember anything like that.'

'Well, in the fifties and sixties, when malls started popping up everywhere and replaced neighbourhood stores, one of the constant fears of mothers everywhere was that they'd lose their children in the crowds. Kids of that generation were brought up in the shadow of that bogeyman, and were always being told to keep close to their moms when they were out shopping. The fear of getting lost or kidnapped in the mall is imprinted in their deepest memories, even if they can't consciously remember anything about it any more.'

He got up and poured two glasses of bourbon, one of which he placed in front of me before he sat back down. He took a puff on his cigar, drank a sip of whisky, inviting me to do likewise with a glance, and then went on.

'Quite a few years ago I carried out an experiment. I took a cross section of students born in that period. Not one of them could remember getting lost in a mall as a child. Then I suggested to them under hypnosis that they'd in fact got lost. What do you think happened? Three-quarters of them subsequently declared that they remembered getting lost in a mall and even described the experience: how frightened they were, how they were found by clerks and taken to their moms, how there were announcements on the overhead speakers about Tommy or

Harry having been found by the cafe. Most of them refused to believe that it was all just a question of hypnotic suggestion combined with their old childhood fears. They 'remembered' the event all too well to be able to believe it never happened. If I'd suggested to somebody born and raised in New York City that he'd been attacked by a gator in childhood, for example, the result would most likely have been null, because they had no childhood memory of being afraid of gators.'

'What are you driving at?' I asked.

I didn't feel like drinking any more and the mere smell of the booze was enough to make me queasy after the dinner I'd forced myself to eat. I was tired and I kept wondering whether the buses were still running.

'Driving at? Well, what I'm driving at is that when I asked you about a childhood memory, you told me about something safe and ordinary, a child playing with a bit of wood on a balcony. But the brain never works like that. There must be a very strong reason *why* you remembered that and not something else, if we presume it's true. Maybe the slat had a nail in it and you hurt yourself, even if you can't remember that part any more. Maybe the balcony was on an upper floor and there was a risk of your falling, and your mother screamed when she found you there. When I started dealing with . . . '

He paused, as if he were wondering whether he ought to continue. He probably decided he ought to, as he went on.

'Some people experience very traumatic

episodes, which turn in time into serious blockages. It's the so-called 'boxer syndrome': after you almost get the life beaten out of you in the ring, it's impossible for you to have enough motivation to become a champ. Your instinct for self-preservation becomes a strong inhibitor. So, if a bunch of students can be persuaded they once were lost in a mall, why couldn't somebody who really experienced such a thing be persuaded that the traumatic event never actually happened and that his mom merely bought him a new toy that day? You aren't cancelling out the effects of the trauma, but you're removing the trauma itself.'

'In other words, you're butchering somebody's memory,' I said, but immediately regretted the forthright way I had put it.

'If there's a big bunch of people who give themselves up to the surgeon's knife for the sake of more attractive breasts, noses and butts, then what could be wrong with cosmetic surgery for the memory? Especially if we're dealing with people who are no better than broken toys, unable to do their job any more or function properly.'

'Isn't what you're talking about brainwashing? And what happens when the memories come back to the surface at the wrong moment? What if a mountain climber's blockage comes back all of a sudden, just as he's hanging from a rope at three thousand feet?'

He looked at me in astonishment and slight alarm. Up until then his tone had been somewhat condescending, but after that I detected a note of fear mingled with his surprise.

'That's a *very* good question. I see you're smarter than I thought — no offence. So, yes, what happens in such a situation? Some people will probably hold the person who 'butchered' the climber's mind responsible, to use your words.'

Just then the phone rang, but he didn't answer it, and I wondered whether it might be Laura. Then he suddenly changed the subject, using his familiar tactic. He probably thought he'd already said too much about his experiments.

'Sorry Laura couldn't come. Maybe we'd have had a more pleasant conversation. You know, I'm aware of your relationship, so you don't need to lie to me about it any more. Laura and I don't have any secrets from each other. She told you about that Timothy, didn't she?'

I knew he wasn't bluffing, so I told him it was true. I felt embarrassed at having been caught red-handed and I told myself that he and Laura had a deeper connection than I'd presumed, sharing a secret place in which I hadn't been admitted even as a guest yet, despite my illusions.

'When I asked you about the nature of your relationship, I'd already known you were together,' he said. 'It was just a test.'

'Which I failed.'

'Let's say rather that you chose to be discreet, and that my question was out of line,' he reassured me. 'How much does Laura mean to you? Or rather, how much do you *think* she means?'

'A whole lot.'

'You didn't hesitate,' he observed. 'So let us hope that everything goes well between the two of you. Has anybody asked you about your visits here yet?'

'No.'

'If anybody does, then tell me immediately, no matter who's doing the asking, will you?'

'Sure.'

'Great, thanks.'

I decided to play his game, so this time I was the one who suddenly changed the subject. 'Have you ever been married?'

'My bio is public, Richard. I'm surprised you've never read it. No, I've never been married. Why? Because when I was young I was only interested in studying and making a career for myself, which was something that happened quite late on. When two people meet when they're young and grow up together, it's easy for them to put up with each other's quirks and habits. When you're older it's almost impossible. Or perhaps I just never met the right person. I was once head over heels in love with a pretty young lady, but it ended quite badly.'

'Why?'

'Maybe you'd like me to tell you the combination to the safe, too? That's enough for tonight. Do you want to know what my earliest memory is?'

'I have a feeling I'm going to find out.'

'Your feeling is correct, buddy. You're cut out to be a medium. Well, I wasn't sitting on a balcony, trying to break off a wooden slat. I was

85

in a large yard full of roses, it was early one beautiful summer and the sun was shining. I was standing next to some rose bushes, with big, red blooms, and at my feet there was a tabby cat. A tall and handsome man — all adults look very tall when you're a toddler — was leaning over me and telling me something. He was wearing a dark uniform and he had a couple of medals pinned to his chest, one of which caught my eye more than the others, probably because it was very shiny. I think it was silver, in the shape of a cross. That young man, with blond hair in a crew cut, was paying attention to me and I was very proud of that.

That's my memory, which I can still see vividly before my eyes. I was born in Germany, if you didn't know, and I'm Jewish. I came to America with my mother and sister when I was four years old. My sister Inge was just a baby. My mother later told me that on that day we'd been 'visited' by some storm troopers, who'd beaten my father very badly; he died in hospital a few days later. But that memory, which masked so painful an event, has remained here in my mind. I prefer to keep my memories, you know, no matter how painful. I sometimes use them the way Catholics use a hair belt: they're abrasive and you tie them around your waist or your thigh. It helps me to never forget what some seemingly normal human beings are capable of doing, and that behind appearances there sometimes lurk monsters.'

He stood up and turned on the light, which dazzled my eyes and caused me to flinch. He went to the window and drew the curtain.

'It's hell outside,' he said. 'And it's almost midnight. Are you sure you don't want to stay over tonight?'

'Laura would be worried,' I said.

'You can call her,' he answered, gesturing towards the hall. 'I'm sure she'll understand.'

'No, that's all right, I'll manage.'

'I'll call you a cab, then. I'll pay the fare. It's my fault you stayed until this hour.'

'It was an interesting conversation,' I said.

'As I told you before, there's no need to lie,' he said and went into the hall to call a cab.

In fact, I hadn't lied. He was probably the most intriguing grown-up I'd met up until then, not only due to his reputation and fame, but also because of his undeniable personal charisma. But at the same time he always seemed stuck inside a sort of glass cubicle, locked up in there by his own incapacity to accept that others weren't just sock puppets in his twisted mind games.

I went to the window. The snow looked like a group of ghosts as it whirled in the glow of the light on the balcony. Then, all of a sudden, I thought I saw a figure in the darkness, ten feet away from the window, a figure that darted to the left, behind the tall magnolias, whose branches were laden with snow. I was almost sure I hadn't imagined it, although visibility was very poor because of the darkness, but I decided not to mention it to Wieder: he seemed stressed enough as it was.

★ ★ ★

He managed to find a cab after a number of attempts, and it took over an hour for me to arrive in front of my house. The taxi spat me out in the snow somewhere near the monument, from whence I continued on foot, sinking up to my knees in the drifts, the frozen wind lashing my face.

Twenty minutes later I was sitting on the couch with Laura, wrapped in a blanket, holding a mug of hot tea.

Suddenly she said, 'Timothy came by three hours ago.' She never used the shorter form — Tim or Timmy — just as she never called me Dick or Richie. 'I think he means to continue with the harassment. I don't know what to do.'

'I'll talk to him. Or maybe we should call the cops, like I told you before.'

'I don't think there's any point,' she said quickly, without specifying which option she was referring to. 'It's a pity you weren't at home. We could have sorted it out on the spot.'

'Wieder insisted I stay for dinner.'

'And you had to go along with it, didn't you? What did you talk about?'

'Stuff about memory, something like that. How about you explain to me why you've turned against him lately? If it hadn't been for you, I'd never even have known him. He offered me a job. He's a respectable professor, and I was just trying to be polite, that was all, including because I know you value your relationship with him. It was you who insisted on my meeting him, remember?'

She was sitting on the small carpet in front of

88

the couch, with her legs crossed, as if she was about to do some meditation. She was wearing one of my T-shirts, the one with the Giants logo, and for the first time I noticed that she'd lost weight.

She apologised for her tone, and then told me that her mother had discovered a lump in her left breast. She'd gone to the doctor and was now waiting for the results of the mammogram. She'd told me very little about her family — nothing but small scraps and snatches of memories — and I'd never really been able to form a coherent picture from the pieces of the jigsaw puzzle she offered me, even though I'd told her everything about my own folks. I was thinking of spending the holidays with my mother and brother, the first Christmas without my dad. I'd invited her, but she'd said she'd rather go to Evanston. There were only a few days left and already I could feel the metallic tang of parting; it was to be our longest time apart since we'd met.

★ ★ ★

The next day I had my photo taken for *Signature* at a small studio downtown. A few hours later I picked up the pictures and sent two of them to the magazine's address, keeping the other two: one for Laura and one for my mom. But I forgot to take them out of my shoulder bag before I went away for the holidays, so I never got the chance to give Laura the photo I'd intended for her. Later, in Ithaca, when I remembered the pictures, I discovered that they'd vanished.

By the time the magazine came out, at the end of January, I was already being harassed by detectives and reporters, so I changed my address and the free copies of the magazine sent through the mail never reached me. I didn't see that issue of *Signature* until fifteen years later, when a friend of mine gave me a copy as a present. He'd come across it in a second-hand bookstore on Myrtle Avenue, in Brooklyn. I never spoke to the editor again. It wasn't until the beginning of the 2000s that I found out by chance that he'd died in a car accident on the West Coast in the summer of 1990.

As Laura might have said, maybe the way the magazine and my literary career slipped out of my grasp was a sign. After that I never published anything again, although for a while I did continue to write.

Professor Joseph Wieder was murdered in his home a couple of days after the evening we'd had dinner together, on the night of 21–22 December 1987. The police never found the perpetrator, despite extensive investigations, but for the reasons you'll discover below, I was one of the suspects.

6

Somebody once said that the beginning and the end of a story don't really exist. They're merely moments that are chosen subjectively by a narrator to allow the reader to look in on an event that began sometime previously and will end sometime after.

Twenty-six years later, my perspective changed. I was to discover the truth about the events of those months — I wasn't looking for this revision, but rather it hit me, like a stray bullet.

For a while afterwards I wondered when exactly it was that my relationship with Laura fell to pieces, and perhaps also my whole life with it, or at least the way I'd always dreamed of living it up until then. In a way, it was when she disappeared from home, without saying goodbye and without my ever seeing her again, the morning after Wieder was killed.

But in fact, things had started to go downhill immediately after that evening when I'd had dinner at the professor's house.

Just like on a snow-covered mountain, where a single sound or a falling stone can trigger a huge avalanche that sweeps away everything in its path, a seemingly banal occurrence was to shatter everything I thought I knew about Laura and, ultimately, about myself.

That weekend I'd decided to go to New York with an acquaintance, Benny Thorn, who'd asked me to help him move some of his stuff and to stay over at his place for the night. He was moving into a furnished one-bedroom apartment and he had to get rid of some surplus belongings that he hadn't managed to sell. Laura told me that she didn't want to spend the night alone, so she was going to stay at a friend's and work on her thesis. The friend's name was Sarah Harper and she lived out in Rocky Hill. I'd been making faster progress on Wieder's library than I'd expected, so I thought that I could afford to skip going there the weekend before Christmas.

But it happened that Benny slipped on ice, took a fall and broke his leg while he was loading his stuff into a hired van, just an hour before he was supposed to pick me up. So he didn't turn up to meet me and he didn't answer the phone when I called him. I left him a message and went back home to wait for him to call. An hour later, after doctors had put his leg in plaster, he called from the hospital and told me that we would have to put off our departure and resort to plan B, which involved renting a storage unit out by the airport and taking his stuff there.

I called the storage company and found out that it was possible to rent a unit for twenty bucks a month, so I spent most of the rest of the day loading boxes into the van, taking it to the storage unit, and then returning the van to the hire company. Meanwhile, Benny had arrived back home in a cab and I reassured him that everything was in order. I promised to bring him some groceries later that evening.

Laura hadn't left her friend's phone number,

so I couldn't tell her I'd put off going to New York. I looked for her at the university, but she'd already left. The only thing I could do was go back home. Once I got home though, I decided to go to Wieder's and left her a note, in the event that she might come home. The keys to the professor's house were kept in an empty jar on our sideboard, along with some loose change, nickels and quarters, and I was getting ready to leave when somebody rang the doorbell.

When I opened the door I saw a man of about my age, tall, thin and haggard. Although it was very cold and snowing, he was wearing only a tweed jacket and a long red scarf, which made him look like a French painter. He seemed surprised that I'd answered, and for a few moments he said nothing, merely gazed at me with his hands thrust inside the pockets of his corduroy pants.

'Can I help you?' I asked, certain that he must have got the wrong address.

He sighed and gave me a sad look.

'I don't think so . . . '

'There's only one way to find out.'

'I'm Timothy Sanders,' he said. 'I was looking for Laura.'

Now it was my turn not to know what to do next. A number of options flashed through my mind. The first would have been to slam the door in his face; the second, to give him a dressing-down before slamming the door; the last, to invite him inside, keep him busy, quietly call the cops and then accuse him of harassment when the patrol arrived.

But to my own amazement I merely said, 'Laura isn't at home, but if you'd like, you can come inside. I'm Richard, her boyfriend.'

'I think that . . . ' he began. He sighed again, cast a look around him — it was already growing dark — and then came in, after stamping the snow from his boots on the doormat.

He came to a stop in the middle of the living room.

'Nice place,' he said.

'Coffee?'

'No, I'm fine. Mind if I smoke?'

'We don't smoke inside, but we could go into the backyard. I wouldn't mind a smoke myself.'

I opened the glass door and he followed me outside, rummaging through his pockets for a cigarette. Finally he fished out a crumpled pack of Lucky Strikes, took out a cigarette and stooped to light it.

'Man,' I said, 'Laura has told me about you.'

He looked at me with an air of resignation.

'I supposed she did.'

'She told me about your relationship, and complained that you've been harassing her. I know you came here a few days ago, when I wasn't at home.'

'That's not true,' he said in a cautious voice.

He was taking such deep drags on his cigarette that he almost finished it in four or five puffs. His hands were unnaturally white, with long, delicate fingers, as if they were made of wax.

'And I know you've been to New York together,' I added, but he shook his head.

'I think there must be some kind of mistake,

94

because we've never been to New York together. To tell you the truth, I haven't been there since last summer. I've fallen out with my folks, and now I have to fend for myself. I've been in Europe for two months.'

He looked me in the eye when he said it. His voice had the same neutral tone, as if he were stating something that ought to have been obvious to anybody, the same as it is obvious that the earth isn't flat.

It suddenly struck me with absolute certainty that he was telling the truth and that Laura had been lying to me. I was gripped by a feeling of nausea and stubbed out my cigarette.

'I'd better get going,' he said, looking towards the kitchen.

'Yes, maybe you should,' I said, realising that I wasn't up to the humiliation of pumping him for information, although I was tempted to do so.

I walked him to the front door. On the threshold he paused and said, 'I'm really sorry. I think I've put my foot in it. I'm sure it's all just a misunderstanding that can be cleared up.'

I lied to him, saying I thought so too. We bid each other goodbye and I closed the door behind him.

I went straight back to the yard, where I chain-smoked a couple more cigarettes, without feeling the cold and without being able to think of anything except Laura's face when she'd told me all those lies. I don't know why, but I remembered one of the first evenings we'd spent as lovers, when we were both sitting on the couch and I ran my fingers through her hair, amazed at how soft it was. I was seething with anger now and thinking about how I might find out where that Sarah lived.

Then, all of a sudden, I told myself that Laura had gone in fact to Wieder's house, and that the story about her staying at that friend's place was just another lie.

She hadn't taken the keys to the professor's house with her, though. I'd found them on the sideboard and put them in my pocket before Timothy Sanders had rung the doorbell. I don't know why, but I was now firmly convinced that she was with Wieder, that if I went there I'd find them together. That everything, absolutely everything, had been one huge lie and that I'd been used for some aim I was unable to uncover, maybe just a victim of some perverse, hateful experiment she'd cooked up with her professor.

Perhaps they'd been laughing at me all the while, as they'd examined me like some pea-brained guinea pig. Maybe the business with the library had been another falsehood, a pretext to keep me there for some twisted reason. I suddenly saw the whole story in a different light. I must have been blind not to have realised that everything she'd ever told me had been lies, without even any great effort to make them sound real.

I went back inside and called for a cab. Then I set out for the professor's house in the snow, which began to fall heavier.

That was where the partial manuscript came to an end. I gathered the pages back together and placed them on the coffee table. The clock on the wall read 1.46 a.m. I'd been reading without a break for more than two hours.

What was Richard Flynn's book intending to be?

Was it a belated confession? Was I going to find out that he was the one who'd murdered Wieder, and that he'd managed to elude police suspicion, but that now he'd decided to confess? He'd mentioned in the online submission form sent alongside his query that the full manuscript had 78,000 words. Something important must have happened after the murder, too — the killing wasn't the end of the book, but rather its opening chapters

I'd lost track of the timeline of events to a certain extent, but it seemed that the fragment, whether deliberately or not, ended at the point when he set off for the professor's house, convinced that Laura had been lying to him, including about the real nature of their relationship, on the very night when the man had been murdered. Even if Flynn hadn't done it, he'd certainly gone to Wieder's house on the evening of the murder. Had he caught the two of them together? Had it been a crime of passion?

Or maybe he hadn't killed him, but he had

come to unravel the mystery so many years later, and this manuscript was intending to unmask the real culprit, whoever it might be. Laura Baines?

I told myself that there was no point in my getting carried away, given that I'd soon find out what it was all about from none other than the author himself. I finished my coffee and went to bed, determined to ask Flynn to send me the full manuscript. True crime books were popular, especially if they were well written and about unusual, mysterious cases. Wieder had been a celebrity at the time, he was still an important figure in the history of American psychology, as Google had informed me, and Flynn wrote in a fluid, gripping sort of way. So I was almost convinced that I was dealing with a good acquisition, for which a publisher would be willing to sign a substantial cheque.

Unfortunately, however, things didn't turn out as I'd wished.

★   ★   ★

I sent Richard Flynn an email on my way to work the very next morning, using my personal address. He didn't get back to me that day, but I presumed that he'd taken advantage of the extended MLK Day weekend to have a short holiday and wasn't checking his messages.

After two or three days with still no reply, I called the cell phone number he'd given me in his letter. I reached his voicemail, but found I was unable to leave him a message because it was already full.

Another couple of days passed with still no reply, and after a few more attempts to reach him on his phone — which by now was switched off — I decided to go to the address he gave in the letter, which was near Penn Station. It was an unusual situation — I mean chasing an author — but sometimes if the mountain won't come to you, you have to go to the mountain.

It was an apartment on the second floor of a building on East 33rd Street. I rang the intercom and eventually a woman's voice answered. I told her I was Peter Katz, looking for Richard Flynn. She curtly informed me that Mr Flynn wasn't available. I explained that I was a literary agent and briefly told her what I was there for.

She hesitated for a few moments, and then I heard the lock buzz open. I took the elevator to the second floor. She was already standing in the doorway of the apartment and introduced herself as Danna Olsen.

Ms Olsen was a woman in her forties, with the kind of face you usually forget shortly after first seeing it. She was wearing a blue housecoat and had ebony hair, most likely dyed, brushed back with a plastic headband.

I left my coat on the rack in the hall and went into the small but very tidy living room. I sat down on a couch upholstered in leather. The apartment looked as though it belonged to a single woman rather than a couple because of the colours of the carpets and curtains and the trifles spread all over the place.

After I told her my story once more, she took a deep breath and spoke quickly. 'Richard was admitted to All Saints Hospital five days ago. He was diagnosed with lung cancer last year, when he was already in the third stage of the disease, so they couldn't operate, but had to start chemotherapy. For a while he responded positively to treatment, but two weeks ago he contracted pneumonia and his condition worsened abruptly. The doctors don't hold out much hope for him.'

I uttered the meaningless platitudes one feels obliged to express in such situations. She told me she had no relatives in the city. She was from somewhere in Alabama and had met Richard a couple of years ago, at a marketing workshop. They'd written to each other for a while, gone on a trip to the Grand Canyon, and then he'd insisted that they move in together, so she'd come to New York. She confessed to me that she didn't like the city, and the job she'd found, at an advertising agency, was below her level of training. She'd accepted it only for Richard's sake. If she lost her partner, she was intending to move back home.

For a few minutes she cried softly, without sobbing, wiping her eyes and nose with paper tissues that she took from the box on the coffee table. After she calmed down, she insisted that she make me a cup of tea and asked me to tell her about the manuscript. She didn't seem to have been aware that her partner was writing a book about his past. She went into the kitchen, made some tea and brought it through on a tray, along with cups and a sugar bowl.

I told her what the partial I'd received by

email was about. I had a copy of his letter with me, which I showed her, and she read it carefully. She looked more and more surprised.

'Richard didn't tell me about it,' she said bitterly. 'He was probably waiting to hear back from you first.'

'I don't know whether I was the only one he wrote to,' I said. 'Have you been contacted by any other agent or publisher?'

'No. For the first day after he was admitted to hospital, I took Richard's calls on my cell phone, then I gave up. Eddie, his brother from Pennsylvania, and the guys from his company know about his condition, but they have my phone number. I don't have the password to his email account, so I haven't been able to read his messages.'

'So you don't know where the rest of the manuscript is?' I asked, and she confirmed that she didn't.

All the same, she offered to look on the laptop Richard had left behind. She took a small Lenovo from a drawer, which she plugged in and turned on.

'He probably set a lot of store by it, if he sent you that letter,' she remarked while she was waiting for the laptop to spit its icons onto the desktop. 'Obviously, even if I find the manuscript, you do understand that I'll have to talk to him first before I can give it to you?'

'Sure.'

'What would it mean in financial terms?' she asked, and I explained that an agent was only a middleman and that a publisher would make a decision regarding the offer's advance and royalties.

She put on a pair of glasses and started to search the computer. I realised I was about to miss another appointment, so I called the guy, excused myself and asked him for a rescheduling.

Ms Olsen informed me that the manuscript didn't seem to be on either the desktop or in the documents files: she'd checked every file, no matter what name it'd been saved under. There weren't any password-protected files. It was possible, she said, that the document was at his office or on a memory stick. There were a few sticks in the same drawer in which she'd found the laptop. She was about to visit Richard at the hospital, so she promised she would ask him where he kept the manuscript. She saved my number in her cell and would call as soon as she found out.

I finished my tea and thanked her once again. I was getting ready to leave when she said, 'Up until three months ago, Richard told me nothing about the whole business, about Laura Baines, I mean. But then one evening somebody called him on his cell and I heard him arguing. He'd gone into the kitchen, so that I wouldn't hear the conversation, but I was surprised by his tone of voice, because usually he never loses his temper. He was furious; I'd never seen him like that before. His hands were trembling when he came back into the living room. I asked him who he'd been talking with, and he told me that it was an old acquaintance from his time at Princeton, someone by the name of Laura — that she'd ruined his life, and that he was going to make her pay for it.'

★ ★ ★

Five days after my visit, Danna Olsen called me to say that Richard had died. She gave me the address of the funeral parlour, in the event that I wished to pay my last respects. When she'd arrived at the hospital, on the day of my visit, her partner was already unconscious because of the sedatives, and shortly thereafter he'd slipped into a coma, so she hadn't been able to ask him about the manuscript. She'd also checked the memory sticks and disks around the house, but hadn't been able to find anything containing the manuscript. The company he'd worked for was going to send his personal belongings from the office in the following days, so she'd also check them.

I went to the funeral, which was held on a Friday afternoon. The city was under deep snow, just like on that day in late December when Professor Joseph Wieder had met his end.

A handful of people in mourning were sitting on a row of chairs in front of the bier, on which the body of the late Richard Flynn lay in a closed coffin. A framed picture, with a black ribbon in the corner, had been placed next to it. It showed a man in his forties, smiling sadly into the camera. He had a long face with a prominent nose and gentle eyes, and his slightly wavy hair was receding at the forehead.

Ms Olsen thanked me for coming and told me that the picture had been Richard's favourite. She didn't know who'd taken it or when. He'd kept it in his bottom desk drawer, which he jokingly called 'the wolf's lair'. She also said to me that she was terribly sorry for not having been able to find the rest of the manuscript, which must have been very important to Richard, given that he'd been working on it during his last months. Then she signalled to a gloomy man, and introduced him to me as Eddie Flynn. He was accompanied by a small lively woman with a silly hat perched on her flame-red hair. She shook my hand, introducing herself as Susanna Flynn, Eddie's wife. We talked for a couple of minutes, just a few steps away from the coffin, and I got the strange feeling that we'd known each other for a while, and that I was meeting them that day after a long absence.

When I left, I thought that I'd never learn the outcome of that old story. Regardless of what Richard had intended to reveal, it seemed that, in the end, he'd taken his secret with him.

Part Two

John Keller

When we are young, we invent different futures for ourselves; when we are old, we invent different pasts for others.

Julian Barnes, *The Sense of an Ending*

1

I started talking to the dead because of a broken chair.

As Kurt Vonnegut, Jr, might have said, the year was 2007 and John Keller was finally broke. That's me — pleased to meet you. I'd taken a creative writing course at NYU and, to be honest, I was going round and round my own illusions like a moth drawn to the dangerous glare of a light bulb. I was sharing a railway attic space on the Lower East Side with an aspiring photographer, Neil Bowman, sending long and pointless query letters to literary magazines in the hope that one of the editors would finally offer me a job. But none of them seemed prepared to take any notice of my brilliance.

Uncle Frank — Mom's elder brother — had struck it rich in the mid-eighties by investing in the IT industry, which back then began to inject its steroids. He was in his early fifties and lived in a swanky apartment on the Upper East Side. In those days he didn't seem to have any business other than buying antiques and hanging out with pretty ladies. He was handsome, sunbed tanned and snappily dressed. He used to invite me to dinner at his house or a restaurant every now and then, giving me expensive gifts, which I'd then sell at half price to a guy called Max who was in cahoots with the owners of some dodgy shop on West 14th Street.

The antique furniture in his living room had been purchased in Italy many years ago. The chairs were made of carved wood and were upholstered in brown leather, and the touch of time gave them the look of wrinkled cheeks. The back of one unlucky chair had fallen off, or something of the sort — I can't really remember the details.

So my uncle called a famous restorer from the Bronx, who had a waiting list which was months long. When he heard that Frank would pay double the usual fee if he let him jump the line, he picked up his toolkit and drove straight to my uncle's apartment. By chance, I was there that day.

The restorer, a middle-aged guy with a shaved head, broad shoulders and inquisitive eyes, dressed in black like a hit man, examined the broken chair, grumbled something, then set up camp on the terrace. It was a beautiful day, the sun was shining, and the buildings of the East 70s were like giant blocks of quartz laved in the morning mist. While the restorer displayed his skills, I drank coffee with Uncle Frank, chatting about girls.

Frank noticed that the repairman had brought a magazine with him, which he'd left on a table. It was called *Ampersand* magazine, had forty-eight glossy pages, and on the third page, which listed the editorial staff, it revealed that the publisher was a company run by John L. Friedman.

My uncle told me that he'd been at Rutgers with Friedman. They'd been pals, but had lost touch with each other a couple of years previously. How about my uncle called him and asks him for a job interview? I knew that connections make the world go round, as well as money, but I was young enough to think that I could make my own way, so I turned him down. And besides, I said to him, as I circumspectly leafed through the magazine, the publication was about the occult, the paranormal and New Age stuff, none of which I had a clue about and in which I didn't have the slightest interest.

Frank asked me to stop being so stubborn. He trusted his old pal's financial skills — even when he'd been at college, he was able to wring money from dry stone — and a good reporter needed to be able to write about any subject. In the end, he concluded, it was more interesting to write about the Great Pyramid than about some ball game or humdrum murder, and in any case, readers were all morons nowadays.

The restorer joined in the conversation at one point, after we'd invited him to have some coffee with us. He told us in a hushed voice that he was convinced that vintage pieces of furniture conserved inside it the positive or negative energies of the people who'd owned it over the years, and that sometimes he was able to sense those energies when he touched an object: his fingers would tingle. I left after Frank grabbed a bottle of bourbon from the bar and the restorer started telling him about a sideboard that brought misfortune to its owners.

Two days after that, Frank called me on my cell phone to tell me that Friedman was expecting me at his offices the next day. All he needed was somebody who knew the alphabet — the editor-in-chief, a slightly deranged man, had filled the office with bizarre people who didn't really know how to write. The magazine had been launched a couple of months before, and it was still struggling to get off the ground.

But there's no point in my spinning out the story.

I didn't want to fall out with Uncle Frank, so I paid Friedman a visit. It turned out that I liked him, and the feeling was mutual. He couldn't give two hoots about paranormal stuff and didn't believe in ghosts, but there was a niche for that kind of magazine, especially among baby boomers.

He offered me a far bigger salary than I was expecting, so I accepted the offer there and then. My first published story was about the restorer, as I felt that I owed him in a way for my entry into the occult press. I worked for *Ampersand* for about two years, during which time I met half of all the city's freaks. I attended voodoo séances in Inwood, and visited haunted houses in East Harlem. I received letters from readers who seemed to be more cuckoo than Hannibal Lecter, and from priests who warned me I was heading for the fires of hell.

Then Friedman decided to shut the magazine and helped me to get a job as a reporter for the *New York Post*, where I worked for four years, until a friend persuaded me to join a new publication devised by some investors from Europe. Two years later, when online papers butchered most of what was left of the printed small dailies, and titles were dying out one after the other, I found myself out of a job. I started a blog, and then a news site, which earned me next to nothing, and I tried to make a living from all sorts of freelance work, nostalgically looking back at the good old days and amazed that in my early thirties I already felt like a dinosaur.

★   ★   ★

It was at that time that a friend of mine, Peter Katz, a literary agent for Bronson & Matters, told me about the Richard Flynn manuscript.

We'd met when I was studying at NYU and became friends. He was quite shy and reclusive — the kind of guy you might mistake for a rubber plant at a party — but very cultivated, and one could learn a whole lot from him. He'd skilfully avoided all the cunning traps his mom had laid for him in collusion with the families of marriageable girls, stubbornly remaining a bachelor. What's more, he'd chosen to become a literary agent, although he came from a long line of lawyers, and that made him a bit of a black sheep in his family.

Peter invited me out to lunch and we went to a place on East 32nd Street called Candice's. It'd been snowing heavily for days, even though it was already the beginning of March, and the traffic was hellish. The sky was the colour of molten lead, about to flow down on the city. Peter wore an overcoat that was so long he kept tripping on its hem, like one of the Seven Dwarfs from *Snow White*. He was carrying an old leather briefcase, which swung in his right hand as he dodged the puddles on the sidewalk.

Over our salads, he told me the story of the manuscript. Richard Flynn had died the month before, and his partner, a lady called Danna Olsen, claimed not to have found any trace of the book.

By the time our steaks arrived, Peter had laid out his challenge. He knew I had enough experience as a reporter to tie together the disparate pieces of information. He'd talked to his bosses and they thought that given the market, the subject had great sale potential. But a fragment of a million-dollar manuscript wasn't worth a penny on its own.

'I'm ready to talk to Ms Olsen and come to an agreement,' he told me, goggling at me with those near-sighted eyes of his. 'She seems to be a practical woman, and I'm sure that the negotiations will be difficult, but I don't think she'd turn down a good offer. Flynn left her all his properties and belongings in his will, apart from a few items that he gave to his brother, Eddie. From a legal point of view, an agreement with Ms Olsen would cover us, do you understand?'

'And just how do you imagine I'm going to be able to track down the manuscript?' I asked. 'Do you think I'm going to discover some secret map on the back of a napkin? Or am I going to fly to a Pacific island and dig beneath the twin palm trees growing to the north-west?'

'Come on, don't be like that,' he said. 'Flynn

112

has already provided lots of clues in the excerpt. We know the characters who were involved, the setting and the time frame. If you don't find the manuscript, you can reconstruct the rest of the puzzle, and the fragment will be incorporated into a new book, which you or a ghostwriter will turn out. In the end, readers are interested in the story of Wieder's murder, and not necessarily in some unknown guy by the name of Richard Flynn. It's all about reconstructing what happened in the course of Wieder's last few days, do you understand?'

That verbal habit of his — the constant repetition of 'do you understand?' — gave me the unpleasant feeling that he doubted my intelligence.

'I do understand,' I assured him. 'But the whole thing might be a waste of time. Flynn probably knew what he wanted to tell the public when he set about writing the book, but we haven't got a clue what we're looking for. We'll be trying to solve a murder that happened over twenty years ago!'

'Laura Baines, another main character, is probably still alive. You can find her. And the case is still on the police files, of that I'm sure. It's a cold case, as the cops say, but I'm sure they've got the file in their archives.'

Then he gave me a mysterious wink and lowered his voice, as if he were afraid somebody might overhear us.

'It seems that Professor Wieder was conducting secret psychological experiments. Just imagine what you could uncover here!'

He delivered that last sentence in the tone of voice of a mom promising an obstinate kid a trip to Disneyland if he does his math exercises.

I was intrigued, but still undecided.

'Pete, has it ever occurred to you that this guy, Flynn, might have just been making it all up? I don't want to speak ill of the dead, but maybe he invented a story about the death of somebody famous so he could sell his project before he passed away. Except that he didn't have time to finish it.'

'Well, I've thought of that possibility. But how can we be sure unless we carry out an investigation? From what I've been able to gather up to now, Richard Flynn wasn't a pathological liar. He really did know and work for Wieder, he did have the keys to his house, and he was treated for a while as a suspect, all of which I found out from the Internet. But I need someone as good as you to uncover the rest of the story.'

I was almost convinced, but I let him sweat a bit. For dessert I ordered an espresso, while he had some tiramisu.

I finished my coffee and put him out of his misery. I told him that I'd accept the assignment, signed a contract with a non-disclosure clause, which he'd brought with him, and then he produced a stack of papers from his briefcase. Handing them to me, he told me it was a copy of the first chunk of Richard Flynn's manuscript, plus the notes he'd written in the meantime and which would provide a starting point for my investigation. Together with my copy of the contract, I thrust the papers into my bag, which I've always carried with me ever since my days as a reporter and which was equipped with all kinds of compartments and pockets.

I walked him to the subway, went home, and spent the whole evening reading Richard Flynn's manuscript.

2

The next evening I met with my girlfriend, Sam, for dinner. She was five years older than me, had majored in English at UCLA and had moved to New York after working at a number of TV stations on the West Coast. She was a producer for the NY1 morning news, so her day began at 5 a.m. and usually ended at 8 p.m., which is when she crashed out, regardless of whether I was around or not. We could rarely talk for more than five minutes without her informing me that she had to take an important call, stuffing the hands-free headset in her ear.

She'd been married for three years to a guy called Jim Salvo, a news anchor for a small TV station in California, the kind of skirt-chaser who, once he hits his forties, is left with nothing but bad habits and a liver drowning in fatty tissue. That's why she told me from the very start that she had no intention of remarrying before forty and that, until then, all she wanted was no strings attached.

Between phone calls, chiding the waitress for not taking our order sooner, and telling me about some argument she'd had with her editors, Sam listened to my story about Richard Flynn's manuscript and seemed excited about it.

'John, this could make a splash,' she said. 'It's like something out of Truman Capote, isn't it? Readers just eat up that kind of stuff.'

It was the best verdict Sam could pronounce on any given topic. To her, anything that didn't stand a chance of making 'a splash' was pointless, whether it be TV news, a book proposal or having sex.

'Yeah, it could, if only I can find the manuscript or some kind of explanation for the murder.'

'If not, then you'll write a book based on the partial you have. Wasn't that what you agreed with Peter?'

'Yes, right, but I'm not really an expert in that kind of thing.'

'Times change and people have to change with them,' she said sententiously. 'Do you think that television today looks anything like it used to fifteen years ago, when I first set foot in a news studio? We all end up having to do things we've never done before. To be honest, I'd like it if you *don't* find that manuscript, so that in a year or so I'd see your name on the cover of a book in the window at Rizzoli.'

After we left the restaurant I went to my lair and got down to work. My parents had moved to Florida two years previously, and my older sister, Kathy, had married a guy from Springfield, Illinois, and moved there after she'd graduated from college. I lived in Hell's Kitchen, or Clinton, as real-estate agents call it nowadays, in the three-bed apartment where I was raised. It was an old building, the rooms were small and dark, but it was mine and at least I didn't have to worry about rent.

I made a start by reading the partial again,

underlining the bits that seemed important in different coloured highlighters: blue for Richard Flynn, green for Joseph Wieder and yellow for Laura Baines. I underlined Derek Simmons's name in blue pen, because near the end Richard claimed that he'd played an important role in the whole affair. I made a separate list of all the other names that were mentioned in the manuscript, which, with a bit of luck, might be turned into sources of information. As a reporter I'd learned that most people love to talk about their past, even if they tend to beautify it.

I mapped out three main directions for my investigation.

The first and simplest was to trawl through the deep lake of the Internet to see what I could bring to the surface about the murder and the persons involved.

The second was to track down the people mentioned in the manuscript, especially Laura Baines, and to persuade them to tell me what they knew about the case. Peter mentioned in his notes that Richard Flynn's partner had told him that shortly before he died, he'd had a tense phone conversation with a woman by the name of Laura, who he claimed had 'destroyed his life' and that 'he was going to make her pay for it'. Was this the 'Laura' from the manuscript?

And the third was to go down to the police archives in West Windsor, Mercer County, and try to look up the statements, reports and interrogation notes collected by the detectives back then. Wieder was a high-profile victim, and the inquiry had probably been carried out by the book, even if it hadn't come up with anything. My status as a freelance reporter wasn't going to help me, but if I got stuck, my intention was to ask Sam to call in the cavalry, hinting at the mighty shadow of NY1.

And so I began with Richard Flynn.

All the information I already had on him matched what I found online. He'd worked for Wolfson & Associates, a small advertising agency, and on the company's site I located a short bio that confirmed some of the details in the manuscript. He'd majored in English at Princeton, graduating in 1988, and taken an MA at Cornell two years later. After a couple of junior positions, he'd moved up into middle management. On other sites I discovered that Flynn had given money to the Democratic National Committee three times, been a member of a sport shooting club, and back in 2007 had declared himself deeply dissatisfied with the services provided by a hotel in Chicago.

After Santa Google finished giving his presents about Flynn, I switched to searching for Laura Baines and was surprised to find nothing at all . . . or almost nothing. There were a number of people with the same name, but none of the ones I could find information on matched the woman I was looking for. I found her listed among the math graduates of the University of Chicago in 1985 and the psychology master's students at Princeton in 1988. But after that there wasn't any clue about what she did or where she lived. It was as if she'd vanished into thin air. I thought to myself that she probably got married and changed her surname, so I had to find another way of tracking her down, assuming she was still alive.

As I'd expected, the richest source of information was on Professor Joseph Wieder. There was a detailed page on Wikipedia, and his biography held a place of honour among all the leading figures who had taught at Princeton over the years. I discovered that on Google Scholar there were more than twenty thousand references to his books and papers. Some of the books were still in print and could be purchased from online bookstores.

Amongst the stuff I'd read, here's what I found out: Joseph Wieder was born in Berlin in 1931, into a middle-class Jewish-German family. In a number of interviews he revealed that his father, a doctor, had been beaten by storm troopers in the spring of 1934, in front of his pregnant mother, dying soon after.

A year later, after the birth of his sister, all three had moved to the States, where they had relatives. At first they'd lived in Boston, and then in New York City. His mother had remarried, to an architect by the name of Harry Schoenberg, who was fourteen years older than her. He'd adopted her children, but they'd kept their biological father's name, as a sign of respect for his memory.

Unfortunately, Joseph and his sister, Inge, had become orphans just ten years later, after the Second World War, with Harry and Miriam Schoenberg perishing during a trip to Cuba. Harry had been a sailing enthusiast, and the yacht they were on, together with another couple from New York, had been lost in a storm. Their bodies were never found.

Having come into a large fortune, the two orphans had gone to live at their uncle's house upstate and embarked on very different lives. Joseph had been studious, attending first Cornell, then Cambridge and the Sorbonne. Inge had become a model, achieving some degree of fame in the late fifties, before marrying a rich Italian businessman and moving to Rome, where she'd settled permanently.

Over the course of his career, Joseph Wieder had published eleven books, one of which had strongly autobiographical content. It was called *Remembering the Future: Ten Essays about a Journey to Myself* and it'd been published by Princeton University Press in 1984.

I also found a load of reports about the murder.

Wieder's body had been discovered by Derek Simmons, mentioned in the story as the handyman who worked at the victim's house and a potential suspect. At 6.44 a.m., 22 December 1987, he called 911 from the professor's house, telling the operator that he'd found him lying in a pool of blood in the living room. The paramedics who arrived at the scene could do nothing, and an assistant medical examiner quickly made the formal pronouncement that the professor was dead.

The coroner discovered at the autopsy that Wieder had died at around 2 a.m., and concluded that the cause of death was the internal and external blood loss resulting from blows with a blunt object, probably a baseball bat, administered by a single perpetrator around midnight. The first blow, forensics presumed, had come when the victim was sitting on the couch in the living room, and the killer had sneaked up behind him, having come in from the front door. The professor, who was in good physical shape, had managed to get up off the couch and tried to flee towards the window overlooking the lake, meanwhile fending off the blows, which had fractured both his forearms. Then he'd turned back in the middle of the room to defend himself, and during the struggle with the attacker, the TV set had fallen off its stand onto the floor. It was there that he'd received the fatal blow in the area of his left temple. (From this the investigators concluded that the murderer was most likely right-handed.) Wieder died two hours later, as a result of cardiac arrest and the severe cerebral injury caused by the final blow.

Derek declared that the front door had been locked when he'd reached the professor's house the next morning, and that the windows had also been locked, with no sign of forced entry. Under those circumstances, it had been supposed that the murderer had keys to the house, which he'd used to get inside, taking Wieder by surprise, and then locking the door behind him after he'd committed the killing. Before leaving, he'd rummaged around the living room. The motive couldn't have been robbery, however. The professor had been wearing a Rolex on his left wrist, and a precious gemstone on the ring finger of his right hand. In an unlocked drawer the police had found around a hundred dollars in cash. None of the valuable antiques in the house had been stolen.

In the living room the detectives had discovered two recently used glasses, suggesting that the victim had had a drink with one other person that evening. The medical examiner had found that the professor had consumed a significant quantity of alcohol before the murder — the alcohol content level in his blood was 0.11 — but there were no traces of narcotics or medication in his body. Joseph Wieder hadn't been involved in any known relationship with a woman. He hadn't had a partner or a mistress, he hadn't been dating anybody, and none of his friends or colleagues had been able to remember him being in a relationship recently. It was therefore unlikely to have been a crime of passion, the detectives had concluded.

★　★　★

Using the reports run by the press, I reconstructed roughly what happened in the period following the murder.

Laura Baines's name wasn't mentioned, not even once, in the newspapers, although Richard Flynn's appeared several times. As I knew from the partial, Flynn had been treated as a suspect for a while, after Derek Simmons had been eliminated from the inquiry, given that he had 'a strong alibi'. There was nothing about Wieder being involved in some clandestine psychological experiments. But it was emphasised continuously that Wieder had been a well-known figure with the New Jersey and New York police forces, as he'd acted as an expert witness in many assessments of the mental health of people accused of felonies.

As for his status as an expert witness in criminal trials, the detectives had treated it as a potential lead from the very beginning. They'd reviewed the cases in which Wieder had testified, particularly those that had had an unfavourable outcome for the accused. But that had quickly proved to be a dead end. None of those convicted due to Wieder's testimony had been released during that time, with the exception of a man called Gerard Panko, who'd been discharged from Bayside State Prison three months before the murder. But almost immediately after his release, Panko had suffered a heart attack. He'd left hospital just one week before the professor was murdered, so as doctors had concluded, he wouldn't have been capable of carrying out the attack by any physical effort — the hypothesis had been discarded.

Richard Flynn had been interviewed repeatedly, but never officially declared a suspect or charged. He'd hired an attorney called George Hawkins, who'd accused the cops of harassment and suggested they were trying to turn Flynn into a scapegoat, covering up their own incompetence.

What was Flynn's version of events? What exactly had he declared to the detectives and reporters? From the articles I found, it seemed that what he'd said at the time was different to what he wrote in his manuscript.

Firstly, he hadn't said anything about Laura Baines introducing him to Wieder. He'd merely said that he'd been introduced to the professor through 'a mutual acquaintance', because Wieder had been looking for somebody suitable to do part-time library work. Flynn had worked at the Firestone Library on campus, and Wieder had needed somebody capable of organising his library using a computer system. Wieder had given him a set of keys in case he wanted to work there when the professor wasn't at home, as he frequently travelled out of town. Flynn had used the keys a couple of times, entering the professor's house when he was away. On two or three occasions, the professor had invited him to stay for dinner, always for two. One Friday, he'd played poker with the professor and two of his colleagues. (That episode didn't appear in the manuscript.) He'd met Derek Simmons and had been told Derek's story by Wieder himself.

He hadn't had any kind of conflict with the professor, and the relationship between them might be described as 'warm and friendly'. The professor had never told him that he felt threatened by anyone or anything. As a rule, Wieder had been easy-going and liked a joke. He'd been happy to talk about his new book, which had been due to be published the following year, and which he'd thought was going to be a big success, both academically and commercially.

Unfortunately for him, Flynn hadn't had an alibi for the night of the murder. At the end of the manuscript, he wrote that he'd set off to the professor's house about twenty minutes or so after the visit from Timothy Sanders, which would mean around 6 p.m. I mapped it out and it'd have taken him another twenty minutes to get there, perhaps longer, because of the weather, and about as long to come back. But he'd told the investigators that he'd gone to Wieder's at around 9 p.m., as he'd wanted to talk to the professor about something to do with the library before he went on Christmas break. He'd also said that he'd got back home at 10 p.m., after having a chat with the professor, and that he'd gone to bed shortly after that. Had he lied during the investigation or was he lying when he'd written the manuscript? Or was it his memory deceiving him?

In those years, as Flynn himself confirmed in his manuscript, the crime rate had been quite high in New Jersey, especially after the sudden influx of meth and crack into the suburbs. A couple of days after Wieder's death, between Christmas and New Year, just two streets away from his house, there had been a double homicide. An elderly couple, Mr and Mrs Easton, aged seventy-eight and seventy-two respectively, had been killed in their home. The detectives had found that the perpetrator had broken in at 3 a.m., murdered the couple and then burgled the house. The murder weapons had been a carving knife and a hammer. Given that the murderer had taken the cash and jewels he'd found in the house, robbery had definitely been the motive and in actual fact there had turned out not to be many similarities with the Wieder case.

This hadn't stopped the cops. They'd taken advantage of the fact that a suspect had been arrested just one week later, as he was trying to sell the jewels stolen from the elderly couple's house to a pawnshop in Princeton. So Martin Luther Kennet, aged twenty-three, an African American with a record and a known drug user, had become the official prime suspect in the inquiry into the murder of Joseph Wieder.

From then on — this was in early January 1988 — Richard Flynn was mentioned only in passing in the press articles about the murder. Wieder's sister, Inge Rossi, had inherited his entire estate, apart from a small sum of money that the deceased had left to Simmons in his will. 'HAUNTED HOUSE UP FOR SALE' was the title of a story published on 20 April 1988 in the *Princeton Gazette* that referred to the house of the late Professor Wieder. The reporter claimed that the property had a sinister reputation after the tragedy, and that a couple of people in the neighbourhood were ready to swear that they'd seen strange lights and shadows moving inside, so the estate agents were probably going to have a hard job selling it.

Martin Luther Kennet had turned down the deal proposed by the Mercer County Prosecutor's Office — he'd have been spared a death sentence if he'd been found guilty — and claimed he was innocent to the very end.

He'd admitted that he was a small-time drug dealer in the university campus area and on Nassau Street, and that one of his occasional customers, whose name he didn't know, had left him the jewels stolen from the Eastons as a guarantee in exchange for a quantity of pot. He hadn't had an alibi for the night of the couple's murder because he'd been at home alone, watching some video tapes he'd rented the day before. When the man who'd left him the jewels hadn't come back to reclaim them, he (not knowing they were stolen) had taken them to the pawn shop. If he'd known where they'd come from, why would he have been so dumb as to try to sell them in broad daylight, at a shop famous for ratting to the cops? As for Wieder, he'd never even heard of him. If he remembered correctly, on the evening of the professor's murder he'd been at an arcade, leaving early the next morning.

But he'd had a public defender appointed by the court, with an appropriate name for a brave fighter against injustice — Hank Pelican. Everybody had wanted to get it over with as quickly as possible and save tax dollars, so after just a couple of weeks the jury had said 'guilty' and the judge had added 'life'. The death penalty had still existed in the State of New Jersey at the time — it was to be abolished in 2007 — but the reporters said that the judge had taken into account Kennet's age when he'd decided not to hand down the death sentence that the prosecutor had been demanding. I said to myself that the evidence presented by the prosecution to Judge Ralph M. Jackson, an old gunslinger with a lot of experience, probably hadn't convinced him at all. Unfortunately, the evidence had been quite sufficient for the jurors.

In any case, the prosecutors had decided not to accuse Kennet of Wieder's murder. They hadn't come up with any other leads. Other stories made the news, so the dust had slowly settled. The West Windsor murder remained a cold case.

★ ★ ★

I watched the 11 p.m. news on NY1, a habit from my days as a reporter, then I made myself a cup of coffee and drank it by the window, trying to connect the information from Flynn's manuscript with what I'd found out on the Net.

The relationship between Professor Wieder and his protégée Laura Baines, which had maybe been more than just a professional one, should have been well known among the professors in the Department of Psychology, so I asked myself why she hadn't been interviewed by the police. She could have had another set of keys cut at any time, even if the ones the professor had given to her had been with Richard Flynn that evening. But nobody seemed to have brought her name to the attention of the cops and press: neither Flynn, nor the professor's colleagues, nor her own colleagues, nor Derek Simmons, who'd also been questioned a couple of times. It was as if the relationship between the two had had to be kept from public knowledge at all costs.

The professor had been a strong guy, who'd worked out and boxed in his youth. He'd survived the first blow and even tried to struggle with his attacker even after his forearms had been fractured. If a woman had been involved, she'd have had to be exceptionally strong to stand up to a counter-attack from such a man, especially one who was fighting for his life. What's more, the very brutality of the killing seemed to point to the murderer being a man. It was unlikely that Laura Baines — who Flynn described as quite slender and not in good shape at the time — could have been guilty. And the most important thing: what would be her motive? Why would Laura Baines have wanted to kill the man who'd helped her and on whom her career had most likely still depended?

Nevertheless, Flynn had told his partner that Laura had 'ruined his life' and that he was 'going to make her pay for it'. Had he suspected her of murder, or had he merely been reproaching her for having dumped him and for leaving him alone to face the music? But his actions didn't seem very logical to me. If Laura was guilty of leaving him in the lurch, why hadn't he taken his revenge during the investigation, when he'd been a suspect and hadn't even had an alibi? Why hadn't he exposed her to the press or tried to shift at least some of the blame in her direction? Why had he protected her then, only to change his mind nearly three decades later? Why had he thought Laura had destroyed his life? He'd escaped from the prosecutor's clutches in the end. Had something else happened after that?

I fell asleep, still thinking about everything, almost certain that beneath the surface the case concealed something much darker and more mysterious than Flynn revealed in the partial manuscript or the police had discovered at the time. I was grateful to Peter for entrusting me with the investigation.

And there was one other detail that was vaguely drawing my attention — a date, a name, something that didn't fit at all. But I was exhausted and falling asleep, and I couldn't quite place it. It was like when you glimpse something from the corner of your eye for a fraction of a second, and afterwards you're not sure whether you really saw it or not.

3

The next morning I drew up a list of people I had to locate and, if possible, persuade to talk to me. Laura Baines was at the top, but I had no idea how to track her down. At the same time, I started to look through my old address books, trying to find a contact or some connection in the West Windsor Township Police Department, which hadn't moved since the time of the incident in the late eighties.

A good few years back, during an enquiry I was carrying out for the *Post*, I'd met a guy called Harry Miller. He was a private detective from Brooklyn who specialised in missing persons investigations. Short and overweight, dressed in a rumpled suit, wearing a necktie so skinny that you could barely see it and a cigarette behind his ear, he was like a character straight out of a forties noir movie. He lived out in Flatbush and he was always looking for solvent customers, given that he was constantly broke. He was a gambler, regularly betting money on the horses, and mostly losing it. I called him on his cell phone and he answered from a noisy bodega, where the clients had to raise their voices to be heard over an old beat.

'Hi, Harry, what it do?' I asked.

'Keller? Long time no see. Well, another day on the Planet of the Apes,' he replied in a surly voice. 'I'm trying to pretend I'm not human, so I

132

won't wind up in a cage. Do the same. Now tell me what's popping, son.'

I filled him in on what the case was broadly about, asked him to jot down two names — Derek Simmons and Sarah Harper — and told him what I knew about the pair. As he was taking notes, I heard the clatter of a plate being set down on his table and he said thanks to someone called Grace.

'Who are you working for now?' he asked suspiciously.

'For a literary agency,' I said.

'Since when have literary agencies gotten involved in this kind of investigation? There must be quite a bit of cash in it, eh?'

'Sure there is, don't worry on that score. I can wire you some dough right now. I've got other names, but I want you to start with these two.'

He seemed relieved.

'I'll see what I can do. Derek seems easy, but all you've given me on the woman, Sarah Harper, is that she got a master's in psychology from Princeton, probably in 1988. Not a lot to go on, dude. I'll call you in a couple of days,' he assured me and hung up after giving me his PayPal details.

I opened my laptop and wired him some cash, and sat back thinking about Laura Baines again.

Six or seven months ago, before Flynn had begun working on his manuscript, something *must* have happened to push him in that direction, something out of the ordinary and significant enough to change his whole view of the events that had taken place in 1987, just as he'd hinted in the query letter to Peter. When she'd met Peter, Danna Olsen had been disturbed enough by his illness to have overlooked some details that might prove highly important to my investigation. I decided that it'd be best to start by having a chat with her and I called her at the number I'd got from Peter. There was no answer, so I left a message on her voicemail, explaining who I was and saying that I'd call back. I didn't get a chance to, because she called me just a couple of minutes later.

I introduced myself and found out that Peter had already talked to her on the phone about me, telling her that I was gathering information about Joseph Wieder's death for a true crime book.

She was still in New York but was planning on leaving in a week or two. She'd decided not to sell the apartment, so she'd contacted an estate agent to rent it out. However, she'd asked the agents to put it on the market only after she'd left — she wouldn't have been able to bear the thought of people poking their noses around the apartment while she was there. She'd donated some stuff to charity and started boxing up the things she meant to take with her. A cousin from Alabama, who had a pick-up truck, was going to come and help her move. She told me all these things as if she were talking to a pal, though her voice was monotonous and robotic, and she took long pauses between words.

I invited her out to lunch, but she told me she'd rather meet me at home, so I set off towards Penn Station on foot and twenty minutes later I rang the intercom at her building.

The apartment looked upside down, like any house on the eve of a move. The hall was full of cardboard boxes sealed with duct tape. The contents of each was inscribed in black marker pen, so I was able to see that most of them were full of books.

She invited me into the living room and made some tea. We drank it while we made small talk. She told me how shocked she'd been when, during Hurricane Sandy, a young woman had picked a fight with her while she'd been waiting in line at a gas station. Back home in Alabama, she'd been told about old floods and hurricanes, but they were epic tales, about neighbours who'd risked their lives to save people, heroic cops and firemen who'd saved folks in wheelchairs in the midst of the cataclysm. In a big city, she said to me, you wondered which you had to fear the most in such cases, the fury of nature or the reaction of other people.

She had a nicely arranged hairdo and healthy skin, set off by the plain black dress she was wearing. I wondered how old she was — she looked younger than her late partner's forty-eight years. She had a small-town air, in a pleasant way. Her words and gestures suggested an upbringing from a time when people used to ask each other how they were in the morning and genuinely mean it.

From the very start she asked me to call her Danna and I did so.

'Danna, you knew Mr Flynn much better than I do from having read the fragment of his manuscript. Did he ever talk to you about Professor Wieder or Laura Baines, or about his time at Princeton when they met?'

'Richard was never a very open person. He was always reclusive and gloomy, usually distant with people, so he had few social acquaintances and not one close friend. He saw his brother very rarely. He lost his pa when he was at college, and his ma died by cancer in the late nineties. In the five years we were together nobody ever visited us and we never paid anyone any visits. His relationships at work were strictly professional, and he wasn't in touch with the people he'd been at college with.'

She paused and poured more tea.

'Once he received an invitation to an event at the Princeton Club on West 43rd Street. It was a kind of reunion and the organisers had found his address. I tried to persuade him that we should go together, but he refused. He curtly told me that he didn't have any pleasant memories of his time at college. He was telling the truth. I know, I've read the fragment of the manuscript — Peter gave me a copy. Though maybe it was that after the episode with that woman, Laura Baines, he reset all his memories, which is what usually happens, and his view of that time became a dark one. He didn't have any kind of mementoes, photos or other knick-knacks to remind him of that time. Nothing but a copy of the magazine he mentions in the manuscript, *Signature*, where he'd published some short stories, which an old acquaintance had given him as a present when he came across it by chance in a bookstore. I've put it in one of the boxes already, but if you like I can dig it out. I don't have any pretensions to being an expert in literature, but his stories struck me as exceptional.

'In any case, I understand why people usually kept their distance from Richard. Probably most of them saw him as a misanthrope and maybe he was to a certain extent. But when you genuinely came to know him, you realised that underneath the stony surface he'd built up over the years, he was a very good man. He was cultivated and you could discuss almost anything with him. He was fundamentally honest and prepared to help anybody who'd have asked him. That's why I fell in love with him and moved here. I didn't agree to be with him because I was lonely or because I wanted to get away from a small town in Alabama, but because I was genuinely in love with him.

'I'm sorry I can't be of more help,' she concluded. 'I've told you a lot about Richard, but it's Professor Wieder you're interested in, isn't it?'

'You said you've read the excerpt . . . '

'Yes, I've read it. I tried to find the rest of the manuscript, especially since I've been curious as to what happened next. Unfortunately I wasn't able to find it. The only explanation is that Richard eventually changed his mind and erased it from his computer.'

'Do you think the woman who called him that evening was Laura Baines? The woman he told you afterwards had 'ruined his life'?'

137

For a while she didn't answer my question. She was lost in her thoughts, as if she'd forgotten I was there. Her eyes travelled around the room, as though she were looking for something, then without another word she got up and went into the next room, leaving the door open. She came back after a couple of minutes and sat down in the armchair she'd just left.

'Perhaps I might be able to help you,' she said in a rather official-sounding voice, which she hadn't used up until then. 'But I want you to promise me something: that in what you'll write, when you write it, you won't do any damage to Richard's memory, regardless of the results of your research. I understand you're interested in Wieder, so Richard's character isn't necessarily relevant to you. You can omit certain things that concern him and him alone. Do you promise?'

I'm not saint material and sometimes, as a reporter, I'd lied a whole sack of crap trying to grab a piece of information necessary for a story. But I said to myself that she deserved me to be honest with her.

'Danna, as a journalist, it's almost impossible for me to promise you something like that. If I find out anything important about Wieder's life and career that was directly connected to Richard, then there's no way I can omit it. But don't forget that he wrote about the events, so he wished to make them public. You say he changed his mind and pressed the delete button. I don't think so. I guess that it's more likely that he hid the manuscript somewhere. He was a practical kind of person. I don't think he'd have toiled

138

over a manuscript for weeks and weeks, during which time he must have thought about every aspect implied by his intention, only then to erase it just like that. I'm almost positive that the manuscript still exists somewhere, and that Richard wanted to see it published right up to his very last moment.'

'Maybe you're right, but all the same, he didn't say anything to me about this project. Could you at least keep me up to date about what you find out? I don't like to nag and in any case I'll be leaving the city, but we can talk over the phone.'

I promised I'd contact her if I discovered anything significant about Flynn, and she took a crumpled piece of paper out of a notebook, which she smoothed and laid on the table between our mugs, pointing at it.

I took it from the table and saw that on it were written a name and a cell phone number.

'On the evening when Richard got the call I told you about, I waited until he was asleep and then I checked out his cell phone's call log. I wrote down the number that matched the time of the call. I was ashamed of acting jealous, but I was very worried when I saw what a state he was in.

'The next day I called the number, and a woman answered. I told her I was Richard Flynn's partner and that I had something important to pass on to her from him, something that oughtn't to be discussed over the phone. She hesitated but then accepted my proposal, and we met not far from here, in a restaurant, where we had lunch.

She introduced herself as Laura Westlake. I apologised for having approached her and told her that I was worried about Richard after I saw his behaviour after their conversation that evening.

'She told me not to worry: Richard and she were old acquaintances from Princeton and they'd had an unimportant disagreement about some past event. She told me that they'd shared a house for a few months, but that they'd been nothing more than friends. I didn't have the courage to tell her what Richard had said about her after their talk, but I claimed that he'd told me they'd been lovers. Her response to that was that Richard probably had an overactive imagination, or maybe his memory was playing tricks on him, and she emphasised yet again that their relationship was entirely platonic.'

'Did she tell you where she worked?'

'She teaches psychology at Columbia. We left the restaurant, went our separate ways, and that was all. If Richard talked to her again after that, he did so without my finding out. The phone number might still be valid.'

I thanked her and left, promising again to keep her up to date on Richard's part in all this.

* * *

I had lunch at a cafe in Tribeca, hooking up my laptop to its wireless. This time, Google was much more generous.

Laura Westlake was a professor at the Columbia University Medical Center and ran a joint research programme with Cornell. She'd taken a master's at Princeton in 1988, and a PhD at Columbia four years later. In the mid-nineties, she'd taught in Zurich, before returning to Columbia. Her bio contained lots of technical details about specialist training and research programmes she'd run over the years, as well as a major prize she won in 2006. In other words, she'd become a big shot in psychology.

I tried my luck and called her office as soon as I left the cafe. An assistant named Brandi answered and told me that Dr Westlake wasn't available at the moment, but wrote down my name and number. I asked her to tell Dr Westlake I was calling in connection with Mr Richard Flynn.

★ ★ ★

I spent the evening in my lair with Sam, making love and telling her about the investigation. Later she was in a nostalgic sort of mood; she wanted more attention than usual, and she had the patience to listen to everything I had to say. She even set her cell to silent, which was very rare, and thrust it into her handbag, which was lying on the floor by the bed.

'Maybe Richard's whole story is just a charade,' she said. 'What if he took a real occurrence and fictionalised the events around it, like Tarantino did in *Inglourious Basterds*, remember?'

'Possible, but a reporter deals in facts,' I said. 'For the time being I'm going on the assumption that everything he wrote is true.'

'Let's get real,' she said. 'The 'facts' are what editors and producers choose to put in the newspapers, on the radio or on the TV. Without us, nobody would have cared that people are slaughtering each other in Syria, that a senator has a mistress or that there was a murder in Arkansas. They wouldn't have a clue that any of those things were happening. People have never been interested in *reality*, but in *stories*, John. Maybe Flynn wanted to write a *story*, and that's all.'

'Well, there's only one way to find out, isn't there?'

'Exactly.'

She rolled on top of me.

'You know, a colleague told me today that she'd just found out she's pregnant. She was so happy! I went to the restroom and cried for ten minutes, I just couldn't stop. I pictured myself old and alone, wasting my life on things that in twenty years won't be worth anything, while I lose sight of the really important stuff.'

She laid her head on my chest and I lightly stroked her hair. I realised that she was sobbing softly. Her change in attitude had taken me by surprise and I didn't know how to react.

'Maybe now you ought to tell me that I'm not alone and that you love me, at least a little bit,' she said. 'That's what would have happened in a chick-lit book.'

'Sure. You're not alone and I love you a bit, hon.'

She lifted her head off my chest and looked me in the eye. I could feel her warm exhalation on my chin.

'John Keller, you're lying your head off. In the

old days they'd have hanged you by the nearest tree for that.'

'Hard times back then, ma'am.'

'All right, I've pulled myself back together, I'm sorry. You know, you seem really caught up in this story.'

'Another reason they'd have hanged me, isn't it? Didn't you say it's a good story?'

'Yes, I did, but you risk winding up in some boarded-up old house on Nobody Street in a couple of months, without being able to make head or tail of anything. Did you think of that?'

'It's just a temporary job, which I'm doing because a friend asked me to. I might not find anything spectacular, nothing to make a splash, as you like to say. A man fell in love with a woman, but for various reasons it turned out badly and he probably lived with a broken heart for the rest of his life. Another man was murdered and I don't even know whether the two stories are all that connected. But as a reporter I learned to listen to my guts and follow my instincts and any time I didn't, I screwed it. Perhaps this story is like one of those Russian dolls, each of them hiding a different one inside. Well, a bit absurd, isn't it?'

'Every good story is *a bit* absurd. At your age, you ought to know that by now.'

We lay there holding each other for a long time, not making love, not even talking, each wrapped up in his and her own thoughts, until the apartment grew completely dark and the noise of the evening traffic seemed to be coming from another planet.

Laura Baines called me the next morning, while I was in the car. She had a pleasant, slightly husky voice, which you could fall in love with even before laying eyes on its owner. I knew she was over fifty, but her voice sounded much younger. She told me that she'd received my message, and asked me who I was and what was my connection with Richard Flynn. She knew he'd died recently.

I introduced myself and told her that the subject I wanted to present was too private to discuss over the phone and suggested we meet.

'I'm sorry, Mr Keller, but I'm not in the habit of meeting strangers,' she said. 'I've no idea who you are or what you want. If you want us to meet, then you'll have to provide me with more detail.'

I decided to tell her the truth.

'Dr Westlake, before he died, Mr Flynn wrote a book about his time at Princeton and the events of the fall and winter of 1987. I think you know what I'm talking about. You and Professor Joseph Wieder are the main characters in his story. At the request of the publisher of the book, I'm investigating the veracity of what's claimed in the manuscript.'

'Am I to understand that a publisher has already bought the manuscript?'

'Not yet, but a literary agency has taken it on, but — '

'And you, Mr Keller, are you a private detective or something of the kind?'

144

'No, I'm a reporter.'

'What newspaper do you write for?'

'I've been a freelancer for two years, but before that I worked for the *Post*.'

'And you think that mentioning the name of that tabloid is a good recommendation?'

She had a perfectly calm and measured tone, almost devoid of inflection. The Midwest accent Flynn talked about in his manuscript had completely vanished. I pictured her in the lecture hall, talking to students, wearing the same thick-rimmed spectacles she wore in her youth, her blonde hair tightly tied in a bun, pedantic and confident. It was an attractive image.

I paused, not being sure what to say next, so she went on, 'Did Richard use real names in the book or did you merely deduce that it refers to Joseph Wieder and myself?'

'He's used real names. Of course, he refers to you by your maiden name, Laura Baines.'

'It gives me a strange feeling hearing that name, Mr Keller. I haven't heard it for very many years. This literary agent, the one who hired you, is he aware that a lawsuit could halt the publication of Richard's manuscript if its contents cause me any material or moral damage?'

'Why do you think that Mr Flynn's manuscript might damage you, Dr Westlake?'

'Don't try to be smart with me, Mr Keller. The only reason I'm talking to you is because I'm curious to find out what Richard wrote in his book. I recall that he dreamed of being a writer in those days. All right, then, I propose a trade

145

— you give me a copy of the manuscript and I agree to meet you and talk to you for a couple of minutes.'

If I did what she asked, I'd be in breach of the non-disclosure clause of the contract signed with the agency. If I refused, I was certain she'd hang up on me. I chose the option that seemed to me the least damaging in that moment.

'I agree,' I said. 'But you should know that the agency only provided me with an excerpt of Richard's manuscript in hard copy, the first few chapters. The story begins at the time when you first met him. There are about seventy pages or so.'

She considered this for a few moments.

'Very well,' she said finally. 'I'm at the Columbia Medical Center. What do you say we meet here in an hour, at ten thirty? Could you bring the pages with you?'

'Sure, I'll be there.'

'Go to the McKeen Pavilion and ask for me at reception. Goodbye now, Mr Keller.'

'Goodbye and — '

She hung up before I could thank her.

I quickly set off back home, cursing Peter in my mind for not having given me the manuscript in electronic form. I picked up the excerpt from home and went looking for a copy shop, eventually finding one three blocks away.

While a sleepy guy with a silver ring in his left nostril and forearms full of tattoos was copying the pages on an old Xerox, I wondered how I should approach her. She seemed cold and pragmatic and I reminded myself not to forget

146

for a single moment that her job was to rake around in people's minds, just as she'd warned Richard about Professor Wieder all those years ago.

4

The Columbia University Medical Center was in Washington Heights, so I skirted the park to 12th Avenue and turned onto NY-9A, then I followed 168th Street. Half an hour later, I arrived in front of a couple of tall buildings linked by glass walkways.

The McKeen Pavilion was on the ninth floor of the Milstein Hospital Building. I gave my name at reception, said Dr Westlake was expecting me, and the secretary called her on the interior line.

Laura Baines came down a few minutes later. She was tall and good-looking. She didn't have her hair tied up in a tight bun, as I'd pictured her, but had a rather simple hairdo, with her wavy locks falling to her shoulders. She was attractive, there was no doubt about it, but she wasn't likely to be the kind of woman you'd turn your head to look at in the street. She wasn't wearing glasses and I wondered whether she'd switched to contact lenses in the intervening years.

I was the only person in reception, so she came straight up to me and extended her hand.

'I'm Laura Westlake,' she said. 'Mr Keller?'

'Pleased to meet you, and thanks for agreeing to see me.'

'Would you like some coffee or tea? There's a cafeteria on the second floor. Shall we?'

We went down seven floors in the elevator,

then through a couple of corridors, before reaching a cafeteria, one of whose walls was made of glass, giving a great view of the Hudson River. Laura had a determined gait, she walked straight-backed, and all the way there she seemed lost in thought. We didn't exchange a single word. From what I could tell, she didn't use make-up, but she was wearing a discreet perfume. Her face was smooth, with hardly a wrinkle and slightly tanned, with well-defined features. I bought myself a cappuccino, and she opted for a tea. The place was almost empty, and the art nouveau-style interior alleviated the feeling of being in a hospital.

Before I could open my mouth, she spoke again.

'The manuscript, Mr Keller,' she said, peeling back the foil on a capsule of milk and emptying its contents into her cup of tea, 'as you promised.'

I took the pages from my bag and handed them to her. She leafed through them for a few seconds, and then carefully placed them on the table to her right, after inserting them back in the folder. I took out a small voice recorder and switched it on, but she shook her head disapprovingly.

'Switch it off, Mr Keller. I'm not giving an interview. I agreed only to talk to you for a few minutes, and that is all.'

'Off the record?'

'Absolutely.'

I switched off the recorder and put it back in my bag.

'Dr Westlake, may I ask you when and how did you meet Richard Flynn?'

'Well, it happened so long ago . . . As far as I can remember, it was in the fall of 1987. We were both students at Princeton and we shared a small two-bed house for a while, out by the Battle Monument. I moved from there before the Christmas, so we lived together for just three months or so.'

'Did you introduce him to Professor Wieder?'

'Yes. I told him that I knew Dr Wieder well, so he insisted on my introducing them, as the professor was a very famous public figure at the time. In a discussion with Richard, Dr Wieder mentioned his library. He wanted an electronic record of it, if I remember rightly. Flynn needed the money, so he offered to do the job, and the professor accepted. Unfortunately, afterwards I understand he had a lot of problems and was even considered a suspect in the case. The professor was brutally murdered. You do know that, don't you?'

'Yes, I know, and actually that's why the agency I'm working for is so interested in this case. Were you and Flynn anything more than room-mates at any time? I don't want my question to sound out of line, but Richard states very clearly in his book that you had a sexual relationship and that you were in love with each other.'

A wrinkle appeared between her eyebrows.

'I find it slightly ridiculous to talk about such things, Mr Keller, but yes, I remember that Richard was in love with me, or rather obsessed with me. But we were never involved in a love affair. I had a boyfriend at the time — '

'Timothy Sanders?'

She seemed surprised.

'Timothy Sanders, that's right. Do you know the name from the manuscript? It means Richard must have had a fantastic memory or maybe he had notes or a diary from that time. I would not have thought that he could remember such details after so many years, but in a way, I'm not surprised. Anyway, I was in love with my boyfriend, we lived together, but then he had to go away to Europe for a couple of months as part of a research programme, and the rent on our apartment was too high for me to pay by myself, so I found another place. During the time Timothy was away, I shared a house with Richard. When he returned, we moved back in together, just before Christmas.'

'You never use the shorter forms of people's names, not even when you're talking about people who are close to you,' I remarked, remembering what Flynn said in the manuscript.

'That's right. I think that diminutives are childish.'

'Richard says in the manuscript that he was somewhat jealous of Professor Wieder and that for a while he suspected that you were having an affair with him.'

She gave a start and the corners of her mouth drooped slightly. For an instant, I got the feeling that I could see her mask starting to crack, but then her poker face rapidly resumed.

'It was one of Richard's obsessions, Mr

Keller,' she said. 'Professor Wieder wasn't married, he didn't have a partner, so some people supposed he must be having an affair and that he was keeping it secret. He was a very charismatic man, although not very handsome, and he had a very protective attitude towards me. I think that ultimately he wasn't very interested in romantic relationships, being completely dedicated to his job. To be frank, I know that Richard had his suspicions, but there was nothing of that nature between Joseph Wieder and myself, apart from a normal student — professor relationship. I was one of his favourite students, that much was clear, but that was all. I also helped him significantly with the project he was working on at the time.'

I asked myself how far I could go without risking her ending our conversation, then plowed ahead.

'Richard also says that the professor gave you a spare set of keys to his house and that you often went there.'

She shook her head. 'I don't think he ever gave me the keys to his house, not that I remember. But I think that Richard was given a set, so that he could work in the library when the professor wasn't at home. That's why he had problems with the police.'

'Do you think Richard could have been capable of murdering Wieder? He was a suspect for a while.'

'I chose for myself a field in which one learns, among other things, how deceptive appearances can be, Mr Keller. Richard harassed me continually after I moved out of that house. He waited for me after my classes, wrote me dozens of letters, phoned me dozens of times a day. After the professor's death, Timothy spoke to him a couple of times, asking him to mind his own business and to leave us alone, but to no effect. I didn't file a complaint about him with the police, because he had troubles enough as it was, and in the end I pitied him more than I feared him. In time things got worse . . . But anyway, one shouldn't speak ill of the dead. No, I don't think he'd have been capable of murder.'

'You've just said that in time things got worse. What did you mean by that? I know from the manuscript that he was jealous. Jealousy is a common motive in such cases, isn't it?'

'Mr Keller, he didn't have any reason to be jealous. All we did was share a house together, as I said. But he was quite simply obsessed with me. The following year, I came to Columbia University, but he found out my address and went on writing to me and phoning me. Once he even turned up here in the city. Then I went to Europe for a while and was able to get away from him that way.'

I was very surprised at what I was hearing.

'In the manuscript, Richard Flynn said something entirely different. He claimed that it was Timothy Sanders who was obsessed with you and kept harassing you.'

'I'm going to read the manuscript, that's why I asked you for it. Mr Keller, for a person like Richard Flynn, the boundaries between fiction and reality don't exist, or else they're very

153

slender. In that period there were times when I genuinely suffered because of him.'

'On the evening when the professor was murdered, did you go to his house?'

'I visited the professor at home for a total of just three or four times in the course of that whole year. Princeton is a small town, and we'd both have had problems if gossip about us had had an opportunity to arise. So no, I wasn't there that evening.'

'Were you interviewed by the police after the murder? I didn't see your name in the newspapers, but Flynn's was all over the place.'

'Yes, I was questioned only once, I think, and I told them that I'd been with a friend of mine the whole evening.'

She looked at the watch on her left wrist.

'Unfortunately I have to go now. It was nice talking to you. Perhaps we can talk again after I read the manuscript and I refresh my memory.'

'Why did you change your surname? Did you marry?' I asked as we stood up from the table.

'No, I've never had time for anything like that. To be honest, I changed my name so that I could get away from Richard Flynn and all those recollections. I cared a lot about Professor Wieder and was devastated at what happened to him. Flynn had never been violent, just a pest, but I was sick and tired of being harassed by him and it seemed as if he'd never stop. In 1992, before I went to Europe, I became Laura Westlake. It's my mother's maiden name, actually.'

I thanked her, and then she picked up the

154

copy of the manuscript and we left the cafeteria, just as it was starting to get busy.

We reached the elevator, got inside, and headed towards the 9th floor. I asked her. 'Flynn's partner, Danna Olsen, told me that one evening she caught him speaking to you on the phone. She contacted you about it and you met with her. Can I ask you what it was you talked about on the phone to him? Had he managed to find you again?'

'I hadn't heard from Richard for over twenty years when, last fall, he suddenly turned up at the door of my apartment. I'm not one to lose control very easily, but I was really shocked, especially when he began babbling a lot of nonsense, and it became clear that he was very agitated, which made me wonder whether he might be mentally ill. He threatened me with some revelations, the nature of which weren't very clear, but seemed to have something to do with Professor Wieder. To be honest, I'd managed to almost forget that I'd once known a young man by the name of Richard Flynn. In the end I asked him to leave. He phoned me two or three times after that, but I refused to meet him, and then I stopped answering the phone. I didn't know he was seriously ill — he didn't mention anything about it to me. Then I found out that he'd died. Perhaps when he'd come to my apartment he was disturbed because of his illness and incapable of reasoning. Lung cancer often has complications, with metastases in the brain. I don't know whether this is what happened in Richard's case, but it's highly likely.'

We got outside, and I asked her, 'Richard also claimed in his manuscript that Professor Wieder was conducting secret research. Do you have any idea what it was about?'

'If it was secret, then it means we weren't supposed to know anything about it, doesn't it? The more you tell me about this manuscript, the more I'm convinced that it's a work of pure fiction. Many departments of every major university do conduct research projects, some of them for federal agencies, some of them for private companies. Most such projects are confidential, because the people paying for them want to reap the results of their investment, don't they? Professor Wieder was working on something of the kind, I guess. I merely helped him with the book he was writing at the time and I was never au fait with whatever else he might have been doing. Goodbye, Mr Keller, I really have to go now. Have a pleasant day.'

I thanked her once again for meeting me and I took the elevator to the ground floor.

As I was walking to the parking lot, I wondered how much of what she said was the truth and how much was lies, and whether it was true that Flynn had been fantasising about their supposed relationship. Behind her apparent calm, she'd given me the impression that she was afraid of what Flynn might have been capable of revealing about her past. It was a feeling rather than anything to do with her body language or facial expressions: like a distinct smell that she couldn't conceal beneath her perfume.

Her answers had been precise — perhaps too

precise — even if she'd repeated a couple of times that she couldn't remember all the details. And how could she have almost forgotten, even after so many years, a guy she'd shared an apartment with, who'd been harassing her for months and had been accused of killing her mentor and friend?

5

Harry Miller called me a couple of hours later, just after I'd met with one of my old sources, a retired homicide detective who'd promised me he'd try to get in touch with somebody from the West Windsor Township Police Department in Jersey. I'd invited him to lunch at Orso on West 46th Street, and I was walking back to my car, parked two blocks away. It was raining and the sky had the colour of cabbage soup. I answered the phone and Harry told me he had some news. I took shelter under the awning of a bodega and asked him what's good.

'Bingo,' he told me. 'Sarah Harper graduated in '89 and she hasn't been very lucky. After college she got a job at a school for kids with special needs in Queens and led an ordinary life for about ten years. Then she had the bad idea to marry a jazz singer called Gerry Lowndes, who made her life a living hell. She got into drugs and ended up doing a year in jail. In 2008 she got divorced and now she lives in the Bronx, in Castle Hill. She seems ready to talk about the old days.'

'Awesome. Can you text me her address and phone number? What did you find out about Simmons?'

'Derek Simmons still lives in Jersey, with a lady called Leonora Phillis. I talked to her, in fact, as the guy wasn't at home. She's looking after him in a way; they live mostly on benefits. I explained that you're a reporter who wants to talk to her man about the Professor Wieder case. She doesn't know what all that is about, but she's expecting a call from you. Make sure you have some cash when you go there. Anything else?'

'Have you got any sources at Princeton?'

'I've got sources all over the place — I'm a true maven, son,' he boasted. 'How do you think I tracked down Sarah Harper? By calling 911?'

'In that case, try to get hold of the names of some people from the eighties for me, people who worked at the Department of Psychology and were close to Professor Joseph Wieder. And not just colleagues. I'm interested in people who were in his group, anyone who knew him well.'

He told me he'd try to find out what I asked, then we talked about baseball for a couple more minutes.

I picked up my car from the garage and went home. I called Sam and when she answered her voice sounded as if she was at the bottom of a well. She told me she had a stinking cold and that after she'd dragged herself to the office that morning, her boss had sent her straight back home. I promised I'd drop by that evening, but she said she'd rather go to bed early, and in any case, she didn't want me to see her like that. After we hung up, I called a florist and ordered a bunch of tulips to be delivered to her. I was trying not to get carried away, as we'd agreed, but as time went by I discovered that I missed her more and more when we didn't see each other for a day or two.

I called Sarah Harper at the number Harry had sent me, but she didn't pick up, so I left her a voicemail. I had more luck with Derek Simmons. His partner, Leonora Phillis, answered the phone. She had a strong Cajun accent, like a character out of *Swamp People*. I reminded her that she'd spoken with a guy named Harry Miller, about my wanting to have a talk with Derek Simmons.

'From what your buddy said, I take it the newspaper will be payin', right?'

'Right, there may be some money in it.'

'Okay, Mr . . . '

'Keller. John Keller.'

'Well, I'd say ya should pay us a visit, and I'll make sure to tell Der-eh' what it's all about. He doesn't much like talkin'. When ya comin' over?'

'Right now, if it's not too late.'

'What time's it now, sweetie?'

It told her it was 3.12 p.m.

'How about five?'

I said that would be fine and made sure once again that she would persuade 'Der-eh' to speak to me.

★ ★ ★

A bit later, as I was entering the tunnel, thinking about my talk with Laura Westlake, I suddenly remembered the detail that had eluded me on that first evening after I'd begun to research the Wieder case — the book the professor had been working on at the time and which was going to

160

be published a few months later. As Richard said in his manuscript, Laura Baines believed that it'd rock the world of science. A 'bomb-shell', as Sam would have said.

But when I'd tried to look it up on Amazon and on other sites that listed the professor's works, there was no mention of it. The last book Wieder had published was a 110-page study on artificial intelligence released by the Princeton University Press in 1986, over a year before he was murdered. Wieder had told Richard that he'd signed a publishing contract for the book he was working on, stirring rumours among his colleagues. So Wieder had already sent the manuscript or a proposal to the publisher before his death, and had maybe received at least part of an advance. Why then was the book never published?

There were two possible explanations, I figured.

The first would be that the publisher had changed their mind and decided not to publish the manuscript. That was unlikely, given that there was a contract, and the mystery surrounding the professor's violent death would probably have boosted sales, cynically speaking. Only some kind of forceful intervention would have made a publisher abandon a project like that. An intervention made by whom? And what did that manuscript contain? Was it linked in any way to the secret research Wieder had been working on? Had he been intending to reveal details about it in his new book?

Another possibility was that the executor of

Wieder's will — from the newspapers I gathered that there had been a will and that he had left everything to his sister, Inge — had opposed publication of the book and had been able to muster the necessary legal arguments. I knew that I ought to try to speak to his sister, although she'd settled in Italy many years previously and probably didn't know very much about what had happened at the time of the murder.

I turned onto Valley Road, made a left down Witherspoon Street, and soon I reached Rockdale Lane, where Derek Simmons and his partner lived, not far from the Princeton police station. I'd arrived earlier than I'd expected. I parked next to a school and went into a nearby cafe, where, over a cup of coffee, I tried to put the new leads that had cropped up in my investigation in order. The more I thought about the professor's book, the more intrigued I was by the fact that it'd never been published.

★ ★ ★

Derek Simmons and Leonora Phillis lived in a small bungalow at the very end of the street, next to a ball field overrun with weeds. There was a small yard in front of the house, with rose bushes that were just beginning to bud. A grimy garden gnome showed me his plaster grin to the left of the front door.

I pressed the bell and heard it ringing somewhere at the back of the house.

A short, brown-haired woman with a wrinkled face opened the door, a ladle in her right hand, mistrust in her eyes. When I told her I was John Keller, her figure brightened a little and she invited me inside.

I entered a dark, narrow hallway, then a living room crammed with old furniture. I sat down on the couch, and the stuffing raised a visible cloud of dust under the weight of my body. I could hear a baby crying in another room.

She asked me to excuse her for a moment and vanished, making soothing sounds somewhere in the back of the house.

I looked at the objects around me. They were all old and mismatched, as if they'd been bought at random from a garage sale or found lying on the street. The floorboards were warped here and there, and corners of the wallpaper were peeling. An old carriage clock was ticking asthmatically on a wall. It seemed that the small sum of cash mentioned in the professor's will was long gone.

She came back holding in her arms a kid who looked to be around one and a half, and who was sucking on his left thumb. The child spotted me immediately and looked fixedly at me with thoughtful, serious eyes. He had strangely mature features and I wouldn't have been surprised if he'd started speaking to me in the voice of a grown-up, belligerently asking me what the heck I was doing there.

Leonora Phillis sat down opposite me, on a wretched bamboo chair. She rocked the kid gently in her arms and told me he was her grandson, Tom. The boy's mom, Ms Phillis's daughter, named Tricia, had gone off to Rhode Island to meet some guy she'd met online, asking her to look after the boy until she got back — that had been two months ago.

She informed me that she'd persuaded Derek to speak to me, but it'd be preferable if we talked about money before that. She lamented that she and Derek were having a hard time making ends meet. Three years ago they'd managed to obtain a small benefit and that was the bulk of their income, apart from the odd jobs that Derek did from time to time. Plus they had to take care of her grandson. The woman wept softly as she told me this, and all the while Tom kept casting me those strange grown-up glances.

We agreed on an amount and I handed over the bills, which she carefully counted before putting them in her pocket. She stood up, sat the child on the chair and asked me to follow her.

We went down a passage and came to a kind of patio, the grimy panes of which filtered the light of the sunset like stained-glass windows. The patio's surface was almost entirely taken up by a huge workbench, on which were lined up all kinds of tools. In front of the workbench was a stool, where a tall, well-built man was sitting, dressed in greasy jeans and a sweatshirt. He stood up when he saw me, shook my hand and introduced himself as Derek. His eyes were green, almost glittering in the wan light, and his hands were large and corny. Although he must have been in his sixties, he stood very straight and seemed to be healthy. His face was furrowed with wrinkles so deep that they looked like scars, and his hair was almost white.

His partner went back inside the house,

leaving us alone. He sat down on the stool and I leaned against the workbench. In the backyard, which was just as small as the front one and enclosed with a weed-infested fence, there was a small swing, its rusty metal frame looming like a ghost from the bald earth covered with scraps of grass and puddles.

'She told me you wanna talk about Joseph Wieder,' he said without looking at me. He took a pack of Camels from his pocket and lit one with a yellow plastic lighter. 'You're the first person to ask me about him in over twenty years.'

He seemed resigned to playing a role, like an old clown, weary and drained of all good tricks and jokes, forced to caper over the sawdust of a poor circus ring to entertain a bunch of indifferent kids chewing gum and vamping on their cell phones.

I told him briefly about what I'd uncovered about him and Professor Wieder, about Laura Baines and Richard Flynn. While I spoke, he smoked his cigarette and stared into empty space, making me wonder whether he was even listening to me. He stubbed out his cigarette, lit another, and said, 'And why are you interested in all that stuff that happened so long ago?'

'Somebody asked me to look into it, and he's paying me to do what I'm doing. I'm working on a book about mysterious murder cases, whose perpetrators have never been caught.'

'I know who killed the professor,' he said in a toneless voice, as if we were talking about the weather. 'I knew it and I told 'em back then. But my statement wasn't worth a damn. Any

165

attorney would have had it thrown out of court, because a few years before I'd been accused of murder and locked up in the nuthouse, so I was a cuckoo, na'mean? I was taking all kinds of pills. They'd have said I was just making it up or that I'd been hallucinating. But I know what I saw and I wasn't crazy.'

He seemed deeply convinced of what he said. 'So you know who killed Wieder?'

'Told 'em everything, sir. And after that I didn't have any idea that anybody would be interested in that story. Nobody asked me anything else, so I minded my own business.'

'Who killed him, Mr Simmons?'

'Call me Derek. It was that boy, Richard. And that bad kitty, Laura, was an eyewitness, if not an accomplice. Now let me tell you what happened . . . '

★   ★   ★

Over the next hour, chain-smoking cigarettes while darkness fell slowly outside, he told me what he'd seen and heard on the evening of 21 December 1987, providing me with all kinds of details that I was surprised he could remember so well.

He'd gone to the professor's house that morning to repair the toilet in the downstairs bathroom. Wieder had been at home, packing his luggage for a trip to the Midwest, where he planned to spend the holidays with some friends. He'd invited Derek to stay for lunch and ordered in some Chinese food. He'd looked tired and

166

worried, confessing to Derek that he'd discovered some suspect footprints in the backyard — it'd been snowing during the night and in the morning the prints were clearly visible. He'd promised that he'd continue to take care of Derek, even if he intended to leave the country for a while, and had told him that it was important for him to keep taking his medication. At around 2 p.m., Derek had left the professor's house and headed to the campus area, where he was going to paint an apartment.

That evening, after nightfall, Derek had gone back home and had dinner. Worried about the state in which he'd left Wieder, he'd decided to check on him. Upon arriving at the professor's house, he'd seen Laura Baines's car, which was parked nearby. He'd been about to ring the doorbell when he heard the voices of people having an argument inside.

He'd gone around the back of the house, by the lake. It'd been about 9 p.m. The lights in the living room had been lit and the curtains were open, so he'd been able to see what was going on. Joseph Wieder, Laura Baines and Richard Flynn were there. The professor and Laura had sat at the table, while Richard had been standing over them and gesticulating as he spoke. He'd been shouting the loudest, reproaching the other two.

A few minutes later, Laura had stood up and left. Neither of the men had tried to stop her. Richard and Wieder had continued to argue after her departure. Eventually, Richard had seemed to calm down. They'd both smoked, drunk

167

coffee and a couple of glasses of booze, and the atmosphere had seemed more relaxed. Derek had been frozen outside and he had been just about to leave when the argument had erupted once more. It'd been just after 10 p.m., as far as he could remember.

At one point Wieder, who up until then had kept his calm, had become very angry and raised his voice.

Then Richard had left and Derek had quickly gone back around the house to catch him and ask him what was up. Although it took him no longer than twenty or thirty seconds to reach the front of the house, Richard had been nowhere to be seen. Derek had looked for him on the street for a couple of minutes, but it'd been as if the earth had swallowed him up.

In the end he'd given up and told himself that Richard had probably broken into a run after he came out. He'd returned to the back of the house to check if the professor was all right. He'd still been in the living room and when he'd got up to open the window and let some air in, Derek had left, afraid that he might be seen there. But as he'd been leaving, he'd noticed that Laura had returned, because her car was parked in more or less the same spot. Derek had thought that she'd come back so that she and the professor could spend the night together, so it'd be better if he got out of there.

The next morning he'd woken up very early and decided to go back to the professor's to double-check if he was all right. He'd rung the doorbell, but nobody had answered, so he'd used his set of keys and found the professor's body in the living room.

'I'm certain the kid didn't leave that night, but hid somewhere nearby, then he went back and killed him,' Derek said. 'But Laura would also have been in the house at the time. The professor was a strong guy, and she wouldn't have been able to put him down by herself. I've always thought that Richard was the one who killed him, and she was either an accomplice or a witness. But I didn't say anything to the police about her; I was afraid that the papers would have taken advantage and tarnished the professor's name. But I had to say something, so I told them that the kid was there and he had an argument with the professor.'

'Do you think that Laura and the professor were lovers?'

He shrugged. 'Don't know for sure, hadn't seen them screwing, but she sometimes stayed overnight, na'mean? The kid was mad about her, I'm sure of that, because he told me. I talked to him quite a lot at the time, when he was working in the library. Told me lots of things about himself.'

'And the cops didn't believe you?'

'Maybe they believed me, maybe they didn't. As I said, my words wouldn't have been worth a damn in front of a jury. The prosecutor didn't buy it, so the cops dropped the lead. If you check it out, you'll see that the statement I gave at the time was exactly the same as what I've just told you. I'm sure they kept those papers.'

'But you remember a lot of details,' I said. 'I

169

thought that you lost your memory.'

'My condition has affected the *past*. It's called *retrograde* amnesia. After that shitty experience in the hospital, I couldn't remember anything that had happened up until then, but my memory has always been fine when it comes to what happened *after* my head injury. I had to relearn my own past, the way you learn things about a different person — when and where he was born, who his parents are, what school he went to, and all that stuff. It was really weird, but I got used to it. In the end, you have no choice.'

He stood up and turned on the light. Sitting there on the patio, I got the feeling that we were like two flies trapped in a jar. I wondered if I should believe him or not. 'There's something else I'd like to ask you.'

'Please go ahead.'

'The professor had a gym in his basement. Did he keep a baseball bat there or anywhere else in the house? Did you ever see anything like that lying around?'

'No. I know he had a couple of weights and a punch bag, though.'

'The cops said that he was probably killed with a baseball bat, but the murder weapon was never found. If the professor didn't have a bat in the house, it means that the killer must have brought it with him. But it's not easy to hide something like that under your coat. Do you remember what Flynn wore that night, when you saw him through the window?'

He pondered for a few moments and then shook his head.

170

'Not sure . . . I know he almost always was wearing a parka, and maybe that was what he wore that night, but I wouldn't go out on a limb.'

'One last question. I know that you were a suspect in the beginning, but then they eliminated you from the inquiry because you had an alibi for the time of the murder. But you're saying that around eleven p.m. you were still in Wieder's backyard and then you went home. From what I know, you were living alone at the time. Can you tell me what your alibi was?'

'Sure. I stopped at a bar near home, which was open till late. I was worried and didn't want to be alone. I probably got there at a few minutes after eleven. The owner was a pal of mine; I used to help him out with small repairs. So the guy told the cops I'd been there, which was true. The police bugged me for a while after that, but then they left me alone, all the more so as I was the last person who'd have wanted anything to happen to the professor. What motive could I have had for killing him?'

'You say you were in that bar. Were you allowed to drink booze at the time, if you were taking all those pills?'

'I didn't drink booze. I still never touch the stuff. When I go to a bar, I have a Coke or a cup of coffee. I went there so I wouldn't have to spend my time alone.'

He stubbed out his cigarette in the ashtray.

'Are you left-handed, Derek? You smoke using your left hand.'

'Yes.'

I talked to him for another few minutes. He

171

told me that his life had taken its course, and finally he'd moved in with Leonora. He hadn't had any more problems with the law, and for the last twelve years he'd no longer been required to present himself to the psychiatric evaluation commission annually.

We said goodbye to each other and he remained in his makeshift workshop. I found my own way back to the living room, where Leonora was on the couch, watching TV with the child asleep in her arms. I thanked her once again, bid her good night and left.

6

Laura Baines called two days later, while I was waiting in line at the bureau on West 56th Street to renew my driver's licence — I needed to update my photo, too — and leafing through a magazine that somebody had left on the chair beside me.

'Mr Keller, I've read the manuscript you gave me and it bears out my suspicion. Richard Flynn made it all up, or almost all of it. Perhaps he was trying to write a novel. Back in the day, writers used to claim that the story they were telling wasn't a figment of their imagination, but that they had unearthed an anonymous manuscript or that the narrator was a real person who'd since passed away, or something of that sort, it helped generate publicity. Or maybe after all these years he'd come to believe that those things really happened. Did you get the rest of the manuscript?'

'Not yet.'

'Flynn never managed to finish it, did he? He probably realised how pathetic it was, and that it might also have unpleasant legal repercussions, so he abandoned it.'

Her voice was calm and kind of triumphant, which pissed me off. If what Derek had told me was true, she'd lied to my face without blinking.

'With all due respect, Dr Westlake, the fact that Professor Wieder was beaten to death with a baseball bat wasn't a figment of Mr Flynn's imagination, and nor is the fact that you decided to change your name after that. Okay, I don't have the full manuscript yet, but I have a lot of other sources, so let me ask you something: you did meet Wieder the night he was murdered, didn't you? Then Flynn turned up. You'd lied to him that you'd be spending the night with a friend and he kicked up a fuss. I know all that for sure, so please don't bother to lie to me again. What happened after that?'

She said nothing for a few moments, and I pictured her as a fighter sprawled on the ring's floor, the referee giving her the count. Probably she'd never expected that I'd be able to discover such details about that evening. The professor had died, so had Flynn, and I was almost certain that she never knew that Derek Simmons had been there within the space of those few hours. I wondered whether she'd deny it or pull another rabbit out of her magician's hat.

'You're a very mean person, aren't you?' she finally said. 'Do you really know where you want to go with this whole story, or are you just playing detective? How do you expect me to remember such details after all these years? Do you intend to blackmail me?'

'Would I have anything on you to blackmail you with?'

'I know a lot of people in this city, Keller.'

'You make it sound like some threat from an old detective movie. Now I'm supposed to say, 'Just doin' my job, ma'am,' give you a sad smile, pull my fedora down over my eyes and lift up the collar of my trench coat.'

'What? You're talking nonsense. Have you been drinking?'

'Are you denying that you were there on the evening of the crime, and that Richard Flynn covered for you by lying to the cops?'

Another long pause, and then she asked me, 'Are you recording our conversation, Keller?'

'No. I don't.'

'Maybe you lost your mind, just like Flynn. Your health insurance, if you have any, should cover a couple of therapy sessions, so maybe now is the time for you to take advantage of that. I didn't kill the man, so who cares where I was on that one evening, after more than twenty years?'

'I do, Dr Westlake.'

'All right then, go ahead and do whatever you like. But don't try to contact me ever again, I mean it. I've tried to be polite and told you everything I have to say, but I don't have any more time for you. If you call me or approach me again, I'll file a complaint for harassment. Goodbye.'

She hung up and I put the cell phone back into my pocket. I felt angry with myself because I'd lost an extremely important source of information for my story — I was sure she'd hold to her threat and would never talk to me again after that conversation. Why did I overreact like that and why was it necessary to put all my cards on the table over a stupid discussion on the phone? Derek Simmons had given me a pair of aces and I'd wasted it.

They called me for the photo a couple of

minutes later, and the guy behind the camera said, 'Try to relax a bit, man. Don't get me wrong, but you look like you're carrying the burdens of the whole world on your shoulders.'

'Well, just a couple of them,' I told him. 'And I haven't even been paid for this yet.'

★ ★ ★

Over the next three weeks, while spring was slowly landing over the city, I talked to a number of people who'd been close to Joseph Wieder and whose contact details Harry Miller had uncovered one by one.

Sam's flu had developed into pneumonia, so she languished in bed most of the time. Her younger sister, Louise, who was studying fine arts, had come from California to take care of her. I insisted on visiting her, but she told me each time to have patience, because she didn't want to be seen like that, with watering eyes and a big red nose.

Peter was out of town most of the time or caught up on business, so I only talked to him over the phone, to keep him up to date about the investigation. He told me that Danna Olsen hadn't yet found any trace of the other chapters of Flynn's manuscript.

I called Laura Baines's ex-schoolmate, Sarah Harper, a few times, but she didn't pick up the phone or answer my voice messages. Nor did I manage to contact the professor's sister, Inge Rossi. I found out her address and phone number, so I called and talked with a housekeeper who could barely string two words of English together. I understood eventually that Signor and Signora Rossi were away for two months, on a long trip in South America.

Harry tracked down Timothy Sanders, but it wasn't good news — Laura Baines's ex-boyfriend had passed away in December 1998, in Washington DC. He'd been gunned down in front of his house and had died on the spot. The police had never managed to find the perpetrator, but they'd concluded that it'd been an armed robbery turned into a killing. He'd taught social sciences at the School Without Walls and had never been married.

My conversation on the phone with Eddie Flynn was short and unpleasant. He was very angry with his late brother's decision to bequeath his apartment to Ms Olsen and told me that he knew nothing about a college professor called Joseph Wieder. He asked me to never contact him again and hung up.

I talked to a couple of Wieder's former colleagues, after making up a story about my being a researcher for a publisher that was doing a biography on Wieder and trying to find out as many details as I could from the people who knew him well.

I met a retired professor from the same department at Princeton, a seventy-three-year-old man by the name of Dan T. Lindbeck. He lived in Essex County, New Jersey, in an imposing mansion in the middle of a small forest. He told me that the house was haunted by the ghost of a woman called Mary, who'd died in 1863, during the Civil War. I remembered the days when I wrote for *Ampersand* and told him about the case of a haunted house I'd visited, while he carefully recorded the details in an old-fashioned spiral notebook.

Lindbeck described Joseph Wieder as an atypical person, a man highly aware of his own importance and totally devoted to his work, a dazzling intellectual, but difficult and distant when it came to personal relationships.

He vaguely remembered that Wieder had been about to publish a book, but he couldn't remember which publisher had bought the manuscript. He pointed out that it was hard to believe that there could have been a conflict between Wieder and the board of trustees on the subject of the publisher, given that the professors were free to publish their works wherever they wished and that any bestselling book by one of them would benefit the institution. He didn't recall any special research programme that the department might have been working on during Wieder's time.

Another two people provided me with interesting albeit conflicting information.

The first was a professor called Monroe, who'd been one of Wieder's assistants. In the late eighties he'd been preparing his doctoral thesis. The other was a woman in her sixties, Susanne Johnson, who'd been Wieder's assistant and very close to the professor. Monroe still taught at Princeton. Johnson had retired in 2006 and was living in Astoria, Queens, with her husband and daughter.

John L. Monroe was a squat, gloomy man, with skin as grey as the suit he was wearing when he received me in his office, after a long and thorough questioning over the phone. He didn't offer me coffee or tea, and throughout our conversation he kept casting me suspicious glances, turning up his nose at the ripped knees of my Nudies when they entered his field of vision. He had a faint voice, as if he had problems with his vocal cords.

Unlike the others, he described Wieder as a shameless maverick who didn't hesitate to pilfer other people's work so that he could always be in the limelight. His theories, claimed Monroe, were dishwater, mere voodoo science for the ignorant public, the kind of seemingly shock revelations that you get on radio and TV talk shows, but which the scientific community viewed with circumspection even back then. The achievements of neuroscience, psychiatry and psychology in the years since Wieder's death had merely highlighted just how shaky Wieder's theories really had been, but nobody would waste their time demonstrating the obvious fact now.

Monroe's words were so venomous that it made me think he'd die if he ever bit his tongue. It was clear that he had no affection for Wieder, and he was probably grateful that somebody was prepared to listen to him sullying the professor's memory.

On the other hand, he remembered the publisher that had been planning on publishing Wieder's book: it was a press from Maryland called Allman & Limpkin. He confirmed that the board had had discussions on the subject. Wieder had been accused of using the university's resources to gather data that he was going to publish strictly in his own interest.

Monroe told me that he had no idea why the book hadn't come out. Maybe Wieder hadn't finished it, or maybe the publisher had asked him to make changes he hadn't agreed with. He explained that in general such things were contracted via what was called a 'proposal', a document in which the author provides the publisher with all the necessary information about his project, ranging from content to target audience. Such a document usually contains no more than two or three chapters of the actual book project, with the rest of the manuscript to be delivered at a later date, agreed on by the two parties. The final contract would be signed only after the finished manuscript was submitted and revised in accordance with the publisher's suggestions.

He hadn't heard of Laura Baines, but he said that Wieder was a notorious womaniser who'd had countless affairs, including some with students. The board hadn't been intending to renew his contract the following year. Everybody had known that Wieder was going to leave Princeton in the summer of 1988, and the Department of Psychology had already started looking for a replacement professor.

★ ★ ★

I invited Susanne Johnson to have lunch with me at a restaurant called Agnanti in Queens. I arrived earlier than the time we'd agreed on, and I sat down at the table and ordered a coffee. When Mrs Johnson arrived ten minutes later, I was surprised to see that she was in a wheelchair. As she later explained, she was paralysed from the waist down. She was accompanied by a young woman, whom she introduced as Violet, her daughter. Violet left after checking that everything was fine, telling us that she'd return to pick her mom up an hour later.

Mrs Johnson proved to be a breath of fresh air, an optimistic woman despite her condition. She told me that ten years ago, during a trip to Normandy, on the trail of her father who'd fought on D-Day as a marine, she'd had a terrible accident in the car she'd hired in Paris. Fortunately her husband, Mike, who'd been in the passenger seat, had escaped almost unharmed.

She told me that not only had she been Wieder's assistant but also his confidante. The professor, Mrs Johnson said, had been a true genius. He'd happened to choose psychology as his area of research, but she was convinced that he'd have shone in any other field. And like any authentic genius, he'd been a magnet for the hatred of the mediocre, who were unable to rise to the same level. He'd had only a few friends at the university and had been constantly harassed under various pretexts. The same enemies had periodically spread all kinds of baseless rumours, such as that Wieder had been a drunk and a womaniser.

Susanne Johnson had met Laura Baines many times; she knew that she was the professor's protégée, but she was certain that they hadn't been involved in an affair. She confirmed that the professor had just finished a book during that period, something about memory. As she was the one who'd typed up the manuscript, because Wieder had used neither a typewriter nor a word processor, she knew for certain that the manuscript had been ready for weeks before his death, and up until now she'd never asked herself whether it'd been submitted to the publisher before his death or why the book hadn't been released.

Over dessert, I asked her whether she knew anything about a secret project that Wieder was supposed to have been involved in. She hesitated for a few moments before answering, but eventually she admitted that she'd known.

I know he was involved in a project to do with therapy for soldiers suffering from post-traumatic stress, but that's all I can remember. I majored in economics, not psychology or psychiatry, so I transcribed the documents mechanically, without thinking much about their content. I won't conceal from you the fact that I believed that Professor Wieder's mental state was shaky towards the end of those experiments, whatever they might have been.'

'So, do you think there was a connection between his death and the project he was working on?'

'I'd thought about it at that time, to be honest. Obviously I know about these things only from what I've read in mysteries or from what I've seen in movies, but I think that if this was planned as a result of his work, they'd have tried to cover their tracks, making it look like a burglary or even an accident. I think he was murdered by an amateur, who was lucky enough to get away with it. But I guess there must have been tensions between the professor and the men he was working for. For about two months before his death, he didn't give me any more documents to type up. He'd probably stopped working with those people.'

She was silent for a few moments, and then she said, 'I was in love with Professor Wieder, Mr Keller. I was married and, although it might seem paradoxical to you, I loved my husband and children. I never told him, and I don't think he ever realised. Probably to him I was just a friendly colleague who was prepared to help him even outside office hours. I hoped that one day he'd see me differently, but that never happened. I was overcome by grief when he died, and for a long time I had the feeling that my world had come to an end. He was probably the most wonderful man I've ever met in my entire life.'

Violet Johnson arrived exactly at that point in our conversation, and she accepted my invitation to stay for a couple of minutes with us. She'd majored in anthropology, but was working as an estate agent, and told me that the market was beginning to recover after the financial crisis of the last few years. She bore an uncannily close resemblance to her mom — when I looked at them, I got the feeling that I was seeing the same person at different stages in her life. I walked them to the parking lot, where Violet had left her car, and we parted after Susanne insisted on hugging me and wished me success.

★ ★ ★

I called the Allman & Limpkin switchboard the very next morning.

I was put through to the acquisitions editor in charge of psychology books, a very nice lady who listened to me carefully and then gave me the number of their archive department. Professor Wieder was a famous figure in the academic world, she told me, so it was possible that his book proposal had been preserved in the archive, especially given that in those days email hadn't existed and correspondence with authors had been by letter.

But I didn't have any luck with the archive department. The person I got through to hung up on me after telling me he wasn't allowed to talk to the press without prior permission from management.

I called the editor I'd spoken to earlier, explained what had happened, and listed once more the questions I was trying to answer: whether Wieder's proposal really existed, whether he'd submitted the full manuscript, and why the book had never been printed. I marshalled the full might of my personal charm, and it seemed to work — she promised to try to find out the answers to my questions.

I didn't hold my breath, but two days later an

email from the editor arrived in my inbox, and she brought me up to date on what she'd found out.

Wieder had sent his editor the proposal in July 1987, with the first chapter of the book enclosed. He'd mentioned in the proposal that the manuscript was complete and ready for submission. The publisher had sent him a contract a month later, in August. Among other things, it'd stipulated that Wieder should start working on the revision of the text with the editor in November. But in November, the professor had asked for another few weeks, saying he'd wanted to polish the manuscript one more time over the holidays. This request had been granted, but then tragedy had intervened. The full manuscript had never reached the publisher.

Attached to the email was a copy of the proposal, a scan of the original typewritten document. It was almost fifty pages long. I set about printing it, watching as the pages were disgorged into the printer's plastic tray one by one. Finally I leafed through them, before fastening them together with a paperclip and laying them on my desk to read later.

★   ★   ★

That evening I tried to draw up a balance sheet of what I'd achieved in my investigation so far and what chances I had of reaching any eventual conclusion.

Half an hour later, looking at the diagram I'd drawn, I came to the conclusion that I was in fact lost in a kind of maze. I'd set out on the trail of Richard Flynn's book, and not only had I not found it, but I was buried under a mound of details about people and events that refused to coalesce into a coherent picture. I got the feeling that I was groping in the dark, in an attic full of old junk, without being able to understand the real meaning of the objects that had been amassed there over the years by people I didn't know and about whom I hadn't been able to discover anything of real meaning.

Many of the details I'd found were contradictory, an avalanche of formless information, as if the characters and events of that time were stubbornly refusing to reveal the truth to me. What was more, when I'd begun the investigation, the central character had been Richard Flynn, the author of the manuscript, but as it'd progressed, he'd begun to fade from sight, relegated to the background, so that the patriarchal figure of Professor Joseph Wieder had stepped to the front of the stage, like the star he'd been throughout his entire career, shoving poor Flynn into a dark corner and reducing him almost to the size of a minor supporting role.

I tried to make a connection between the character of Laura Baines in Flynn's manuscript and the woman I'd met at the Columbia University Medical Center, but I just couldn't do it. It was as if there were two different images, one real, one imaginary, and it was impossible to superimpose them.

I tried to compare the Flynn I knew indirectly from the manuscript — a young student at

Princeton, full of life, who'd dreamed of becoming a writer and had already published his first short stories — with the reclusive, solitary man who'd lived a dull life with Danna Olsen in a modest apartment, a misanthrope robbed of his dreams. And I tried to understand why that man, who'd already been dying, had used up the last months of his life writing a manuscript which he'd eventually taken with him to the grave.

I tried to picture Wieder, characterised by some as a genius, but by others as an imposter, locked up with his own ghosts in that huge, cold house, as if haunted by some unknown guilt. Wieder had left behind him the mystery of a missing manuscript, and, in a twist of fate, that's exactly what had happened in the case of Richard Flynn nearly three decades later. I'd set out seeking a missing manuscript, hadn't found it, but had ended up instead stumbling on the trail of yet another lost book.

I tried to lend consistency to all the characters that my investigation brought back from the past, but they were just shadows without any definite outline, flitting about within a story whose beginning, ending and meaning I was unable to uncover. I had in front of me a puzzle, but none of the pieces fitted the others.

Paradoxically, the more I'd delved into the past, driven by the abundant but contradictory information, the more important the present had become to me. It was as if I'd descended into a tunnel and the circle of light diminishing above my head would have been the vital element reminding me that I had to ascend back to the surface, because that was where I came from and where, sooner or later, I should return.

I spoke to Sam on the phone almost every day, and she told me that she was getting better. I discovered that I missed her more than I'd have believed before starting the investigation and before her illness had separated us. The more deceptive the shadows around me proved to be, the more real our relationship seemed to become, and it gained a consistency that it hadn't possessed previously, or which I'd perhaps refused to accept.

That was why it came as such a shock, what happened next.

I was just about to leave the house to meet Roy Freeman, one of the police detectives, now retired, who'd worked on the Wieder case, when my phone rang. It was Sam, and without any introduction she told me straight out that she wanted us to break up. Furthermore she pointed out, 'break up' perhaps wasn't the right term, given that she'd never thought that we'd had a 'serious' relationship, but rather a friendship without strings.

She told me she wanted to get married and have kids, and a guy she knew had been pursuing her for quite a while. He looked, she said, like he might be a suitable lifelong partner for her.

She told me all this in a tone of voice that sounded as though she were a casting executive informing an unsuccessful candidate that another actor was more suitable for a role.

I wondered whether she could have cheated

188

on me with that colleague of hers, but then I realised that it was an idle question: Sam wasn't the kind of person who didn't thoroughly explore all her options before making a decision.

As she explained that she'd used the days she'd spent ill in bed thinking about what it was she really wanted, I knew that most likely her relationship with that guy had been going on for quite a while.

'It was you who said you wanted a light relationship, with no strings attached,' I said. 'I respected your wishes, but that doesn't mean I didn't want something more.'

'Then why didn't you tell me till now? What stopped you?'

'Maybe I was just about to.'

'John, we know each other too well. You're just like all other men — you only realise how much a woman means to you the instant you lose her. Did you know that while we were together I was afraid that one day you'd meet a younger woman and run off with her? Did you know how much it hurt me that you never invited me to meet your friends or that you never introduced me to your parents, as if you wanted to keep our relationship a secret? I said to myself that I'm nothing more than an older lady who you occasionally liked to have sex with.'

'My folks are in Florida, Sam. As for my friends, I don't think you'd like them very much: some guys from the *Post*, and two or three pals I knew at college, who are now overweight and tell me, after having a couple of shots, stories about how they cheat on their wives.'

'I was talking about as a matter of principle.'

'And I was talking about how things really are.'

'I don't think there's any point in us starting the blame game. That's the ugliest part of the end of a relationship, when you remember all your frustrations and start slinging mud.'

'I wasn't blaming you for anything, really.'

'All right, I'm sorry. I just — '

I heard her coughing.

'You okay?'

'They told me that I'll be rid of this cough in two or three more weeks. I have to hang up now. Perhaps we'll keep in touch. Please take care of yourself.'

I wanted to ask her whether she was sure she didn't wish us to meet up right away, to talk face to face, but I didn't get the chance. She hung up and after I stared at the phone for a few moments, as if I couldn't understand what it was doing in my hand, I did the same.

As I walked to my meeting with Roy Freeman, I realised that I wanted to get the whole investigation over with as quickly as possible.

I knew that if I hadn't allowed myself to get caught up in it and tried to play detective, maybe I'd have been attentive enough to see the signs of the approaching storm in my relationship with Sam. Her decision to break up with me was the last straw, even though I wasn't able to explain why.

I wasn't superstitious, but I got a distinct feeling that the story of Richard Flynn concealed some kind of spell, something like the curse of the mummy's tomb. I was determined to call Peter and tell him I wanted out, because it was clear to me that I wasn't ever going to get to the bottom of what happened that night with Professor Joseph Wieder, Laura Baines and Richard Flynn.

7

Roy Freeman lived in Bergen County, over the bridge, but he'd said he had some business to take care of in the city, so I'd made a reservation at a restaurant on West 36th Street.

He was tall and skinny, with the look of an actor who's cast in supporting roles, the kind of ageing cop who unostentatiously backs up the alpha hero in his fight against the bad guys, and who gives you the impression — although you don't know why, because he only has one or two lines in the movie — that you can rely on him.

His hair was almost completely white, so too his carefully trimmed beard, which covered the entire lower half of his face. He introduced himself and we started talking. He told me he'd been married to a woman named Diana for almost twenty years. They had a son, Tony, but whom he hardly ever saw. His ex and son had moved to Seattle after the divorce, in the late eighties. His son had graduated from college and was a news anchor at a local radio station.

Freeman didn't hesitate to tell me that he was 100 per cent to blame for the break-up, as he'd been too caught up in his work and used to drink too much. He was one of the first police detectives in New Jersey to join the force straight out of college, back in 1969, and some of the other guys in the department had it in for him because of that, especially given that he was also an African American. And whoever claimed that by the mid-seventies racism had been almost eradicated from the force, especially in small-town departments, was a liar, he stressed. Of course, even before then they'd started making movies with black actors cast as judges, prosecutors, college professors and chiefs of police, but the reality had been different. But the pay was good — an officer on patrol got almost twenty thousand a year back then — and he'd dreamed of becoming a cop since childhood.

The West Windsor Township Police Department, he told me, had had around fifteen officers in the early eighties, most of them aged around forty. There had been just one woman in the agency, a recent recruit, and apart from a Hispanic officer, José Mendez, all the others had been white. It'd been a grim period for New Jersey and New York: the crack epidemic had begun, and even if Princeton hadn't been in the thick of the wave, it didn't mean that the cops had had an easy life there. Freeman had worked in Princeton PD for a decade, and in 1979 he'd been transferred to West Windsor, Mercer County, at an agency that had been set up just a couple of years before.

He was happy to talk to me and confessed that he'd been leading quite a reclusive life since his retirement and that it was common for an ex-cop not to have many confidants.

'Why are you interested in this case, John?' he asked.

He suggested that we call each other by our first names. Although there was something about

193

his tone and his appearance that intimidated me a bit, without my being able to explain why, I agreed and told him the whole truth. I was tired of inventing stories about imaginary biographies and panoptic histories of unsolved murders, and was sure that the man in front of me — who'd been kind enough to accept our meeting without even knowing me and who'd shared with me painful details about his life — deserved my full sincerity.

So I told him that Richard Flynn wrote a book about the period and sent it to a literary agent, but the rest of the manuscript was nowhere to be found. Having been hired by the agent in question, I was researching — or investigating, one might say — the case in an attempt to reconstruct the facts. I'd already talked to a large number of people, but I hadn't come up with anything concrete so far, nor could I grasp what it was all about.

He pointed to the large buff-coloured envelope he'd brought with him.

'I paid a visit to the agency and made some copies for you,' he said. 'We didn't start computerising our records until the early nineties, so I had to comb through the boxes in the archive. None of them are classified, so it was easy. Take the papers with you and read them,' he urged me, and I put the envelope in my bag.

Then he walked me briefly through what he remembered: how he'd arrived with forensics at Wieder's house, about the storm in the press, and how there hadn't been any plausible clues to allow them to form a working theory.

'There were lots of things about the case that just didn't add up,' he said. 'The professor had a quiet life, didn't do drugs, wasn't mixed up with hookers, and didn't hang out in bad places. He hadn't had any recent conflicts with anybody, lived in a good neighbourhood, and his neighbours were decent folks, who had all known each other for years, academics and big shots at corporations. And then, all of a sudden, this guy is beaten to death in his own home. There was lots of valuable stuff inside, but nothing was missing, not even the cash or the jewellery. But I can remember that somebody did search the place in a hurry. There were opened drawers and papers scattered all over the floor. But the only fingerprints we found belonged to known persons: a kid who looked after the professor's library and a janitor who had access and was there often.'

'About those papers on the floor,' I said. 'Were any of them picked up as potential evidence?'

'I can't remember details like that . . . You'll find everything in those photocopies. But I remember that we found a small safe in the house and nobody knew the combination, so we had to bring in a locksmith. He broke it open, but all we found was some cash, deeds, photographs, that kind of stuff. Nothing related to the case.'

'The professor had just finished writing a book and it seems that the manuscript vanished.'

'It was his sister who dealt with his belongings. She arrived about a couple of days later from Europe. I remember her well. She acted like a movie star or something. She wore an expensive fur coat and a lot of jewels, like some diva, and she talked in a foreign accent. She was quite a sight, let me tell you. We asked her a couple of questions, but she just said that she and her late brother hadn't been very close and she knew nothing about his life.'

'Her name is Inge Rossi,' I said. 'She's been living in Italy for a long time.'

'Maybe . . . She's probably got the manuscript you're talking about, or maybe somebody else took it. After a couple of days we cleared all our stuff out of there. His sister didn't complain about anything being missing, but I doubt she knew much about what her brother kept there. As I told you, she said to me they'd never visited each other over the past twenty years or so. She was in a hurry to be done with it all as quickly as possible, and went back straight after the funeral.'

'I know that a young guy was one of the suspects, Martin Luther Kennet, who was later sentenced for the murder of an elderly couple.'

'The Eastons, that's right, a grisly murder . . . Kennet got life and he's still in Rikers Island. But he wasn't accused of the professor's murder — '

'Yes, I know, but he was treated for a while as a prime suspect in the Wieder case, wasn't he?'

He shrugged. 'You know how it goes sometimes . . . Wieder was a celebrity, the press jumped on the story, which went national for a while, so there was pressure on us to solve the case as quickly as possible. We also worked with the Sheriff's Office, and the Mercer County Prosecutor's Office assigned a detective from the Homicide Unit, a guy named Ivan Francis. That guy was a ladder-climbing type, if you know what I mean, with very strong political backup. We the local cops, were just small potatoes, so that guy and the prosecutor pulled all the strings.

'My opinion, which I wasn't afraid of expressing at the time, was that the kid, Kennet, had nothing to do neither with the Easton murder nor with Wieder's case, and I'm dead-ass serious. The prosecutor also tried to make him the prime suspect in the Wieder case, as you said, so all the other leads were more or less gradually abandoned. But that was just plain stupid, and we all knew it. Maybe that kid wasn't too bright, but he wasn't so dumb as to try to sell the rocks he stole from the victims to a pawnshop just a couple of miles away from the crime scene. What the heck? Why didn't he go to New York, or to Philly? He was a small-time dealer, true, but he didn't have any previous convictions for violence. He also had an alibi for the night of the professor's murder, so the possibility that he might have been the perpetrator in the Wieder case shouldn't even have been taken into consideration.'

'I read something about that in the newspapers, but are you sure that — '

'It was exactly how I'm telling you, he'd been in an arcade. There weren't security cameras in those days, but two or three guys initially confirmed that they'd seen him there during the interval in which the killing had been done. Then

197

Ivan Francis went to see them, so they changed their initial statements. In addition, Kennet's public defender was a moron, who didn't want to argue with anybody. Get it?'

'So the Richard Flynn lead was dropped quite quickly?'

'Yes, right, that was a lead too. It wasn't the only one that was dropped 'quite quickly', as you put it. I can't recall all the details, but I think he was the last person to see the professor alive, so we interviewed him a few times, but we didn't catch him out on anything. He admitted he'd been there that night, but he claimed he'd left two or three hours before the time of the murder. Does he confess to anything in that book?'

'Like I said, most of the manuscript's missing, so I don't know where he was going with the story. What you didn't know at the time, because Richard Flynn and Derek Simmons, the other witness, kept their mouths shut about it, was that a grad student by the name of Laura Baines could also have been there that evening. The handyman told me that she and Flynn met with the professor and that they had an argument.'

He smiled. 'Never underestimate a cop, John. I know that people sometimes think we're just doughnut-munching idiots who couldn't even find their dick in their pants. Of course we knew everything about the girl you're talking about, who was apparently shacking up with the professor, but in the end nothing could be proven. I interviewed her, but she had a solid alibi for the whole evening, as far as I remember,

so she couldn't have been at the scene
— another dead end.'

'But that guy, the handyman — '

'As for the handyman's statement . . . well
. . . What's his name?'

'Simmons, Derek Simmons.'

He suddenly stopped talking and stared into
empty space for a couple of seconds. Then he
took a small prescription bottle out of his pocket,
opened it and swallowed a green pill with a sip of
water. He looked embarrassed.

'Sorry about that, but . . . Well, yes, his name
was Derek Simmons, right. I can't remember
what he declared, but there wasn't much we
could do with his statement anyway. The guy was
ill, he had amnesia, and I don't think he had all
the tiles on his roof, if you know what I mean.
But anyhow, besides the gossip, we didn't have
any proof that the professor and that girl were
lovers, and her alibi was strong.'

'Can you remember who confirmed it?'

'It's all in the papers I gave you. I think it was
a schoolmate, a girl.'

'Sarah Harper?'

'Told you, I can't remember all the details, but
you'll find all the names in the papers.'

'Laura Baines had a boyfriend, Timothy
Sanders. Maybe he was jealous, thinking that his
girlfriend and the professor were having an
affair. Did somebody interview him?'

'Laura Baines wasn't a suspect, as I told
you, so why should we have interviewed her
boyfriend? Why, did you find something about
that guy?'

'Nothing related to the case. He was shot dead many years ago in DC. They said it was a robbery turned into a murder.'

'Well, I'm sorry to hear that.'

We'd finished eating and we ordered coffee. Freeman looked tired and absent, as if our conversation had emptied his batteries.

'But why wasn't Flynn officially charged?' I continued.

'Don't remember, but I think a headhunter like Francis had good reasons not to bring him up before the jury. The guy was a student with a clean record, minding his own business. He didn't do drugs or drink excessively, as far as I can remember, he wasn't violent, so he didn't fit the profile of a potential murderer. Oh, yes, and he passed the polygraph, did you know that? People like that don't suddenly go out and commit murders, not even under intense emotional pressure. Some people just aren't capable of killing another person, not even to save their own lives. I read about a study a few years ago that concluded that most of the guys in the Second World War shot into the air rather than at the Germans or Japanese. It's a hell of a difficult thing to beat somebody to death with a bat, not like in the movies. Even if you think the other guy's raped your daughter. I don't think that guy was our man.'

'Roy, do you think a woman would have been able to do that? Physically, I mean.'

He thought for a few moments.

'Well, smashing a guy's head in with a baseball bat? Don't think so. Women kill far less frequently than men do, and they almost never commit murders as violent as that. When they kill, women use poison or other bloodless methods. Maybe a gun. On the other hand, in forensic science there are patterns, but no certainties, so a detective should never exclude any hypothesis. As far as I remember, Wieder was a strong guy, in good shape, and young enough to fight back if necessary. Yes, he'd been drinking before he was murdered. Alcohol content level can reveal a lot of things about the condition of a victim in the moment of the attack, but not everything. With the same alcohol content level, one might have almost normal reflexes, while another might be unable to defend himself. It varies from one individual to another.'

'Was Simmons considered a suspect?'

'Who's Simmons? Oh, sorry, the handyman, the guy with a screw loose . . . '

'Yes. In the past he was accused of murdering his wife and found not guilty by reason of insanity. Why wasn't he a suspect?'

'He was very cooperative and had an alibi, so he was considered a potential suspect only at first, like everybody connected in one way or another with the victim. He was questioned a couple of times, but seemed harmless and we dropped it.'

★   ★   ★

He'd come by train and I gave him a lift back home, to New Jersey. While I drove, he told me about a cop's life in those days. He lived in a

201

one-storey old house surrounded by pine trees at the end of a dirt road, not far off the turnpike. Before I left, he asked me to keep him up to date with my investigation, and I promised to let him know as soon as I found anything interesting. But I already knew I was going to abandon the whole thing.

Still, I read in the evening the papers he'd brought me, but I didn't discover much I hadn't known already.

Richard had been interviewed three times, and on each occasion he'd given clear and straight answers. And as Freeman had said, he'd even agreed to take a polygraph test, which he'd passed.

★ ★ ★

Laura Baines's name was mentioned only in a general report about Wieder's connections and acquaintances. She hadn't been cited as a suspect or a witness, and was only questioned once. It seems that there had been some suspicions that she could have been at the scene that evening, leaving the house at around 9 p.m., when Richard had arrived. But Richard and Laura had both denied it. Flynn and the professor had had a drink together, and the former had claimed that Laura hadn't been there.

Later, searching for more information online, my mind half absent, I thought of Sam: the way she used to smile at me, the changeable colour of her eyes, and the small birthmark on her left shoulder. I had the strange feeling that my memories of her had gradually started to obscure themselves already, hidden one by one in that secret chamber of wasted chances, whose key you threw away because the recollections behind its door were too painful.

I didn't fall asleep until nearly morning. I could hear the deep breathing of the city, where millions of dreams and stories wove together to form a gigantic ball that slowly rose into the sky, ready to burst at any moment.

★   ★   ★

I'd tried a number of times over the previous couple of weeks to get hold of Sarah Harper. She finally called me back the day after I met Freeman, just as I was getting ready to call Peter and wrap up the whole investigation. Harper had a nice voice and told me that she wanted to see me as soon as possible, because she was about to leave town for a while. She'd remembered talking to Harry Miller a couple of weeks ago, and wished to know what I wanted from her.

To be honest, I wasn't interested in meeting her. I'd talked to too many people by then, who'd all told me conflicting stories, and the break-up with Sam was too great shock to allow me to focus on something that had happened so many years ago, something in which I'd lost almost all interest and curiosity. All of a sudden, the events had become like drawings without any depth, like illustrations in a children's book, two-dimensional and incapable of arousing any

203

enthusiasm in me. I had no interest in going all the way up to the Bronx to meet a junkie who'd probably tell me yet another pack of lies, in the hopes of getting a quick payout so she could score.

But she offered to come into the city to meet me, so I agreed. I gave her the address of a pub by the corner and she told me she'd be there in about an hour and that I'd be able to recognise her by her green travel bag.

She arrived ten minutes late, just as I was drinking my espresso. I waved to her and she came over, shook my hand and sat down.

She looked completely different from what I'd imagined. She was short and frail, with an almost teenage body and very white skin, which matched her apricot-coloured hair. She was dressed plainly, in a pair of jeans, a long-sleeved 'Life is Good' T-shirt, and a distressed denim jacket, but she looked very tidy and gave off a subtle scent of expensive perfume. I offered to buy her a drink, but she said she'd been dry for a year, after her last stint in rehab. She assured me that she'd also been off drugs since then too. She pointed to her bag, which she'd placed on the chair next to her. 'As I told you over the phone, I'm leaving for a while,' she said. 'And I thought I'd better talk to you beforehand.'

'Where're you going?'

'To Maine, with my boyfriend. We're going to live on an island. He's taken a job with a foundation that looks after wildlife sanctuaries. I've been waiting to do something like this for a long time, but I wanted to be very sure that I was all right and ready before I left, if you understand what I mean. I'm going to miss New York. I've lived here practically my whole life, but it's a fresh start, isn't it?'

She seemed comfortable talking to me, though we'd only just met, and I thought that she probably still attended support groups like AA. Her face was almost wrinkle-free, but she had deep circles under her turquoise eyes.

'Thank you for agreeing to talk to me, Sarah,' I said, after I'd told her briefly about Richard Flynn's manuscript and my investigation surrounding the events of late 1987. 'Before anything else, I'd like to warn you that the agency I work for doesn't have a large budget for this sort of research, so — '

She interrupted me with a wave of the hand. 'I don't know what that guy Miller told you, but I don't need your money. I've managed to save a bit of cash recently, and where I'm going I won't have much need for it. I agreed to meet you for a different reason. It has to do with Laura Baines — or Westlake, as she calls herself now. I thought it'd be better for you to know a few things about her.'

'I'm going to get another espresso,' I said. 'Would you like one?'

'A decaf cappuccino would be great, thanks.'

I went to the bar and ordered our coffees, then returned to the table. It was Friday afternoon and the pub was beginning to fill up with noisy people.

'You were talking about Laura Baines,' I said. 'How well do you know her?'

205

'I barely know her. We talked for half an hour, and a couple of times on the phone, that's all.'

'And what impression did she make on you?'

'Not a very good one, to be honest. I got the feeling she lied to me when I asked her about what happened back then. It's just a feeling, but I think she's been hiding something.'

'Laura and I were good friends; we shared an apartment for a while, until she moved in with her boyfriend. Although she came from the Midwest, Laura was free-spirited, extremely cultured, and had an allure that made her attractive not only to boys but also to girls. She made lots of friends straight away, was invited to every party and was remarked upon by her professors. She was the most popular student in our class.'

'What was her relationship with Wieder, exactly? Do you know anything about that? Some people told me they had an affair, and that's what Richard Flynn hinted at in his manuscript. But she claims there was never anything romantic between them.'

She thought for a few seconds, biting her lower lip.

'I'm thinking now how to put it clearly . . . I don't believe there was anything physical between them, but they meant a lot to each other. The professor didn't seem like the kind who was into younger women. He just had an energy about him. We all admired him and cared about him. His courses were awesome. He had a great sense of humour, and he gave you the feeling that he knew what he was talking about and really wanted you to learn something, rather than just doing the job he was paid for. Let me give you an example. Once, at some fall fireworks — there were all kinds of stupid rituals back then, and some of them probably still exist — almost the whole of our class had gone together with a couple of professors to the field in front of the Art Museum, waiting for it to get dark and for the artillery to begin. Within half an hour, almost every student was standing in a group around Wieder, who wasn't even saying anything.'

'Some of his former colleagues claim he was a womaniser and that he drank too much.'

'I don't think so, and Laura never mentioned anything like that to me. I'm inclined to believe that it was just gossip. In any event, Laura had a boyfriend at the time — '

'Timothy Sanders?'

'Yes, I think that was his name. I've never had a good memory for names, but I think you're right. Laura seemed to truly care about him, if she was really capable of caring about anyone. But apart from her relationships with that boy or with Wieder, Laura had started to show me a different face, which gradually frightened me.'

'What do you mean?' I asked.

'She was extremely, extremely . . . fierce. Fiercely determined, that's the word, but at the same time very calculating. At that age, almost none of us — students, I mean — took life very seriously. Flirting with a boyfriend was more important to me than my future career, for example. I wasted a lot of time on unimportant things, buying trifles or going to the movies, I stayed up so many nights talking nonsense with friends.

'But Laura was different. Once, she told me that she'd given up athletics at the age of eighteen, realising that the prizes she'd won until then weren't enough to guarantee her a place on the team for the LA Olympics, and four years later she'd have been too old to stand any chance of being chosen for the team. I asked her what one thing had to do with the other and she was amazed at my question. She said, 'What is the point of working hard if you don't have an opportunity to prove you're the best?' Do you understand what I'm saying? For her, sport was only a means to an end, which was public recognition. That's what she wanted above all, or maybe it's the only thing she's ever wanted: for other people to acknowledge that she was the best. From what I could gather, ever since early childhood her sense of competition was overdeveloped, and in time it turned into an obsession. No matter what she did, she had to be the best. No matter what she wanted, she had to achieve it as quickly as possible.

'And she didn't even realise it. She saw herself as an open, generous person, ready to sacrifice herself for others. But whoever stood in her way was an obstacle to be rid of.

'I think that's why her relationship with Wieder was important to her. She was flattered that she'd been noticed by the most charismatic professor, a genius admired by everybody. His attention made her feel special — she was the chosen one, she was unique among that gaggle of girls who all looked at Wieder as a god. Timothy was just a boy who followed her around like a puppy and who she slept with every now and then.'

It seemed as if the effort of talking was exhausting for her, and two red blotches had appeared on her cheeks. She kept clearing her throat, as if it were dry. She'd emptied her cup of coffee, so I asked her if she wanted another, but she said she was fine.

'I think that's why she befriended me in the beginning. Although I was born and raised in the city, I was naive and bowled over by her, which confirmed to her that there was no point in her having any complexes about being a hick who'd made it to the East Coast. She took me under her wing, in a way. Like Sancho Panza, I followed her no matter what, mounted on my donkey, as she blazed her way to fame and glory. But she wouldn't tolerate the slightest gesture of independence. Once, I bought a pair of shoes without asking her advice. She managed to convince me that they were the ugliest shoes in the world and that only somebody completely devoid of taste would wear such a thing. I gave them away.'

'Okay, she was a cold and calculating bitch, but so are a lot of other people. Do you think it's possible that she was involved in Wieder's death? What motive might she have had?'

'The book that Wieder had written,' she said. 'That damn book.'

★ ★ ★

She told me that Laura had helped the professor with a book, and he'd drawn on her knowledge in math to create models to evaluate behavioural changes brought about by traumatic events.

Sarah's impression was that Laura had come to overestimate her contribution. She had been convinced that if she hadn't helped him, Wieder would never have managed to finish the project. So she'd asked him to give her credit as co-author, and the professor — as she'd delightedly told Sarah — had agreed to it. At the time, Timothy had gone to Europe to do some research at a university there, and Laura had moved into the house which she'd shared with Richard Flynn, after staying for a short while in the one-bed apartment Sarah had rented. She'd later told Sarah that Flynn, the guy she was sharing the house with, was a deluded daydreamer, and that he was madly in love with her, a situation Laura had found amusing.

But one day Laura, who'd visited the professor's house quite often, had found a copy of the proposal he'd sent to a publisher. Her name had been nowhere to be found on the document, so she'd realised that the professor had been lying to her and hadn't had the slightest intention of making her a co-author.

That's when, Sarah said, her friend had started showing her ugliest side. She hadn't had fits of hysteria, she hadn't broken stuff, she hadn't screamed — it would have been better if she had. Instead, Laura had asked Sarah to stay

210

at her place overnight, and she'd sat for an hour or two staring into space, saying nothing. Then she had started to figure out a battle plan, like a general determined to completely annihilate the enemy.

Laura had known that disagreements had arisen between the professor and the people he'd been working with on a secret project, so she'd begun to confuse his mind, making him think he was being followed and that people were searching his house when he was out. In fact it was Laura herself who'd been doing it — she'd move things around, leaving other subtle signs of intrusion, in a kind of sadistic game.

Secondly, Laura had led the professor to think that she was in love with Richard Flynn, whom she'd introduced him to, in an attempt to make him jealous. She'd been trying to get Wieder to delay his submission of the manuscript and in the meantime persuade him to go back to their former understanding.

The professor, Sarah said, probably had realised that what Laura was demanding was ludicrous. She hadn't even finished her master's degree, but she'd have been on the cover of a major academic work — and he'd have got the flack, with his career being seriously damaged as a result.

I remembered what Flynn had written in his manuscript about his first meeting with Wieder. If Sarah Harper was telling the truth, he'd been just a patsy. His only role had been to make the professor jealous, a simple sock puppet in Laura's show.

'On the night of the professor's murder, Laura came to my apartment,' Sarah went on. 'It was around three a.m. I'd gone to bed early, because the next day I was going home for the holidays, and a friend had offered to give me a ride to New York.

'She seemed scared and told me that she'd had an argument with Richard Flynn, who'd taken her flirting seriously and become obsessed with her. She'd collected all her stuff from the house, which was in the trunk of her car outside. In any event, Timothy had come back a couple of days previously and they were going to move in with each other again.'

'Richard claimed that Laura had told him she intended to spend that day with you and to stay at your apartment overnight.'

'As I said, she arrived early in the morning. I've got no idea where she'd been up until then. But she begged me to say we'd been together the whole evening, if anybody asked. I promised I would, thinking she was talking about Richard Flynn.'

'Where did you live at the time, Sarah?'

'In Rocky Hill, about five miles from campus.'

'How long do you think it'd have taken Laura to get there from the house she was sharing with Flynn?'

'Not long, even if it was night-time and the weather was very bad. They lived somewhere on Bayard. About twenty minutes or so.'

'And it had taken her about half an hour to get from the professor's in West Windsor back to Flynn's house, given the weather. Plus another

212

hour to pack her stuff — that means two hours. If my information is correct and she did go back to Wieder's house that night, it means she left there at around one a.m., and not at nine p.m., as Flynn declared to the police. In other words, *after* Wieder was attacked . . . '

'I knew even then that something wasn't right and that Laura was lying. Usually she was very self-confident, but that night she was *frightened*, that's the word. I'd just been woken up and I could hardly wait to get back into bed, so I didn't want to hear all the details of her story. We'd grown apart by then and, to be honest, I no longer wanted her friendship. I made up a bed for her on the couch and went back to sleep, after letting her know that I'd be leaving early the next day. But when I woke up at seven a.m., she'd already left. I found a note saying she'd gone to Timothy.

'I left at around eight a.m., and found out about what had happened listening to the radio in my friend's car. I asked him to pull off the highway — we were on the Jersey Turnpike — and I remember that I got out and threw up. I immediately wondered whether Laura had been somehow involved in the professor's death. My friend wanted to take me to the hospital. I tried to calm down and after I got back home, I spent the holidays in bed. The police called me between Christmas and the New Year, and I got back to New Jersey and made a statement. I told them that Laura had been with me that day, from lunchtime until the next morning. Why did I lie for her, knowing she might be involved in

213

something so serious? I don't know. I think that she dominated me and I wasn't really capable of refusing her anything.'

'Did you talk to her after that?'

'Right after I'd been interviewed by the police, we had coffee together. She kept thanking me and assuring me that she had nothing to do with the murder. She told me that she'd asked me to testify so that she wouldn't be harassed by cops and reporters. More than that, she told me that the professor had finally accepted her contribution to the book, promising to mention her name as a co-author, which sounded a bit strange to me. Why would he suddenly have changed his mind, just before being murdered?'

'So you didn't believe her?'

'No, I didn't. But I was down, both physically and mentally, and all I wanted was to go home and forget about everything. I decided to take a sabbatical and I didn't start classes again until the fall of 1988, so Laura wasn't there any more when I returned. She called me a few times at home in that period, but I didn't want to talk to her. I lied to my parents that I'd had a bad break-up and I went to therapy. The next year, when I returned to Princeton, the whole story about Wieder's murder was yesterday's news and almost nobody talked about it. No one asked me anything about the case after that.'

'Did you ever see or talk to her again?'

'No,' she said. 'But last year, by chance, I found this.'

She unzipped her bag and took out a hardback book, which she pushed over the table to me. It was by Laura Westlake, PhD. There was a black-and-white photo of the author on the back of the dust jacket above a brief bio. I laid my eyes on the photo and saw that she hadn't changed much over the past two decades: the same common features, tied together only by an expression of determination that made her look already very mature.

'I found this book in the library of the rehab centre where I stayed. It was published in 1992. I recognised the photo on the cover and realised she'd changed her name. It was her first book. As I later found out, it'd been received with unanimous praise and her entire subsequent career has been built on it. I have no doubt that it's the book Wieder was going to publish.'

'I wondered why that book was never published,' I said. 'It seemed that the manuscript had vanished after the murder.'

'I'm not sure whether or not it played any part in the professor's murder, but I presumed she'd stolen the manuscript she was talking about before the killing. Maybe she manipulated that guy Flynn into committing the murder, and she stole the book. So I did something else . . . '

Leaving a trace of lipstick, she wiped her lips with a napkin, which she took from the holder on the table, and she cleared her throat.

'I found out Flynn's address. It wasn't easy, as he lived in the city and there are a lot of Flynns in this town, but I knew that he'd majored in English at Princeton and graduated in 1988, so in the end I tracked him down. I put a copy of the book in an envelope and sent it to him, without any covering letter.'

'He probably didn't know that Laura had stolen Wieder's manuscript, and still thought that it was a love triangle that turned out badly for everybody.'

'That's what I think, too, and then I found out that Flynn had died. I don't know whether my sending him the book led him to put the whole story on paper, but maybe it was his way of getting revenge on Laura for lying to him.'

'So, Laura got off scot-free, thanks to you and Richard, who covered for her.' I knew it sounded harsh, but it was true.

'She was the kind of person who always knew how to take advantage of the feelings of the people who cared about her. Anyway, do what you like with the information I've given you, but I'm not prepared to make any official statement.'

'I don't think it'll be necessary,' I said. 'As long as the rest of Flynn's manuscript is missing, the whole thing is just a bubble.'

'I think it's better this way,' she said. 'It's an old story that's no longer of any interest to anybody. To be honest, not even to me. I have my own stories that I'm going to think about in the years to come.'

I parted with Sarah Harper and thought how ironic it was that perhaps I'd managed to untangle the threads of the whole affair just after it'd ceased to have any importance to me.

I wasn't interested in making sure justice prevailed. I've never been a fanatic in the service of the so-called truth, and I was smart enough to know that truth and justice don't always mean the same thing. At least in one respect, I agreed with Sam — most people prefer simple and nice stories rather than complicated and unuseful truths.

Joseph Wieder had died almost thirty years previously, and Richard Flynn was six feet under too. Probably Laura Baines had built her career on lies, and maybe on a murder. But people have always worshipped and called heroes people cut from the same cloth — glancing through a history textbook is enough to prove that.

On the way home I pictured Laura Baines ransacking the house in search of the manuscript, while Wieder had been lying in his own blood on the floor. What had Richard Flynn, who'd perhaps wielded the baseball bat, done in the meantime? Had he still been there or had he left? Had he been trying to get rid of the murder weapon? But if he had done it for Laura, why had she dumped him, and in that case, why had he continued to cover for her?

Or maybe that train of events existed only in Sarah Harper's mind, a woman who'd been going down step by step, while her former friend had been building a spectacular career for herself. How many of us are really able to be happy for others' success and don't secretly dream of making them pay sooner or later for what they've got? Take a look at the news, guys.

But my questions were no longer important, along with all the other details. Maybe I just liked to believe that Laura Baines, that cold, calculating woman, had performed one of those pool tricks where you hit one ball, which in turn hits another and another. Richard Flynn, Timothy Sanders and Joseph Wieder had been nothing but pool balls to her, striking up against each other until she'd achieved her aim.

And the most ironic thing of all would have been that a man like Wieder, a man who after all enjoyed so much rummaging through people's minds, had ended up being put in a mortal checkmate by one of his students. In this case, Laura Baines would genuinely have deserved her later success if she'd proven to be a more skilled vivisectionist of the human mind than her mentor.

★　★　★

The next day I met up with Peter at Abraçeo, in the East Village.

'How's it going?' he asked. 'You look tired, man. Has something happened?'

I told him I'd finished the job I'd been hired to do and handed him a written summary. He just put the envelope in his silly briefcase without paying much attention to it. I gave him the copy of Laura Baines's book, too.

He didn't ask me anything else, looking as if his mind was on other things. So I started talking, telling him about a possible version of what had happened in the fall and winter of 1987. He listened to me absently, fidgeting with a sachet of sugar and taking a sip of tea from time to time.

'You may be right,' he said finally, 'but you do realise how difficult it'd be to publish something

218

like that without any solid evidence, don't you?'

'I'm not talking about publishing something,' I said, and he seemed relieved. 'I compared the chapter in the proposal Wieder sent to Allman & Limpkin with the first one in Laura's book. They're virtually identical. Obviously that might be evidence that she stole the manuscript from the professor, or else it might just show that they worked together on the book and that her contribution was a very significant one. In any case, it wouldn't be proof that she killed him in order to steal his manuscript, with Richard Flynn as an accomplice. A written testimony on the part of Flynn would have been something else.'

'I find it hard to believe that the man who sent me the manuscript was a killer,' Peter said. 'I'm not saying that he couldn't have committed the murder, but . . . ' He looked away. 'Do you think his manuscript was a confession?'

'Well, yes. He didn't have long to live, he didn't much care about the reputation he'd leave behind, and he had no heirs. Maybe Laura Baines had lied to him and manipulated him into murdering Wieder, then left him to face the music by himself, whilst building a career on the result of the murder he'd committed. When he received the book and it dawned on him what had really been at stake, he realised what had in fact been going on during those months. He'd destroyed his life for a lie. He'd been tricked from the very start to the very finish. Maybe at the time she'd promised she'd go back to him, that their break-up was just a precaution, so as

219

not to give rise to further suspicion.'

'All right, it's an interesting story, but the manuscript has disappeared, and you don't seem prepared to write a book,' Peter said, getting back to the subject in hand.

'Yes, that's the way things stand. It looks like I've wasted your time.'

'No problem. To be honest, I don't think any publisher would be willing to take on all the legal complexities of publishing such a project. By the sound of it, Laura Baines's lawyers would make mincemeat out of them.'

'I agree, man. Thanks for the coffee.'

I went home, collected all the documents to do with my investigation of the past few weeks, put them in a box and tossed them in a closet. Then I called Danna Olsen and told her that I hadn't been able to discover anything new, and that I'd agreed to drop the whole thing. She said she thought it was better that way: the dead should be left to rest in peace, and the living left to get on with their lives. I thought to myself that her words sounded like an epitaph for the late Richard Flynn.

*   *   *

That evening I visited Uncle Frank, on the Upper East Side and told him the whole story.

Do you know what he said, after carefully listening to me for about an hour? That I'd thrown away the most interesting story he'd ever heard. But he'd always been overenthusiastic.

We chewed the fat, drank a couple of beers

220

and watched a ball game on TV. I tried to forget Sam and all those stories about lost books. It seemed to work, because that night I slept like a baby.

* * *

A couple of months later, a former colleague from the *Post* who'd moved to California called me and offered me a job as a scriptwriter for a new TV series. I accepted and decided to let my apartment before heading to the West Coast. Trying to make some room in the closets, I came across the papers about Wieder's case and I phoned Roy Freeman to ask him if he wanted them. He told me he had news.

'Thanks for thinking of me — I was about to call you too,' he said. 'It seems we've had a confession.'

My heart skipped a beat.

'What do you mean by that? It was Laura Baines, wasn't it? Did she confess?'

'Well, as far as I know it wasn't her. Listen, why don't you come over for a cup of coffee? Bring the papers and I'll tell you the whole story.'

'Sure, what time?'

'Whenever you like, I'm home and not going anywhere. Remember where my place is? Okay then, and please don't forget those papers, there's still something that bothers me.'

Part Three

Roy Freeman

Who states distinctly what things he saw and what things he heard from others. For this book will be a truthful one.

Marco Polo, *The Travels*, Book 1, Prologue 1

1

Matt Dominis called me on one of those evenings that make you feel sorry you don't have a cat. After we finished talking, I went out onto the front porch and lingered there for a couple of minutes, trying to put my thoughts together. It was getting dark, a few stars shone in the sky, and the traffic on the highway echoed in the distance like the buzzing of a swarm of bees.

When you finally discover the truth about a case that has obsessed you for a while, it's like losing a travelling companion. A talkative, prying and perhaps even ill-mannered companion, but one you've grown used to having around when you wake up in the morning. And that had been the Wieder case to me over the past few months. But what Matt had told me placed a heavy lid on all the hypotheses I'd come up with in all those many hours spent in the small office I'd fixed up in the spare bedroom. And I told myself that things couldn't just end like this, that there was still something that didn't fit, even if everything my friend had said was true.

★　★　★

I got back inside and called Matt back and asked him if it'd be possible for me to talk to Frank Spoel, who'd confessed to the murder of Professor Joseph Wieder, a few months before he was scheduled to be executed. Matt was a veteran at Potosi Correctional Center and the director did him the favour after he found out that the visitation request came from a detective who'd worked on the case in the late eighties. I wanted to see the guy with my own eyes, hear with my own ears his story about the West Windsor murder. I wasn't convinced that he was telling the truth; I suspected that perhaps he was just trying to get attention, after he'd heard that an author from California wanted to put his name in a book. Wieder had been murdered immediately after Spoel had been released from a mental institution and was hanging in New Jersey, so he'd probably read about the murder in the papers at the time.

John Keller paid me a visit, bringing all the papers he had about the case. He didn't know that I'd started to dig back into Wieder's murder after our conversation in the spring and we talked about Spoel's confession over coffee. He told me that he'd lost his girlfriend because of that story.

'I don't believe in hoodoo, but there's something like a jinx about this case,' he said, 'so you should watch yourself. I'm glad I dropped it, and I don't want to be involved in this stuff again, now or ever. Anyway, it seems it's over, isn't it?'

I told him that it seemed that way and wished him good luck with his new job. But I wasn't sure at all that the truth about Wieder's case had finally come to light. So after two weeks, when Matt called back and told me that everything

226

was arranged, I bought a plane ticket online for the following day and packed a small duffel bag.

The cab picked me up at 5 a.m. and half an hour later I was at the airport. Matt would be waiting for me in St Louis, ready to take me to Potosi.

During the flight I was sitting next to a salesman, the kind of guy who, even if he were about to be executed, would try to persuade the firing squad to buy a new vacuum cleaner. He introduced himself as John Dubcek, but it wasn't until ten minutes later he noticed that I was too absorbed in my newspaper to be really listening to him.

'I'll bet you're a high school teacher,' he said.

'You'll lose the bet. I'm not.'

'I'm never wrong, Roy. History?'

'Not even close, sorry.'

'Hey, I've got it: math.'

'Nope.'

'All right, I give up. I know a quiet little place by the airport and I'll buy your breakfast. I bet you skipped breakfast this morning. I don't like eating alone, so you'll be my guest.'

'Thanks, but a friend is picking me up.'

'Okey-dokey, but you haven't told me what you do for a living.'

'I'm an ex-cop, retired detective.'

'Wow, I'd never have guessed it. Know that joke about the three police officers who walk into a bar?'

He told me one of those dull jokes and I didn't get the punchline.

After we landed, he gave me his business card,

which was so gaudy it looked more like a small Christmas card, and loftily told me he could get hold of anything I could possibly think of; all I had to do was call him and tell him what I needed. As I was walking to the exit, I saw him talking to a girl dressed up like a country singer, in Levi's, a gingham shirt, leather vest, and a cowboy hat perched on her long blonde hair.

★ ★ ★

Matt was waiting for me by a newspaper stand.

We went outside the airport to a coffee shop nearby. I wasn't due at the Potosi Correctional Center for another couple of hours.

We'd been colleagues for eight years at the West Windsor Township Police Department. In the early nineties he'd settled in Missouri, but we'd remained friends and spoke on the phone every now and then, keeping each other up to date about what was happening, and two or three times I'd visited him and we'd gone hunting. Matt had been working at the Potosi Correctional Center for eleven years, but he was on the verge of retirement. A lifelong bachelor, he'd married a colleague called Julia just two years previously, and they'd invited me to their wedding. We hadn't seen each other since then.

'It looks like marriage agrees with you,' I told him, pouring a sachet of sugar into a cup of coffee the size of a soup bowl. 'You look younger.'

He gave a sad smile. He'd always had the downtrodden air of a man convinced some

228

catastrophe was about to overtake him. As he was tall and well built, we'd nicknamed him Fozzie in the department, after the bear on *The Muppet Show*. It was a friendly nickname, not a scathing one — everybody liked Matt Dominis.

'I can't complain. Julia's great and everything's going fine. But I'm now at that age when all I want is a good retirement, to enjoy my golden years. Before you know it, a stroke may come and I'll be wetting myself like a baby. I wanna take a trip to Louisiana, or have a long vacation in Vancouver. Maybe we'll even go to Europe, who knows? I'm sick of watching over those dickheads all the time. But she says we should wait.'

'I've been retired for three years, and apart from a trip to Seattle, when my granddaughter was born, and another two trips here, I haven't been anywhere, pal.'

'Okay, I get what you're saying. Maybe I won't go to Louisiana or dogged Vancouver. But I wanna get up in the morning, drink my coffee and read my paper without knowing I'm gonna be spending the rest of the day with convicts in a goddamn concrete box. Speaking of Seattle, how are Diana and Tony?'

Diana was my ex-wife, who moved to Seattle after the divorce, and Tony was our son, who was just about to turn thirty-eight. It was obvious that Tony blamed me for the divorce, and he never stopped criticising me for it. He always used the expression 'You blew it'. I knew he was right, and that I'd indeed blown it. But I like to think that people should sometimes forgive other people. As far as I was concerned, I'd paid a heavy price for my stupidity back then, and had lived alone for nearly thirty years.

Tony had got married three years ago, and my granddaughter, Erin, was one and a half. I'd seen her just once, immediately after she was born.

I told Matt a few funny stories about her, which I'd heard from Diana, but then he abruptly changed the subject.

'What do you think about what happened with this guy, Frank Spoel? After all these years — '

'As chance would have it, a reporter contacted me about three months ago in connection with the same story, so I started looking over the case again.'

'What a coincidence . . . '

'What got into him, to spill the beans all of a sudden? How long has he got before the execution?'

'Fifty-eight days. But thirty days before the injection he's going to be moved to Bonne Terre Prison, which is where they carry out executions in this state; it's about half an hour from here. What got into him? As I told you on the phone, he got a visit from some guy from California, a professor writing a book about the criminal mind, or something like that. The guy was interested in how Spoel ended up being a killer. Up until then it was known that Spoel committed his first murder in 1988, in Carroll County, Missouri, when he stabbed an old man who'd made the mistake of picking him up on Route 65. He was twenty-three at the time, and had already done two years' hard time in the Trenton Psychiatric Hospital, back in Jersey. After being arrested for a mugging, he'd been declared insane. The guy has nothing more to lose — he's been in prison since 2005, the Missouri Supreme Court rejected his appeal two months ago, and Governor Nixon would rather put a gun in his own mouth than pardon a creature like that. He's decided to put his business in order, so that history will record the truth and nothing but the truth about his great life . . . Pardon me a moment, please.'

He extricated his huge body from between chair and table and headed off to the bathroom. I felt tired and asked the waitress to bring more coffee. She gave me a smile as she poured it. The name on her badge was Alice, and she looked about the same age as my son. I glanced at the Ninja Turtle-shaped clock on the wall — there was still plenty of time.

'As I was saying,' Matt continued after he sat back down at the table and the waitress poured him another cup of coffee, 'Spoel got it into his head to persuade this guy from California that it'd all started with some crazy thing that Professor Wieder did to him years ago.'

'You mean he's saying that he murdered Wieder, but the victim was to blame?'

'Well, it's a bit complicated. As I was saying, when he was twenty, Spoel had an altercation with some guys and he stole some cash from one of them and beat him up pretty badly. His attorney asked for a psychiatric test, which Wieder performed. Spoel was found not competent to stand trial and committed to a hospital. His attorney assured him that in two or three months he would ask Wieder to test him again and that he'd be released. But he was locked up for two years, because Wieder opposed his release.'

'Like I said, I reviewed the case recently, after that reporter got in touch. It was a lead I considered at the time: possible revenge as a result of cases Wieder had dealt with in his capacity as an expert. But the name Frank Spoel never cropped up.'

'Who knows, maybe because he was just a small-time crook at the time, a twenty-one-year-old kid? You didn't think he was important. But he'll tell you what it's all about. I couldn't care less about stories told by morons like him. Anyway, I'm glad you came. Will you be staying at our place overnight?'

'I'm in the middle of repairing my home, so I want to finish before the rains come. Another time, buddy. Let's go, shall we?'

'We've got plenty of time, relax. The traffic on the I-55 is light at this hour. It'll take us an hour and a half to get there.' He let out a deep sigh. 'Spoel's complaining about being sent to the nuthouse when he was sane, but usually it's the other way round. Did you know that a third of the guys behind bars in maximum-security prisons have a screw loose? Two months ago I was in Chicago, at a training session on criminality. There were all kinds of hotshots there from agencies in DC. Apparently, after a two-decade cycle when criminality was in retreat, we've entered the opposite cycle. Since the psychiatric hospitals have become over-crowded, a complete nut stands every chance of being thrown into a jail among ordinary inmates. And people like me, who guard them, have to deal with specimens like that every day.'

He cast a glance at his watch. 'Shall we saddle up the horses?'

★ ★ ★

As we drove onto the interstate, I started thinking about Frank Spoel, whose case I'd studied before I set off for St Louis. He was one of the most dangerous murderers on death row. He'd killed seven people — eight, if it was true that he'd also killed Wieder — in three states before they caught him. He'd also committed four rapes and countless muggings. His last two victims had been a woman, aged thirty-five, and her daughter, aged twelve. Why had he done it? The woman had hidden some cash from him, he said. Spoel had picked her up in a bar two months before, and they'd been living together in a trailer by the river.

As Matt had said, the investigators were to later discover Frank Spoel had committed his first known killing in 1988, when he was just twenty-three years old. He'd been born and raised in Bergen County, New Jersey, and had committed his first serious crime at the age of twenty-one. He'd been released from the psychiatric hospital two years later and had headed to the Midwest, where he'd done all kinds of odd jobs for a while. His first victim had been a seventy-four-year-old man from Carroll County, Missouri, who'd given Spoel a lift in his truck on Route 65. The loot? A couple of bucks, an old leather jacket and a pair of boots that had happened to fit him.

He'd decided then to go to Indiana, where he'd committed his second murder. Then he had taken up with a gang from Marion, who'd specialised in burglaries. After the gang members had gone their separate ways, he'd returned to Missouri. It was interesting that for eight years after that he hadn't committed a single crime, working in St Louis in a pizza shop. Then he'd gone to Springfield and worked at a gas station for another three years. But suddenly he'd started all over again. He'd been arrested in 2005, after he'd been pulled over by a routine highway patrol.

At the time of the Wieder murder, I'd been reaching the end of my divorce and I'd found myself living all alone in a house that was far too big for me. Like any genuine alcoholic, I'd used that as an excuse to pour even more bottles down my throat and cry on the shoulder of anybody willing to listen. With the last remnants of my lucidity, I'd tried to do my job, but I'd always presumed that I'd made a hash of the Wieder case, along with some other cases from that time. The chief, Eli White, had been a very good man. If I were him, I'd have kicked me out of the service with references so bad that I wouldn't even have been able to find work as a nightwatchman in a mall.

Matt opened the windows and lit a cigarette as we drove down I-55, across the prairie. It was early summer and the weather was fine.

'When was the last time you were in a jail?' he asked, talking loudly to make himself heard over Don Williams, who was moaning on a country music station about a girl who never knew him at all.

'I think the last time was in the fall of 2008,' I said. 'I took a statement from a guy on Rikers, in connection with a case I was working on. It was a bad place, pal.'

'You think where we're going is any nicer? Every morning when I start my shift I feel like breaking something. Why the hell didn't we become doctors or lawyers?'

'I don't think we were smart enough, Matt. And I wouldn't have liked cutting people up.'

2

The Potosi Correctional Center was a red-brick giant, surrounded by barbed-wire electric fences, which lay in the middle of the prairie like a huge beast caught in a trap. It was a maximum-security prison, where around eight hundred inmates eked out their days, along with a hundred guards and auxiliary personnel. The few scraggy trees that flanked the visitors' parking lot were the only splotch of colour in that sad landscape.

Matt parked the car, then we went to the staff gate on the west side, passed through a courtyard paved with blood-red stone chips, and then entered a corridor that bored into the depths of the building. Matt saluted the men in uniform we met on the way, hulking, hard-faced men who'd seen all too much.

We went through a frame detector, collected our personal belongings from the plastic trays and arrived in a windowless room with a linoleum floor, where a number of tables and chairs were screwed to the floor.

An officer called Garry Mott gave me the usual instructions. speaking with a strong southern accent: 'The meetin' will last an hour sharp. If ya wanna end it soonah', tell the officers accompanyin' the inmate. Physical contact of any kind ain't allowed durin' the meetin', and any object ya wish to give the inmate or which he

236

might wish to give to ya has to be inspected first. Durin' the meetin', y'll be under constant camera surveillance and any information ya obtain may later be used in legal proceedings.'

I listened to the speech, which I was already familiar with, and then he left. Matt and I sat down.

'So this is where you work,' I said.

'It's not the happiest place in the world,' he said grimly. 'And thanks to you, one of my days off has gone down the drain.'

'I'll buy you a good lunch when we get out of here.'

'Maybe you should buy me some booze.'

'Then you'll have to drink it by yourself.'

'You can signal that way,' he said, pointing with his chin towards the corner where a camera was staring at us. 'Julia's on duty in the monitoring centre.'

He stood up.

'I've got to scoot. I've got some shopping to do. I'll be back in an hour to get you out of here. Play nice and make sure nobody gets hurt.'

Before he left, he waved at the video camera, and I pictured his wife sitting on a chair looking at banks of video screens in front of her. She was a strong woman, almost as tall as Matt, born and raised somewhere in the Carolinas.

I waited for a few minutes, and then I heard the buzz of the door. Frank Spoel made his entrance, flanked by two armed officers. He was wearing a grey jumpsuit. On the left side of his chest there was a white label with his name on it. His hands were cuffed behind his back and his legs were shackled with a chain, which shortened the length of his steps and rattled whenever he moved.

He was short and scrawny and if you'd met him on the street, you wouldn't have looked at him twice. But lots of the guys who end up behind bars for blood-curdling killings look just like him — an almost regular dude, like a mechanic or a bus driver. Before the eighties you could recognise criminals by the tattoos they'd had done in jail, but after that everybody started inking their hides.

Spoel sat down on the chair opposite me and grinned, flashing teeth as yellow as scrambled eggs. He had a sandy-coloured moustache, which drooped down on either side of his mouth to join a beard. He was going bald and the few remaining strands of hair covering his scalp were plastered down with sweat.

One of the officers said, 'You're gonna be a good boy, aren't you, Frankie?'

'Otherwise I can kiss my parole goodbye, right?' Spoel answered without turning around. 'What do you think I'm gonna do?' he continued rhetorically. 'Lob my dick out and open the cuffs?'

'Mind your mouth, princess,' the officer replied and then, to me, 'We'll be right by the door if you need us. If he starts playin', we're here in one sec.'

The two went out, leaving me alone with the inmate.

'Hey,' I said. 'I'm Roy Freeman. Thanks for agreeing to talk to me.'

'You a cop?'

'Ex-cop. I'm retired.'

'Could have sworn you a cop. In '97, I met a freak by the name of Bobby, back there in Indiana. He had a dog named Chill that could sniff out a cop even if he wasn't in uniform, know what I'm saying? A great mutt, that dog of his. Never could work out how it did it. It'd start barking whenever it got scent of a cop.'

'One hell of a dog,' I agreed.

'Yeah . . . I heard you're interested in that old New Jersey story.'

'I was one of the police detectives assigned to the Wieder case, the professor who got beaten to death.'

'Yeah, I remembered his name . . . Got a cigarette?'

I hadn't smoked for fifteen years, but taking Matt's advice I'd brought a carton of Camels with me. I knew that in jail, cigarettes were the main unit of currency, after drugs and sleeping pills. I reached into my bag and pulled out the carton, showed it to him, and then put it back.

'You'll get it after I leave,' I said. 'The guys have to check it.'

'Thanks. I don't have anybody on the outside. I haven't seen my folks for more than twenty years. Don't even know if they're still alive. In four weeks I'll be gone and I'd be a liar if I say I'm not scared. So, you wanna know what happened, right?'

'You claim you killed Joseph Wieder, Frank. Is it true?'

'Yes, sir, it was me. To be honest, I didn't

239

wanna do it, I wasn't a killer. Not back then anyway. I just wanted to beat him up a bit, if you know what I'm saying. I mean for the hospital, not for the morgue. The guy had done me a bad turn and I wanted to get even. But it ended up badly and I became a killer. But after two years in that nuthouse, nothing should have surprised me any more.'

'How about you tell me the whole story? We've got an hour.'

'The guys outside will be busy washing my Jag in the meantime,' he said, cracking a lame smile, 'so why not? I'm going to tell you what I told the other guy, the one who said he was writing a book.'

⋆　⋆　⋆

At the age of fifteen, Frank Spoel had dropped out of high school and started hanging out with some guys who ran an arcade. He'd been their errand boy. His dad had worked at a gas station and his mom had been a housewife; he had a sister who was five years younger. Two years later, his family had moved out of Jersey and Frank never saw them again.

At twenty, he'd already seen himself as a hustler, and had been mixed up in all kinds of petty crimes: he took stolen goods to fences in Brooklyn, and sold smuggled cigarettes and fake electronic goods. Sometimes he collected small amounts of cash for a loan shark, and sometimes he pimped for a couple of hookers.

In the gangs there're always lots of petty guys

like him, the little fish in a complex chain which goes from the streets of poor neighbourhoods all the way up to multimillion-dollar houses with swimming pools. Most of them end up in the same position: chasing after the next twenty-dollar bill, getting older and older and less and less important. Some of them rise through the ranks and get to wear expensive suits and gold watches. And a few end up committing felonies, rotting away in the joint, forgotten by everybody.

In the fall of 1985, Spoel had sold two boxes of cigarettes to a couple of guys in Princeton, and they'd paid for them with some French perfume. He'd later discovered that more than half of the bottles of perfume had been fakes, so he'd set off to demand his cash back. He'd found one of the guys, there had been a fight, he'd beaten him up and taken all the cash he'd found in his pockets, but a police patrol had happened to be passing by so he'd been arrested for mugging. He hadn't said anything about the cigarettes, because that would have got him into deeper trouble.

The court had assigned Spoel a public defender called Terry Duanne. By chance, the guy he'd beaten up had had a clean record. He was the thirty-eight-year-old owner of a small shop, married with three kids. Spoel, on the other hand, was a school drop-out and had already received a number of warnings for breaking the law. Duanne had tried to reach an agreement with the victim, but nothing had come of it.

Given the alternative of being tried as an adult, which meant between five and eight years

241

hard time, and having a medical expert declare him temporarily insane, Frank had been advised by his attorney to take the second option. Duanne had hinted that he knew the expert in question well and that in a couple of months Frank'd be discharged from hospital. Trenton Psychiatric Hospital wasn't the most pleasant place in the world, but it was better than Bayside Prison.

Joseph Wieder examined Frank Spoel and had come to the conclusion that he was suffering from bipolar disorder and had recommended that he be committed to a mental hospital, so a few days later he'd been taken to Trenton, confident that in a couple of months he would be out.

'Why weren't you discharged?' I asked.

'Ever been in a nuthouse?'

'No.'

'Don't ever go there. It was horrible, man. Shortly after I got there, they made me drink a cup of tea, and I woke up two days later, not even knowing my fuckin' name. There were guys there who'd start howling like wild animals or jump on you and beat you up for no reason. One guy ripped off a nurse's ear with his teeth as she was trying to feed him. The things I saw there, man . . . I heard that up until the sixties they used to pull all the patients' teeth out, claiming that it was to prevent infection. Infection my ass . . . '

He told his story. He'd been beaten up, by both the guards and the inmates. The warders, he claimed, were corrupt, so if you had cash you could get hold of anything you wanted, but if not, you were dead meat.

'People think that if you're doing hard time the thing that's most on your mind is women,' he said. 'But I tell you it ain't like that. Sure, you miss getting laid, but the most important thing is cash, believe me. If you've got no money, then you're as good as dead — nobody's interested in you, except the ones who're going to kick your ass. And I didn't have a penny, man. In the joint you can work to earn some cash, even if your folks aren't sending you dough. But in the nuthouse you just spend all day staring at the walls if you haven't got anybody on the outside to send any dough. And nobody sent me a dime.'

Three weeks after his admission, Spoel said, he'd been taken to a special ward, where there had been another ten inmates or so, all of them aged between twenty and thirty, all of them violent offenders. He'd later found out that he and the others were being given experimental medication, as part of a programme coordinated by a professor named Joseph Wieder.

'I talked to my lawyer a couple of times, but he just strung me along. In the end, he told me straight out that in a year he could apply to the judge to have me discharged or sent to a hospital with lower security. I couldn't believe what was happening to me. Two guys had ripped me off, I'd beaten one of them up and took eighty dollars from his wallet, money that didn't even cover my losses from the cigarettes, and there I was, locked up in the nuthouse for at least a year.'

'Didn't you get an opportunity to talk with Professor Wieder?'

'Sure, he sometimes came to our ward. He asked us all kinds of questions, made us pick colours, filled in questionnaires, stuff like that. We were just guinea pigs, man, white rats, you know? Told the guy straight out, 'That shit Duanne told me he knew you, so I agreed to the nuthouse just to get out of anything more serious. But I'm just as sound in the head as you are. What's the problem?' The guy just looked at me with those dead-fish eyes of his — I can almost picture them even now — and do you know what he said? That he didn't know what I was talking about, that I was there because I had mental issues, and that it was in my own interest to take the treatment, so I'd stay there as long as he saw fit. Bullshit.'

Then Spoel told me that he'd started having terrible nightmares, not even sure whether he was awake or dreaming, and that the pills he was being given had done him more harm than good. Most of the guys on the ward had had terrifying headaches, and as the treatment had gone on, many of them had ended up spending most of their time tied down to their beds, hallucinating. Most of them vomited back up what they ate and had skin rashes.

A year later he'd been visited by another attorney, called Kenneth Baldwin. The guy had said he'd taken over the case from Duanne, who'd left New Jersey. Spoel had told Baldwin how he'd ended up there and what the original agreement had been. He didn't know whether the new lawyer had believed him, but even so he'd applied for a judge to re-examine his client's case. Spoel had found himself again face to face with Wieder who turned down his request to be discharged and refused also to approve his transfer to the Marlboro Psychiatric Hospital, which had an easier regime. Spoel had been sent back to Trenton.

'About six months before I got the hell out of there,' he went on, 'we were moved to other wards, and the experimental ward was closed down. They changed my treatment and I began to feel better. I didn't have nightmares or headaches any more, but I still used to wake up not knowing who I was. My nerves were crawling, even if I tried to hide it and keep on everybody's good side, to show I wasn't insane. How could they do that to me, man? All right, I wasn't a good boy, but I hadn't killed anybody and I wouldn't even have beaten up that guy if he hadn't ripped me off. They treated me like an animal, and nobody gave a shit.'

When his case was examined the next time, Spoel had seen that Wieder was no longer on the commission. His request for a discharge under legal supervision had passed, and a couple of weeks later he'd left the hospital.

That had been in October 1987. When he'd got out, he hadn't even known where he was going to live. All his belongings had been sold for rent by the landlord of the dump where he used to live before being busted. The guys from his gang hadn't wanted to know him any more, afraid that they would attract the cops' attention if they hung out with him. One guy alone, a Chinese American he'd met before he got sent to

Trenton, had taken pity on him and given him food and shelter for a couple of days.

A few weeks later, he'd managed to get a job as a dishwasher at a diner near Princeton Junction, and the owner, a nice guy, had let him sleep in the storeroom. He'd started following Wieder straight away, who lived nearby in West Windsor. He'd been determined to move away and start a new life, but he hadn't wanted to leave before taking his revenge on the professor. He was convinced that Wieder, along with Duanne and maybe some other accomplices, had been running some kind of scheme and supplying subjects for secret experiments, and that he'd fallen into their trap. He was going to make them pay. But as Duanne was nowhere to be found, Wieder would have to be the one to foot the bill.

He'd found Wieder's address and seen that he lived alone in an isolated house. Originally he'd been planning on beating him up on the street, under cover of darkness, but after he'd staked out the professor's house he'd decided that it was the best place for the attack. He hadn't intended to kill him, he'd just wanted to beat the crap out of him, Spoel stressed again, so he'd got hold of a baseball bat from some kids and had wrapped it in an old towel to soften the blows. He'd hidden the bat on the shore of the lake by the professor's house.

At the time, he said, he'd become friends with one of the bartenders, a guy from Missouri called Chris Slade. Slade had been looking to get out of Jersey and he'd found a job at a trailer park in St Louis, so he'd suggested that Spoel should go with him. He'd wanted to leave straight after the winter holidays, so that had made events move more quickly than they might otherwise have.

Spoel had staked out Wieder's house over the course of a number of evenings. At 10 p.m. the diner closed, so by about 10.30 he would be hiding in the back garden, watching the house. He'd noticed that two people came to the house quite often — a young guy, who'd looked like a student, and a tall, well-built, scruffily bearded guy, who'd seemed to be some sort of handyman. But neither of them stayed overnight.

'On December twenty-first I resigned from the bar and told the owner I was headed for the West Coast. As I was leaving, he gave me my cash and two packs of cigarettes. I didn't want to be seen around the area, so I headed up to Assunpink Creek, where I hid out in a woodshed until it got dark, and then I set off for the professor's house. I think I got there at around nine p.m., but the professor wasn't alone. He was with the young guy and they were both drinking in the living room.'

I asked Spoel whether he remembered what the young guy had looked like, but he said he wouldn't be able to describe him, telling me that he'd looked the same as all the other spoiled kids who lived off their parents' cash on campus. About three days before the attack, when he'd been staking out Wieder's house, the young guy had almost seen him through the window; he'd looked straight at him before he managed to hide. Luckily for him, it'd been snowing heavily, so the guy had probably thought he was mistaken.

'I think it must have been a guy by the name of Richard Flynn,' I said. 'Are you sure there wasn't a young woman with them?'

'Positive. It was just the two of them. Like I said, I got there at around nine. The young guy didn't leave until around eleven, and the professor was alone in the house after that. I waited another ten minutes or so, to make sure the young guy was gone. I thought of ringing the bell and punching Wieder as he opened the door, but he made my job even easier — he opened the windows that looked out onto the backyard, and then he went upstairs. So I sneaked inside the house and hid in the corridor.'

Wieder had come back down into the living room, closed the windows and sat on the couch, looking through some papers. Spoel had crept up behind him and hit him over the head with the baseball bat. The blow hadn't been very hard, probably, because the professor had managed to get up and turn towards him. Spoel had gone around the couch and started hitting the professor wildly, ten or twelve times, before he fell to the floor. Spoel had been wearing a mask, so he hadn't been afraid that Wieder might recognise him. He'd been about to search the place for cash when he'd heard somebody opening the front door. He opened the glass door, ran around the house and fled into the snowstorm.

He'd tossed the bat into the half-frozen stream and hid in the woodshed near Assunpink Creek overnight. The next morning he'd met Slade at Princeton Junction and they'd set off for

Missouri. He'd later found out that the professor had died.

'I probably hit him harder than I thought,' he concluded. 'So that's how I ended up being a killer. Know what? After that, whenever I did anything bad, it was like I was waking up from a dream and I couldn't believe that I was the one who'd done it. I was always convinced I'd lost my mind because of the pills they gave me in that shithole. I'm not saying it just to make out I'm not to blame; in any case, there wouldn't be any point now.'

'You were on parole,' I said. 'Didn't anybody raise the alarm when you left New Jersey? Didn't they come looking for you?'

'I have no idea, man. I just left. Nobody asked me any questions after that, and I didn't get into trouble with the law again until 2005, when they pulled me off the highway for speeding. I told my attorney that I'd been a patient in Trenton years ago, so he asked for a psychiatric test. The expert appointed by the court ruled that I was sane enough to stand trial, so I was tried and convicted. And do you know what the irony is? When I was sane — and I'm telling you I *was* sane — I ended up in the nuthouse. But when even I was convinced that I wasn't sound in the head, they refused to send me to the nuthouse and decided to give me the injection instead.'

'It's been a good few years since then and maybe you don't remember everything too well, so let me ask you once again: are you sure that the professor spent that evening with a white guy about twenty, and with nobody else? Maybe you couldn't see very well — it was snowing outside, you were hiding in the backyard, and maybe you didn't have a good line of sight — '

'I'm positive, man. You said you were assigned to the case . . . '

'Right.'

'Then maybe you remember what the place looked like. The living room had two large windows and a glass door, opening up onto a backyard and the lake. When the lights were on and the curtains were open you could see everything in the room perfectly. The professor and that guy were both eating at the table. They talked, the young guy left, and Wieder was left alone.'

'Did they have an argument?'

'I don't know. I couldn't hear what they were saying.'

'You say it was eleven p.m. when the young guy left?'

'About eleven, I'm not very sure. It might have been eleven thirty, but no later than that.'

'And ten minutes later, you attacked Wieder.'

'Like I said, first I got inside the house and hid, then he came back down into the room, and that was when I whacked him. Maybe it wasn't ten minutes, maybe it was twenty, but no longer than that. My hands were still frozen when I hit him the first time, that's why I botched the blow, so I can't have been hiding indoors long.'

I looked at him and wondered how it was that his name had completely eluded me when I'd been investigating the possibility that the murder had been an act of revenge carried out by one of the professor's former patients.

True, the list of cases in which Wieder had testified as an expert was very long. And the prosecutor had been dumb and disorganised. He'd sent us every which way and then had changed his mind the next day about what leads we were supposed to follow up, so maybe I hadn't got the chance to check everything down to the last detail. The reporters had been harassing us, writing all kinds of crazy stuff in the newspapers. And I'd been driving around with a bottle of booze hidden in my car, wondering whether I was drunk enough to get kicked out of the force. When I thought back on that period, I wondered how interested I'd really been in who'd killed Joseph Wieder — all I'd been bothered about at the time was taking pity on myself and looking for excuses for my behaviour.

'So, you don't have the faintest idea who it was you heard entering the professor's house after you hit him?'

'No, I split straight away. I wasn't expecting anybody to turn up at that hour, so I got out of there as fast as I could and didn't look back. I thought that all I'd done was to give him a good beating. There were plenty of junkies in the area, so the cops would believe it was an attempted burglary. I didn't think it would be a big deal that some guy had got beaten up, and anyway, I'd be far away by then. But he died, and that changed everything, right?'

'You don't know whether there was more than one person at the door?'

251

He shook his head. 'Sorry, I've told you everything I know.'

'Wieder didn't die straight away, but two or three hours later,' I said. 'If somebody did arrive at around midnight, that person ought to have called an ambulance, but didn't. Maybe you just thought you heard the door. There was a strong wind that night and maybe it just rattled on its hinges.'

'No,' he said decisively. 'It was like I said. Somebody unlocked the door and walked into the house.'

'And that somebody left him there to die on the floor?'

He gave me a long look, wrinkling his forehead, which made him look like a confused monkey.

'I didn't know that . . . So, he didn't die instantly?'

'No. This unknown person could have saved him by calling for an ambulance. It wasn't until the next morning, by which time it was too late, that the handyman called 911. Wieder had been dead for a few hours by then.'

'That's why you're interested in who showed up?'

'Yes. During the attack, did Wieder say anything? Did he call for help, or ask who you were or anything like that? Did he utter any names?'

'No, he didn't call for help. Maybe he croaked something, I can't remember. At first he tried to defend himself, and then he fell and just tried to shield his head. But he didn't cry out, I'm

252

sure of that. Anyway, there was nobody around to hear him.'

The two armed officers came in and one of them signalled to me that our time was up. I was just about to say 'See you later' to Spoel, but then I realised that it'd have been a bad joke. In eight weeks the guy would be dead. I thanked him once again for agreeing to talk to me. We stood up and he made a move as if he wanted to shake hands, but then turned on his heel and, flanked by the officers, walked away with that stumbling gait caused by the shackles.

★   ★   ★

I remained alone in the room. I pulled the cigarettes out of the bag and held on to them, so that I wouldn't forget to give them to the officers on the way out.

Who had turned up at the professor's house at midnight and found him slumped on the floor, but hadn't called an ambulance? That person hadn't rung the bell or knocked on the door, but had used a key to get in, if Spoel was telling the truth. After so many years, one's memory can play tricks. Anyway, one thing was for sure — what he'd told me certainly didn't match up with what Derek Simmons had said at the time, and had repeated to that reporter a few months ago.

At the end of the investigation he'd carried out, John Keller had written a kind of summary of all the information he'd gathered; there was a copy of it in the papers he'd brought over to my house. He suspected that Laura Baines had been in the house at the time of the murder, and that she'd stolen the professor's manuscript, which he'd just finished and had been about to send to his publisher. Keller supposed that Laura and Richard could have been accomplices, because Laura wouldn't have been physically capable of killing Wieder by herself. He believed that Flynn had most likely wielded the bat, but that Laura Baines had been the moral author of the murder, the mastermind and the only one who'd stood to gain from it.

But if Spoel was telling the truth, then Laura Baines hadn't needed Flynn as an accomplice to the murder. Arriving there by chance after the attack, she'd have found the professor lying on the floor and could have taken advantage of the situation to steal the manuscript, closing the glass door through which Spoel had jumped and locking the entrance door behind her. Derek Simmons had stated that in the morning, when he'd arrived at the professor's house, he'd found the windows and doors closed.

And then I remembered another important detail, mentioned in the medical examiner's report. The coroner had been puzzled by one thing: of all the blows that Wieder had suffered during the struggle, only one had been fatal. It was probably the last blow, to the left temple, when the victim had already been lying on the floor and possibly unconscious. Spoel said he'd wrapped his baseball bat in a towel. A bat wrapped in a towel wouldn't have been so devastating a weapon. But what if the last blow, the one that killed Wieder, had been delivered by a different person?

★ ★ ★

Matt arrived a few minutes later and we went back out the way we'd come. I left the cigarettes for Frank Spoel at the gate and we went to the parking lot. The sky had cleared and now stretched over the prairie without one shred of cloud cover. A hawk hung high in the air, now and then letting out a shrill cry.

'You okay, buddy?' Matt asked me. 'You're as pale as death.'

'I'm fine. The air in there probably doesn't agree with me. Know any good restaurants nearby?'

'There's Bill's Diner, about three miles from here, on I-55. Wanna go there?'

'Told you I was going to buy you lunch, didn't I? I've still got four hours till my flight.'

He drove in silence to the place he'd mentioned, while I mulled over Spoel's story.

It was strange to me that his confession didn't fit Derek Simmons's story. Simmons had also claimed to be hiding in the backyard. If that's really what had happened, then it'd have been impossible for him and Spoel not to have seen each other. The backyard was big, but the only place where you could have hidden without being seen from inside, while at the same time having a view of the living room window, was somewhere on the left, on the side opposite the lake, where at the time there had been some

255

dwarf ornamental pine trees, about ten feet high, and a clump of magnolias.

'You're thinking about what the guy said, right?' asked Matt as we pulled into the parking lot opposite the diner.

I nodded.

'You can't even be sure he wasn't just making it all up. Trash like that would lie their heads off just to get some cigarettes out of it. Maybe he invented it all just to get some attention, or hopes that the execution will be delayed if they reopen the Wieder case. The killing was in a different state, so maybe he hoped he'll be sent to New Jersey to be tried for the murder, which means years in court and more tax dollars gone with the Swanee. His lawyer tried something like that already, but nothing came of it. A good thing too, if you ask me.'

'But what if he isn't lying?'

We got out of the car. Matt took his baseball cap off and ran his hand through his silver hair before putting it back on again.

'You know, I've been thinking about that guy from California, the one writing that book about murderers. I've lived among criminals all my life. At first I tried to put them in jail, and then I tried to keep them there for as long as the jury and the judge decided. I know them well and there's not much to say about them: some are born that way, just like one's born with a talent for drawing or basketball. Sure, they all have a sad story to tell, but I don't give a damn.'

We went inside the diner and ordered our lunch. During the meal, we talked about this and that, without mentioning Spoel. After we finished, he asked, 'What's gotten into you with all this stuff, anyway? Ain't you got anything better to do?'

I decided to tell him the truth. Matt wasn't a man who deserved to be lied to, and I was sure that he wouldn't look at me with that pitying expression I couldn't abide.

'About six months ago I went to see the doctor,' I said. 'I'd started to forget things, especially street names, even though I'd always had a good memory. I tried to do exercises: which actor was in which movie, who sang a particular tune, what the score was in some ball game, stuff like that. I noticed I was also having problems with names, so I went to the doctor. He ran some tests, asked me all kinds of questions, and two weeks later he gave me the big news.'

'Don't tell me it's — '

'All right, I won't tell you.'

He gave me a look, so I carried on.

'It's Alzheimer's, yes, in the early stages. I haven't started forgetting to go to the toilet yet, or what I ate last night. The doctor told me to keep my mind active, to do exercises; he gave me a book and some videos to help me. But I remembered that reporter who was interested in the Wieder case. I'd been to the department and got hold of some papers for him from the archive. He sent me what he'd found out, so I said to myself that it seemed like a good idea to keep my mind busy with something like that, something actually interesting and important,

257

rather than trying to remember ancient ball games. I realised that I'd always thought I'd blown the case, because at the time I was just a lousy drunk. So, after that I called you and came here.'

'I'm not sure I did a good thing, digging up the dead like that. I only told you for the sake of conversation, by the by, I wasn't expecting you to come out here because of it. I'm really sorry to hear about — '

'It's important for me to know what happened back then and how I let the murderer get away. In a year or two, but not more than three, I won't know who Wieder was any more or even remember that I used to be a cop. I'm trying to clear up the mess I made, all the shit that happened because of me, most of which I'm still paying for.'

'I think you're being too hard on yourself,' he said, flagging the waitress and asking her to bring more coffee. 'We all had good and bad periods. I can't remember you ever not doing your duty. We all respected you, Roy, and thought you were a good man. Okay, we all knew you liked a drink, but we had to shield ourselves the best we could from the things that went on around us, didn't we? Let the past lie and start looking after yourself.'

He paused before asking, 'Did he give you a course of treatment? The doctor, I mean, pills and stuff?'

'I'm taking some pills. I do everything the doctor tells me to, but I'm not holding out much hope. I've been reading up about Alzheimer's online, so I know there's no cure. It's just a matter of time. When I'm no longer able to look after myself, I'll go to an old folks' home.'

'Sure you don't want to stay overnight? We could talk some more.'

'I'd lose money if I changed the ticket now. But maybe I'll come back out here at some point. I haven't got much else to do.'

'You're welcome any time, you know that. But no more visits to the jail.'

'I promise.'

⋆ ⋆ ⋆

He drove me to the airport. I got this weird feeling that it'd be the last time I'd ever see him, despite our conversation, and after he started walking back to the entrance I watched him navigate his way through the crowd, like a cruiser among rowing boats, until he vanished outside.

Three hours later I landed in Newark and took a cab home. On the way, the driver put on a CD of old Creedence Clearwater Revival and as I listened I tried to remember my first days together with Diana: how we'd met at a picnic; how I'd lost her number and then bumped into her by chance as I'd been coming out of a cinema with some buddies; how we'd made love for the first time in a motel on the Jersey Shore. Strangely, those memories seemed more vivid than the visit I'd just made to Potosi.

I'd long since noticed that when you're intensely caught up in something, one part of your brain keeps chewing it over, even when

259

you're thinking about something else. I paid the cab and as I was opening my front door, I decided that Spoel's story that he'd killed Wieder was true — it had to be, he had nothing to lose — and that for one reason or another Derek Simmons had been lying to me when I'd questioned him almost thirty years ago. Now I had to find out why.

3

I paid Simmons a visit two days later, after having called him first. I found his address among the papers I'd received from John Keller. Simmons lived near the Princeton Police Department, and I got there around 3 p.m., just as some rainclouds were shedding their load on the shingled rooftops.

Before the meeting I'd tried to remember his face, but I couldn't. He was in his early forties when I'd investigated the case, so I expected to find a wrecked man. I was wrong — if you ignored the deep wrinkles on his face and the white hair, he had a much younger appearance.

I introduced myself and he told me that he vaguely remembered me — the guy who looked like a priest, not like a cop. I asked him where the woman I'd read about in Keller's notes, Leonora Phillis was, and he said that she'd gone to Louisiana to look after her mom, who'd had surgery.

We went into the living room and I sat on the couch, while he brought me a cup of coffee that had a taste of cinnamon. He explained it was a trick he'd learned from Leonora, a Cajun technique. He fixed a cup of coffee for himself and lit a cigarette, dragging closer an already full ashtray.

'I don't think I'd have recognised you if I'd bumped into you on the street,' he said. 'To be

261

honest, I tried to forget the whole thing ever happened. Do you know that a reporter came here asking me about it a couple of months ago?'

'Yes, I know, I spoke with him too.'

I told him the story of Frank Spoel, referring to the notes I'd jotted down in the notepad I'd been using to organise all the information I had, like I did in the old days. He listened to me carefully, without interrupting, sipping his coffee from time to time and lighting one cigarette after another.

When I finished he didn't comment, but just asked me if I wanted more coffee. The ashtray was so full of butts that it was on the verge of spilling over onto the mahogany table between us.

'Now do you understand why I wanted to talk to you?' I asked.

'No,' he answered calmly. 'Nobody has asked me anything about it for almost thirty years, and now everybody seems interested. I don't get it, na'mean? It doesn't give me any pleasure to talk about what happened back then. The professor was the only pal I had.'

'Derek, do you remember what you said in your statement at the time? And what you told the reporter not long ago?'

'Sure.'

'What you said doesn't add up with what Spoel told me. He claims that on the evening of the crime he was hiding in the backyard, behind the house. You stated that you were hiding there at the same time, nine p.m. How could you have missed each other? You said that the professor

262

was there with Laura Baines, and Richard Flynn, who started an argument with Wieder; then you said Laura left, though you saw her car parked nearby later. But Spoel said nothing about Laura Baines. He claims that the professor was with Richard Flynn, and that he didn't notice any disagreement between them.'

I'd written down in my notebook all the discrepancies between the two versions, point by point.

'So what?' he said, not seeming the least bit interested. 'Maybe the guy forgot what happened in the meantime or maybe he's lying. Why would you believe him and not me? What do you want from me anyway?'

'It's not hard to guess,' I answered. 'One of you isn't telling the truth, and now I'm inclined to think it's you. What I'm interested in is why you'd lie to me.'

He grinned, but without any trace of amusement.

'Maybe I'm not lying, but I just can't remember that night well. I'm old: isn't it normal to forget when you get old?'

'I'm not just talking about what you told Keller a couple of months ago, but also what you told the police at the time, immediately after the murder,' I said. 'The two accounts are practically identical. And you told Keller that Wieder and Laura were having an affair, remember?'

'Maybe they were. How do you know that they weren't?'

'You're the only person who had claimed back then that Laura Baines and the professor were lovers. And because Flynn was in love with her, it'd have given an investigator a reason to presume he'd murdered Wieder in a fit of jealousy — a possible motive.'

'That's what I've always thought, that they were lovers. And I still believe that Richard only pretended to leave that night, but then he came back and murdered the professor. If you weren't able to prove it, then that's your problem, na'mean? As for their relationship, maybe you didn't ask the right people.'

'You weren't hiding behind the house that night, were you, Derek? Why did you try to frame Flynn?'

He suddenly seemed angry and agitated.

'I didn't try to frame anybody, man. It was exactly like I said: I was there and saw all three of them in the living room.'

'So you're saying you stood in the snow for almost two hours? What were you wearing?'

'How the hell should I know? Don't remember.'

'How come you didn't see Spoel and he didn't see you?'

'Maybe he's lying and he wasn't there, or maybe he got the time wrong. Why should I care?'

'Why did you claim Laura Baines was there?'

'Because I saw her, and her car was parked nearby. You keep making me repeat the same things, like a parrot, man.'

He stood up abruptly.

'I'm sorry, but I promised a customer that I'd finish fixing his car by this evening. It's in the garage. I've got to go. I don't feel like talking to you, no offence, but I don't like your tone. Now it's time to play ball. Thank you for your cooperation.'

'What did you say?'

'Yankees versus Baltimore Orioles: I was there when the announcer said it after the catcher — Thurman Lee Munson — got killed in that plane crash. Now, FYI, I'm not going to talk to anybody about Wieder unless that person's got a warrant. I'll see you out.'

I left, feeling almost ridiculous, like a kid playing detective who'd just been kicked out of the house by one of the 'suspects'. I'd used to be a cop once, but those times were long gone. Now I was only an old man fooling around, no shield or gun in his belt. I got into my car and tossed the spiral notebook in the glove box.

As I turned onto Valley Road, with the windscreen wipers barely able to cope with the downpour, I asked myself where I wanted to go with the whole story. I was almost sure Derek was lying, and that he'd also been lying in the statement he'd made immediately after the murder, but there was nothing I could do about it. Matt had told me that Spoel's attorney had tried to have the case reopened, but without success. I was nothing but a senile ex-cop fooling around.

For the next couple of days, I worked on repairing the roof of my house and painted the living room, while thinking about the case.

That Saturday I cleared the backyard, and on Sunday I crossed the river and visited a former colleague in the city, Jim Foster, who'd survived a heart attack and had been released from hospital a couple of weeks earlier. It was a beautiful day, so we went for a walk and then sat down for lunch at a restaurant near Lafayette Street. He told me all about the drastic diet he was on. I asked him whether he remembered anything about the Joseph Wieder case and he was a little taken aback, saying the name didn't ring a bell.

'He was that professor at Princeton who was murdered in his own home in December 1987. A death row inmate in Potosi, Missouri, is claiming he killed him. The guy's name is Frank Spoel and he was just twenty-two at the time. I dealt with the case back then.'

'I never did like the name Frank,' he said, looking at the Italian sausages on my plate. 'As a kid I read *Gone with the Wind* and there was a character called Frank, whose breath stank. I don't know why that detail stuck in my head, but I always remember it when I hear the name. Why are you still interested in this story?'

'Have you ever had a case you were obsessed with, one that you remember all the time, even years later?'

'I had many cases, Roy.'

'Yes, I know, but I've realised after all these years that this case still troubles me. I mean, I have the feeling there's something more down there, something important, waiting for me, you know? I'm not talking about *Law & Order* crap, but about justice, about the sensation that if I failed, it'd be for good.'

He thought for a few moments.

'I think I know what you're saying . . . After I moved to the NYPD in the nineties, I worked in narcotics for a while. It was back when we were working with the Feds, battling the Westies in Hell's Kitchen and Gotti's boys. There was no time to get bored. The ex of an Irish boss, a young lady named Myra, told us she was ready to spill the beans if we gave her protection. I arranged to meet her in a bar on West 43rd Street, called Full Moon. I went with a colleague, Ken Finley, who was killed in a gun fight with some guys from Nicaragua down in Jersey a year later. Now, the lady showed up, we ordered drinks, and I told her what the witness protection programme involved, if she was ready to work with us. Then she said she had to go to the ladies' room, so I waited. My team and I sat for ten minutes or so, and then we realised that something was wrong. I asked the barmaid to go into the ladies' and look for her, but she wasn't there. Finally I talked to the manager and we did a search. Nothing, man. There were no windows and the only way out was down the john or through the air shaft, which wasn't even big enough for a toddler. We couldn't understand what was going on: our table was by the toilets, so if she'd come out, we'd have seen her. Plus, the joint was almost empty, and nobody else had gone in or out of the toilet in the meantime.'

'Whatta story . . . Did you ever find out what happened?'

He shook his head.

'Perhaps I didn't feel like thinking about it. It

makes my hair stand on end even now. It was like she'd vanished into thin air, just a few feet away from me, and I did nothing. She was never found, dead or alive. For years I've beaten my brains trying to understand how it could have happened. Probably every cop has a monkey like that on his back, Roy. Maybe you shouldn't think too much about yours.'

After I walked Jim back to his home, I went to the parking lot where I'd left my car. As I was passing McNally Jackson Books, I saw a small poster announcing that Dr Laura Westlake was going to be giving a lecture there on Wednesday afternoon, which was in three days' time. I wouldn't have dared approach her in a private setting, so I thought that maybe I'd be able to have a few words with her after the book signing. The fact that I'd come across that poster was like a sign to me, so I decided to take my chances.

There was no photo on the poster, so that evening I tried to find one on the Internet. I vaguely remembered her — a tall, slim and self-confident young lady who'd answered all my questions calmly during the interview back then — but I couldn't bring her face to my mind. I found a few recent photos and studied them for a couple of minutes, noticing her high forehead, cold gaze and the harsh expression of her mouth. She wasn't pretty in a lot of ways, but I could understand why Richard Flynn had so madly fallen in love with her.

★　★　★

Three months earlier, at John Keller's request, I'd gone to the archives of the West Windsor Township Police Department and made some copies of the documents from the Wieder case. Now I went to the Princeton Police Department and asked about the Simmons case, when Derek had been accused of murdering his wife. Richard Flynn had mentioned the case in his manuscript only in passing, saying that he'd heard the details from Laura Baines. There was nothing wrong with taking a look at the file. The murder had taken place in 1982, a few years after I'd moved to the West Windsor department.

I talked on the phone to Chief Brocato, whom I knew from back in the day, when we'd worked together, and he let me look through the archives without asking too many questions. A guy in reception gave me a visitor's badge, and then I went down to the basement, where the archives were kept, alongside the evidence room.

As far as the layout of the archives went, nothing had changed since the time I'd worked there. An elderly officer, Val Minsky, whom I also knew, put an old cardboard box in my arms and took me to a makeshift office, where there was a table with a lamp, a tired old Xerox machine, two chairs and some empty shelves. He told me to take my time to look over the paperwork I'd requested, and left me to it, after pointing out that smoking wasn't allowed.

Over the next hour, as I read the file, I told myself that Flynn's account, although brief, was accurate.

Derek Simmons hadn't admitted to the

murder, and the judge's ruling had been not guilty by reason of insanity, following an examination carried out by Joseph Wieder. After his arrest, Simmons had been held in New Jersey State Prison, and had then been committed to the Trenton Psychiatric Hospital, which is where the accident that caused his amnesia had happened.

A year later, having recovered physically, he'd been moved to the Marlboro Psychiatric Hospital, from where he'd been released from two years later. It was also Joseph Wieder who'd written the expert assessments that led to the judge deciding to move Simmons to Marlboro and later to release him. After his release under supervision, there was just one more document in the file: in 1994, the judge's order lifting the supervision, also following an expert assessment.

I jotted down the names of the other two experts who, along with Wieder, had signed the report that got Simmons out of jail in 1983. One of them was called Lindsey Graff, the other John. T. Cooley.

Then I noticed a list of phone numbers.

Simmons hadn't been arrested straight away; instead he'd been taken in eight days after his wife's death. The list contained the numbers of the phone calls made and received at the Simmons family home from a week before the murder up until Derek's arrest. I copied out the list and put it in my briefcase.

One of my buddies who'd dealt with the Simmons case, Nicholas Quinn, had died of a heart attack in the nineties. The other guy on the paperwork had probably joined the department after I'd left. His name was Ian Kristodoulos.

I gave back the box of papers to Officer Minsky, who asked me whether I'd found what I was looking for.

'Don't know yet,' I said. 'Do you know Detective Kristodoulos, one of the guys who worked on the case? I knew the other one, Quinn, but he died about fifteen years ago.'

'Sure I know him. He moved to the NYPD about five years ago.'

'Do you have any idea how I could get hold of his number?'

'Gimme a sec.'

'Thanks a lot, Val.'

'Anything for a buddy.'

Minsky made a few calls, sprinkled with jokes about cheating wives and drunk moms, during which he kept winking at me like he had a twitch. Finally his wrinkled, reddish face revealed a triumphant expression, and he wrote a cell phone number on a Post-it and handed it to me.

'He hasn't retired yet, apparently. He's with the Sixty-seventh Precinct in Brooklyn, on Snyder Avenue. Here's the number.'

I entered Kristodoulos's number in the memory of my cell phone, thanked Minsky and left.

* * *

I arranged to meet Ian Kristodoulos that afternoon at a cafe near Prospect Park, and in the meantime tried to track down the two experts.

After much searching online, I found out that

there was a psychiatrist named Lindsey Graff who had a practice in the city, on East 56th Street. The practice also had an Internet site, where I had a look at Ms Graff's bio. There was a 99 per cent chance that I'd hit on the right person — between 1981 and 1985, Lindsey Graff had worked as an expert for the Office of the State Medical Examiner, after which she'd taught at NYU for six years. She'd opened the clinic with two colleagues in 1998.

I called the clinic and tried to get an appointment, but the assistant told me that Dr Graff wouldn't be available until around mid-November. I told her that I had a special problem, so I'd like to speak to Dr Graff over the phone. I left her my number and she said she'd pass on the message.

I still hadn't managed to track down John T. Cooley when I arrived to my meeting with Kristodoulos that afternoon. The man was short and stocky, dark-haired, the kind that grows a day's worth of beard just an hour after shaving. Over the next hour, he told me in an unfriendly voice what he remembered about the Simmons case.

'It was my first important case,' he said. 'I'd been with the department a year and a half and had only dealt with small stuff up to then. I asked Quinn to take me on as his partner when it happened. You know how it is, you never forget your first murder case, the same as you never forget your first girlfriend. But that scumbag Simmons got away with it.'

He said that he'd never doubted that Derek

Simmons had killed his wife, the motive being that she'd been having an affair. Simmons had seemed sane, but very cunning, so the result of the psychiatric evaluation had disgusted the entire department.

'The evidence was solid, so if it'd gone to trial he'd have got life without parole, no doubt about it. But there was nothing we could do. That's the law — nobody can override the expert's verdict. They took him to the hospital, and he got out of there in a couple of years. But I don't think God was napping, because some guy hit him over the head while he was in the hospital and then he really did lose his mind, from what I've heard. They changed the law just a year later, in 1984, after the guy who'd attempted to kill President Reagan was found not guilty by reason of insanity, when Congress passed the Insanity Defence Reform Act.'

After I left Kristodoulos and got home, I carried on looking for some trace of Cooley, but without any success. Lindsey Graff didn't call me but I wasn't really expecting her to.

At around 10 p.m., while I was watching an old episode of *Two and a Half Men*, Diana called.

'You promised to do me that favour I asked you,' she said after we exchanged the usual pleasantries. It was two or three weeks since we'd last spoken.

I remembered what she was talking about: I was supposed to track down a certificate from a company she'd worked for years ago; she needed it for her retirement application. I mumbled an excuse and promised to do it the very next day.

'I was just checking,' she said. 'There's no rush. Maybe I could fly out for a week or so and do it myself in the next few days. You okay?'

Every time I heard her voice I got the feeling that we'd broken up just a few days before. I told her I was fine, that I'd get her the certificate, but that I'd quite simply forgotten and only just remembered now. And then I understood why she was really calling, and asked her, 'Matt called you, didn't he?'

She didn't say anything for a couple of seconds. 'That bigmouth didn't have any right to — '

'Roy, is it true? There's no doubt? Have you asked for a second opinion? Is there anything I could do for you?'

I felt embarrassed, as if Diana had found out something shameful about me. I told her I'd never be able to accept her pity. And I didn't think it'd be the best thing for her to spend her last years with a zombie who couldn't even remember his own name.

'Dee, I don't want to talk about it. Not now, not ever.'

'I'd like to come over for a couple of days. I've got nothing else to do apart from filling in this damned application, and even that can wait.'

'No.'

'Please, Roy.'

'I'm living with someone, Dee.'

'You never said anything about it till now.'

'She moved in last week. We met two months ago. Her name's Leonora Phillis; she's from Louisiana.'

'Leonora Phillis from Louisiana . . . You might

274

as well have said Minnie Mouse from Disney-land. I don't believe you, Roy. You've lived alone ever since we split up.'

'I'm serious, Dee.'

'Why are you doing this, Roy?'

'I have to hang up now, sorry. I'll get you that certificate, I promise.'

'I'm coming over, Roy.'

'Don't do that, Dee. Please.'

I hung up, lay down on the couch, clenching my eyelids until it hurt and my eyes started to water.

Interracial couples weren't common in the early seventies, not even in the north-east. I remembered the looks we used to get when we went into a bar, some of them hostile, some of them outraged. There were also complicit looks, as if Diana and I had fallen in love with each other just to prove some point. We'd both had to deal with it, and I'd at least been able to console myself that I'd never have to spend Christmas with my in-laws in Massachusetts. But later I'd lost everything when I hit the bottle. When I'd been drinking, I wasn't just coarse; I was really mean. I'd liked to insult her, to blame her for everything, to say stuff I'd known would hurt her the most. And even after all that time, when I remembered the way I'd been back then, I still felt my stomach turn in disgust.

Forgetting all of that was going to be the only good thing my illness would bring — I'd stop thinking about those years, because I wouldn't even remember they'd ever existed.

I'd managed to give up drinking three years

after the divorce, with the help of many AA meetings, a halt in a clinic in Albany; I'd also hard to work my way back from two relapses. But I knew that I'd remained an alcoholic and that I'd be an alcoholic until the very end. I knew that the moment I walked into a bar and ordered a cold one or a Jack's, I'd never be able to stop. I'd sometimes been tempted to do it, especially right after I retired, when I used to think that nothing was of any importance any more. But each time I'd told myself that it'd be the ugliest kind of suicide possible; there were other ways, quicker and cleaner.

I got dressed and went for a walk in the park, which was about three hundred feet from my house. It was on a hill and in the middle there was a large glade with wooden benches that I liked to sit on. From there I could see the lights of the town — it made me feel as if I was floating over the rooftops.

I stayed there for about half an hour, watching the people walking their dogs or taking the short cut to the bus stop at the bottom of the hill. Then I slowly walked back home, wondering whether I'd done the stupidest thing in the world when I'd told Diana not to come and see me.

4

On Wednesday afternoon I arrived at McNally Jackson Books at 4.45 p.m., quarter of an hour before the start of the event. Laura Baines had published her new book on hypnosis less than a month before, and the lecture that afternoon was part of her promotional tour. I bought a copy of the book and took a seat downstairs. Almost every chair was taken.

Early that morning I'd stopped off at the company from which Diana needed the certificate. A clerk had promised me that she'd send it in an email attachment the next day, so I'd texted Diana to tell her the problem had been solved. But she hadn't replied, and I'd thought she must have had her cell phone switched off.

Laura looked better than in the photos I'd found on the Internet, and she was obviously an experienced public speaker. I listened to her with interest, even though I was on tenterhooks, wondering how many seconds it'd take her to send me packing once she realised who I was and why I was there.

She finished the lecture, and after a short Q&A session a line formed for signings. I was the last person to hand her a copy and she looked at me questioningly.

'Freeman, Roy Freeman,' I said.

'For Freeman, Roy Freeman,' she said with a smile and then signed the book.

'Thanks.'

'And I thank you. Are you a psychologist by chance, Mr Freeman?'

'No, I'm an ex-police detective, homicide. I investigated the death of Professor Joseph Wieder almost thirty years ago. You probably don't remember me, but I took an interview with you back then.'

She stared at me, opened her mouth to say something and then changed her mind, running her left hand through her hair. She looked around and saw that I was the last person wanting an autograph. She placed the cap back on her fountain pen and put it in the handbag on the chair next to her. A middle-aged woman whose hair was dyed violet was watching dutifully from a few feet away.

'I think I'll walk a little with Mr Freeman,' she told the violet woman, who looked at her in amazement.

'Are you sure — '

'I am quite sure. I'll call you tomorrow morning. Take care of yourself.'

I helped her into her coat, then she picked up her handbag and we left. It had grown dark and the air smelled like rain.

'Debbie is my agent,' she said. 'Sometimes she behaves like a mama bear, you know. Did you enjoy the lecture, Mr Freeman?'

'It was very interesting, really.'

'But that wasn't what you came for, is it?'

'I was hoping to get the chance to talk to you for a few moments.'

'Usually I don't agree to talk to anybody after

a lecture, but in a way it's like I've been expecting you.'

We were passing Zanelli's Cafe and she accepted my invitation to go inside. She ordered a glass of red wine and I asked for a coffee.

'I'm listening, Mr Freeman. After I agreed to talk to a reporter about this story a couple of months ago, I realised that the postman always rings twice. I knew that I was going to meet somebody who'd ask me about a time long gone. Call it female intuition. Do you know Richard Flynn tried to write a book about the Wieder case?'

'Yes, I know. I read an excerpt from that manuscript. John Keller, that same reporter, gave me a copy. But in the meantime something occurred and that's why I wanted to talk to you.'

I told her about Frank Spoel and his version of what had happened that night. She listened carefully, without interrupting me.

'The reporter probably didn't believe me when I told him that I wasn't involved in a love affair with Richard Flynn,' she said, 'and nor with Professor Wieder, of course. But anyway, what that man says does seem to fit what happened, doesn't it?'

'Dr Westlake, I don't think Frank Spoel killed the professor. Somebody who had the keys to the house entered while he was there. The professor was still alive at that point. That person almost came face to face with Spoel, who managed to escape through the glass door at the last moment. I repeat: the professor was still alive. Spoel just wanted to teach him a lesson. But when a man's already unconscious on the floor and you hit him hard over the head with a baseball bat, it means you intend to kill him. Anyway, the person who showed up didn't call an ambulance. Why? I think that person acted like an opportunistic predator, taking advantage of the situation. Wieder was unconscious on the floor, the glass door was open, so it was possible that somebody had broken in, beaten him up and fled. That person would have been accused of the murder.'

'And you want to ask me if I was that person, the opportunistic predator, as you put it?'

I didn't answer, so she went on, 'Mr Freeman, that evening I didn't go to the professor's house. I hadn't been there for a couple of weeks.'

'Ms Westlake, that friend of yours, Sarah Harper, supplied you with a false alibi and lied to us. And you lied to us too. John Keller talked to her and gave me his notes. Harper is in Maine now, but she could testify if necessary.'

'I suspected you knew that. Sarah was a very fragile human being, Mr Freeman. If you'd turned the screws on her back then, she'd have caved in immediately and told you the truth. I took that risk when I asked her to tell you we'd been together. But I was trying not to get in the newspapers, not to be bullied by the press. I didn't want all kinds of dirty insinuations about the professor and me to be made. That was all. I wasn't afraid of being accused of the murder, but merely trying to avoid a scandal.'

'So where were you that afternoon, after you left lectures? Richard Flynn claimed in his manuscript that you weren't with him. And you probably weren't with your boyfriend, Timothy Sanders, otherwise you would have asked him to testify — '

'That afternoon I was at a clinic in Bloomfield, where I had an abortion,' she said curtly. 'I'd got pregnant by Timothy when he was just about to go to Europe. I told him the news when he came back and he didn't seem at all enthusiastic. I wanted to solve the problem before I went home for the holidays, because I was sure my mother would notice what was happening. I didn't even tell Timothy where I was going and went to the clinic alone. I arrived home late and had a terrible argument with Richard Flynn. He wasn't a big drinker, but I think he was drunk. He'd spent the evening with the professor and claimed that he'd told him I was his lover. I packed my bags and went to Sarah's. In any event, I was planning to move from there after the holidays. Do you understand why I didn't want to tell you where I'd been that day, and why I asked Sarah to say that we'd been together? I was pregnant, people gossiped about a love affair with the professor, so the press could have made a connection between — '

'The reporter, Keller, reached the conclusion that you stole Wieder's manuscript and published it under your own name.'

'What manuscript?'

'The manuscript of your first book, published five years later. In his project, Flynn said that you'd told him about a very important book Wieder was working on, which would be a real game changer, something about the connections between mental stimuli and reactions. Actually, it was the subject of your first book, wasn't it?'

'Yes, it was, but I didn't steal the manuscript from the professor,' she said, shaking her head. 'The manuscript you're talking about didn't even exist, Mr Freeman. I'd given the professor an outline for my dissertation and the opening chapters. He was very enthusiastic about my idea and had provided me with some extra materials, after which things gradually became mixed up and he came to think of it as his own work. I found the proposal he'd sent to a press, in which he'd claimed that the manuscript was ready for submission. In fact, he didn't have a proper book project, but only those chapters from my work and an incoherent blend of excerpts from his older books — '

'May I ask you when and how did you find the proposal you're talking about?'

She took a sip of wine, cleared her throat, and then said, 'I guess he'd asked me to put some of his papers in order, without knowing that the proposal was among them.'

'And when was that? You've just said that you hadn't been there for quite a time.'

'Well, I can't remember when I found the proposal, but that was the main reason why I started to avoid visiting him. He'd fallen out with the people he'd been working with, and he was unable to concentrate on finishing another book. At the same time, he wanted to impress the university where he intended to start work the following year. He wanted to go back to

Europe for a while.'

'And which university was that?'

'Cambridge, I guess — '

'Who were these mysterious people he was working for?'

'Well, they weren't quite as mysterious as the professor would have liked to believe. From what I know, he collaborated with the research department of a military agency, which wanted to study the long-term effects of psychological traumas suffered by subjects forced to act under extreme circumstances. In the summer of 1987, the contract expired, period. But the professor was inclined to act like a drama queen sometimes. In a way, he liked to believe that he was being pressured by that agency, mixed up in all kinds of secret affairs, and bullied for knowing too much. Maybe it was an unconscious way of compensating for the fact that, to be honest, his career was in decline. A couple of years before the tragedy, the radio and TV talk shows and the interviews in the newspapers had become more important to him than his scientific career. He was flattered when people recognised him on the street, and at the university he felt superior to the other professors. He'd become a star, in other words. But he'd neglected the genuinely important part of his work, and that had an effect — he had nothing new to say and he began to realise it.'

'But Sarah Harper — '

'Sarah had serious problems, Mr Freeman! Don't think that she took a sabbatical because Professor Wieder was killed. We lived together for a year and I knew her well.'

'Right, so the book you published wasn't Wieder's project?'

'Of course it wasn't! I published my book once I was able to finish it, after my PhD thesis. Today I think it was clumsily conceived, and I'm amazed by the notoriety it gained at the time.'

'But the first chapter of your book is one hundred per cent similar to the chapter sent by the professor to a publisher. Keller got a copy of the professor's proposal. You've said that you saw it.'

'That's because he'd stolen it from me, I told you.'

'So Wieder was about to steal your work . . . Why hadn't you tried to do something? When you found that copy, the proposal was already sent to the publisher. If he hadn't been killed, probably he'd have published the book under his name — your book, I mean.'

'If I'd accused such an important figure of intellectual fraud, I'd probably have been considered paranoid. I was a nobody; he was one of the most appreciated psychologists in the country.'

She was right. But on the other hand, she was a very determined person and this was her life's work we were talking about, a chance for her to be recognised as the best. It wasn't difficult for me to imagine what she'd have done if somebody had tried to hurt her one way or another, especially concerning her career.

'Okay, so let's get back to the night the professor was murdered. That evening, after you argued with Flynn and left, did he remain at home?'

She didn't answer immediately.

'No,' she eventually said. 'He took his coat and left the house before I did.'

'Do you remember what time it was?'

'I got home at around eight p.m., and he arrived immediately after ten. I think he went out again at around eleven.'

'So he'd have had time to get back to West Windsor by around midnight.'

'Yes.'

'Had he called a cab before leaving?'

'Probably, I can't remember.'

'Did he argue with the professor that evening?'

'I don't remember very well . . . He seemed very angry. He left slamming the door after I'd told him that if the professor had asked me to sleep with him, I'd probably have done so, but he'd never asked. That was the truth. At first, I found it amusing that Richard was in love with me, but it'd become tiresome. He was treating me like I'd cheated on him or something. I wanted to put a stop to it once and for all. Unfortunately I wasn't successful. He harassed me for a long time after that, even after we'd both left Princeton.'

'There were papers scattered all over the place and the drawers were open, as if the killer or someone else had been looking for something in a hurry. But it wasn't Spoel, because he left the room using the glass door after hearing someone at the entrance. Okay, maybe it was Flynn, who'd have had time to get back there. But if so, why would he have been interested in those papers?'

'I don't know, Mr Freeman. I've told you everything I remember.'

'When he called you last year, did he confess anything to you? Did he tell you anything you didn't know about what'd happened that night?'

'No, not exactly. He was upset and didn't make much sense. All I could gather was that he was accusing me of being involved in Wieder's death, and that I'd used him to achieve my sordid goal. He was pitiful rather than frightening.'

She hadn't said she was sorry for Flynn's tragic end or even the professor's death, not once. Her voice was dry and analytical and I assumed her pockets were full of carefully prepared answers.

We left the bar and I helped her find a cab. I'd almost left the signed book behind on the table, but she'd smiled and pointed out that it wasn't suitable reading for the customers of such a place.

'What do you intend to do now,' she asked me before getting into the car, 'about the whole story?'

'No idea,' I said. 'Probably nothing. After Spoel confessed, his attorney tried to reopen the case but without success. He's going to be executed in a few weeks — end of the road. It looks like the case will stay cold.'

She seemed relieved. We shook hands and she got into the cab.

I checked my phone and noticed that I'd

received a text from Diana. She said that she'd be arriving the next evening and gave me the number of her flight. I answered that I'd pick her up from the airport, headed for the garage where I'd left my car and drove home.

★ ★ ★

The next morning I came across the phone number almost by chance.

I'd made a copy of the list of calls made and received on Derek Simmons's phone before and after his wife's murder, and I decided to have a look at it. There were twenty-eight in all, listed in five columns: the number, the address, the number of the subscriber, and the date and length of the call.

One of the addresses looked familiar and caught my attention, but the name didn't ring a bell — Jesse E. Banks. The call had lasted for fifteen minutes and forty-one seconds. Then I remembered what the address was, so I checked a few other things. It was obvious that back then, in 1983, this name and number hadn't been relevant to the investigators, but to me they were very important. But in December 1987, when I'd begun investigating Wieder's death, it hadn't even entered my head to connect one case to another, when one had happened four years earlier.

Then it hit me. I remembered the expression used by Derek Simmons the other day when he'd stopped our conversation, which had intrigued me at the time, and I checked some details on Wikipedia.

I spent the next two hours tying together all the details of the two cases, the Simmons case and the Wieder case, and everything began to fit. I called an assistant with the Mercer County Prosecutor's Office and we met for a long talk, with all my papers on the table. He phoned Chief Brocato, fixed all the details, and then I went home.

I had a Beretta Tomcat .32, which I kept in the closet downstairs. I took it out of the box, checked the safety and trigger, and inserted the clip which held seven rounds. I'd been given it as a leaving present by the department when I retired and I'd never used it. I wiped the oil off with a rag and put the gun in my jacket pocket.

★ ★ ★

I parked near the police station and waited behind the wheel for ten minutes, telling myself that I still had time to change my mind, to turn back, to forget about the whole thing. Diana would be arriving in a couple of hours, and I'd already made a reservation at a Korean restaurant in Palisades Park.

But I couldn't let it lie. I got out of the car and set off towards the house at the bottom of the road. An old Percy Sledge song was going round and round in my head: 'The Dark End of the Street'. The gun in my pocket kept banging against my hip at every step, giving me the feeling that something bad was going to happen.

I climbed the wooden steps and rang the bell.

Derek Simmons opened the door a few moments later and didn't look at all surprised to see me.

'Well, you again . . . Come on in.'

He turned on his heel and vanished down the hall, leaving the door open.

I followed him, and when I went into the living room I noticed two large suitcases and a duffel bag next to the couch.

'Going somewhere, Derek?'

'Louisiana. Leonora's mom died yesterday and she has to stay there for the funeral and to sell the house. Said she didn't want to be there alone, so I thought a change wouldn't do me any harm. Coffee?'

'Thanks.'

He went into the kitchen, fixed the coffee and returned with two large mugs, one of which he set in front of me. Then he lit another cigarette and studied me with the blank expression of a poker player trying to guess the other guys' cards.

'What do you want from me this time?' he asked. 'Got a warrant in your pocket or just glad to see me?'

'Told you I retired years ago, Derek.'

'You never know, man.'

'When did you get your memory back, Derek? In '87? Sooner? Or did you never lose it and just faked the whole thing?'

'Why do you ask?'

' 'Now it's time to play ball. Thank you for your cooperation.' You said you were in the stadium when the announcer said that, after that eight-minute standing ovation in memory of

Thurman Lee Munson, who'd died in a plane accident in Ohio. But that was in '79, Derek. How did you know that in '79 you'd been in the Bronx, in the stadium, and that you'd heard it with your own ears?'

'Told you that after the accident I'd tried to learn everything about myself and — '

'Bullshit, Derek. You can't learn something like that, you can only remember it. Did you keep a diary in '79? Did you write it down? Don't think so. And another thing: why did you call Joseph Wieder on the morning you'd allegedly found your wife's body? When did you first meet him, in fact? When and how did you arrange with him to get an expert's opinion in your favour?'

For a while he just sat there smoking and watching me carefully, without saying anything. He was calm, but the wrinkles on his face looked slightly deeper than I remembered. Then he asked, 'Are you wearing a wire, man?'

'No.'

'Mind if I check?'

'Let me show you I'm clean.'

I stood up, turned back the lapels of my jacket, then slowly unbuttoned my shirt and turned around.

'See, Derek? No wires.'

'Okay.'

I sat back down on the couch and waited for him to start talking. I was sure that he'd been waiting a long time to tell somebody the whole story. And I was also sure that once he left town he was never coming back. I'd come across plenty of guys like him. There comes a moment when you know that the man in front of you is ready to tell the truth, and in that moment it's as if you hear a click, like when you dial the right combination to open a safe. But you can't rush things. You've got to let them take their own course.

'You're one hell of a cop . . . ' He paused. 'How did you find out I talked to Wieder on the phone that morning?'

'I looked at the calls listing. Wieder had only just bought the house, and the phone number hadn't been transferred to his name yet. The former owner, a guy by the name of Jesse E. Banks, had passed away, and the house had been sold through an estate agency. The police who checked the calls reached a dead end, so they dropped the lead. Even if they'd found Wieder's name, it didn't have any relevance to the case at the time. All the same, you were reckless. Why did you phone Wieder from your home number, Derek? Weren't there any phone booths nearby?'

'I didn't want to leave the house,' he said, stubbing out his cigarette, which he'd smoked down to the filter. 'I was afraid of being seen. And I had to talk to the guy quick. I didn't know whether they'd arrest me on the spot when the patrol got there.'

'You killed her, didn't you? Your wife, I mean.'

He shook his head.

'No, I didn't, even though she'd have deserved it. It was exactly like I said — I found her there in a pool of blood. But I knew she'd been cheating on me . . . '

Over the next half-hour he told me the following story:

After he'd been admitted to a mental hospital during his last year of high school, his life had fallen apart. Everybody had thought he was crazy, and his schoolmates had avoided him after he'd got out. He'd given up on the idea of going to college and had got a menial job. His father had upped sticks and left. Since his mother had died when he was very young, he was completely alone and for about ten years he'd lived like a robot, taking medical treatment. They'd told him he'd have to stay on medication for the rest of his life, but there were nasty side effects. In the end, he'd stopped taking the pills.

Then he'd met Anne, nine years after he finished high school, and everything had changed, at least in the beginning. He'd fallen in love with her, and she'd seemed to be in love with him. Anne, he said, had grown up in an orphanage in Rhode Island and had left at the age of eighteen. She'd slept rough on the streets, got mixed up with some gangs, and by the age of nineteen she'd become a hooker in Atlantic City. She'd hit rock bottom shortly before she met Derek, in the parking lot of a motel in Princeton, where he'd been repairing the heating system.

Anne had moved in with him and they'd become lovers. About two weeks later, two armed tough guys had turned up at the door and told him the girl owed them money. Derek hadn't said anything. He'd gone to the bank, withdrawn five thousand bucks, everything he'd saved, and given them the money. The guys had taken it and said they'd leave her alone after that. About two months later, before Christmas, Derek had proposed to Anne and she'd accepted.

For a while, Derek said, things had seemed to be going well, but two years later everything had started to go to hell. Anne had got drunk and cheated on him whenever she'd got the chance. She hadn't had relationships, rather it'd just been a string of casual sexual encounters with strangers, and she hadn't seemed to care whether Derek found out or not. She'd kept up appearances in public, but when they'd been alone together she'd changed her tune — she'd insulted him and humiliated him, calling him a crazy and a failure, and chiding him for their cheap existence and for his not being able to earn more money. She'd accused him of not giving her a more interesting life, and had constantly threatened to leave him.

'She was a real bitch, man. When I told her I wanted us to have kids, do you know what she said? That she didn't want some retards like me. That's what she told the guy who'd picked her up in a parking lot and married her. Why did I put up with it all? Because I had no choice — I was crazy about her. She could have done anything, but I still wouldn't have left her. In fact, I was always worried she might leave me for some moron. When I walked down the street, I got the feeling that everybody was laughing at me. When I met guys around town, I'd always wonder whether they'd screwed her. But I still couldn't kick her out.'

But after a while her behaviour had changed, and he'd realised that something had happened to her. Anne was dressing better, putting on make-up. She'd stopped drinking and had seemed happier than ever. She'd started to ignore Derek completely. She would come home late and go out early in the morning, so they barely saw each other and didn't even talk. She couldn't even be bothered to argue with him.

It hadn't been long before he'd found out what was going on.

'I'll cut the shit,' he said. 'I followed her and saw her going into a hotel room with an older guy. Believe it or not, I didn't say anything to her about it. I just prayed he'd dump her and that it'd be all over. I remembered how horrible it'd been when I was alone, before I met her.'

'Who was the guy?'

'Joseph Wieder. He was rich, powerful and famous. And he didn't have anything better to do than to get mixed up with my wife, a woman about thirty years younger than him. I never found out for sure how the hell they'd got together. A lot of professors and students from university used to hang around that coffee shop where she was working, so probably that's how they'd met each other. I was a bit crazy, that's true, but not a idiot — I knew that Wieder would do everything he could to avoid getting involved in a scandal.'

So on that morning when his wife had been killed, Derek had called the professor whose home number he'd found previously rummaging through Anne's stuff. He'd told him about the murder and that the police would probably try to make him the scapegoat, given the circumstances. He'd said he'd drag Wieder into the mess, because he knew they'd been lovers. He'd also said that he'd been admitted to a mental hospital long ago, so it'd be a piece of cake for Wieder to arrange for him to be found not guilty by reason of insanity and committed to a forensic psychiatric hospital.

Finally he'd got busted, accused of murdering his wife. Being declared legally insane, he'd been committed to the Trenton Psychiatric Hospital. Wieder had visited him many times, under the pretext that he had a particular professional interest in his case. He'd promised that within three months Simmons would be transferred to the Marlboro Hospital, in much better conditions. But before that could happen, Simmons had been attacked in Trenton by one of the other patients.

'When I came out of the coma, I didn't recognise anybody and I didn't even know how I'd ended up in hospital. I couldn't even remember my own name. They did all kinds of tests on me and they concluded that I wasn't faking my amnesia. I really couldn't remember anything. To me, Wieder became a friendly, caring doctor, touched by the terrible situation I was in. He told me that he was going to treat me free of charge and have me moved to Marlboro. I was overwhelmed by his kindness.

'I stayed at Marlboro for a few months,

without recovering my memory. Sure, I began to find out things, who I was, who my parents were, what high school I went to, stuff like that. None of it was good — mom's death, the mental hospital, a wretched job, a cheating wife, and an accusation of murder. I gave up on finding out. The guy I'd been was a loser. I decided to start over when I got out.

'It was Wieder who was in charge of the panel that agreed to my release. I didn't even have anywhere to go, so he found me a place to stay, not far from his house, and he gave me a job as a handyman at his house. The house looked good, but it was old, and things always needed repairing. I don't know whether you know this, but with retrograde amnesia you only forget about stuff connected with your identity, but not the rest, the skills you have. You don't forget how to ride a bike, but you can't remember when you learned, if you know what I mean. So, I knew how to repair things, but I didn't have a clue when the hell I'd learned how.'

To him, Derek went on, Joseph Wieder was a saint. He'd made sure he took his treatment, he'd paid him a tidy wage every month for the repairs he did, he'd taken him fishing, and they'd spent the evening together at least once a week. Once, he'd taken him to the university and hypnotised him, but he hadn't told him the result of the session.

One evening in the middle of March 1987, Derek had been at home, flicking through the channels, looking for a movie to watch. After a while he'd come across a news item on NY1, about a guy from Bergen County who'd killed himself. Hey, that's Stan Marini, he'd said to himself when he saw the guy's photo on the screen. He'd been about to change the channel when he'd realised that Stan had been one of the maintenance crew guys when Derek had worked for Siemens. Stan had got married around the same time as him and had moved to New York.

He'd also understood what it meant. He was remembering something that nobody else had told him about and which he hadn't read about.

'It was just like down there in Texas when they strike oil and it springs shooting up out of the ground. A lid had been lifted off of all that stuff buried in my mind, and now *bang!* it was all coming to the surface. I can't even describe the feeling, man. It was like watching a movie at a hundred times the normal speed.'

He'd wanted to call the man he regarded as his benefactor straight away, but then he'd decided it was too late in the evening to bother him. He'd been afraid he'd forget everything again, so he'd found a notebook and started to write everything that came into his mind.

He stood up and asked me whether I wanted to go out into the backyard. I preferred to stay where I was, because I didn't know whether he had a gun hidden somewhere, but I didn't want to upset him so I followed. He was almost as tall as me and much stronger. In the event of a struggle, I wouldn't stand any chance unless I used the gun in my pocket. I wondered if he'd noticed it.

I followed him out into an untidy backyard, with tufts of grass sprouting on the patches of bare earth and fragments of paving stones with a rusty swing in the middle. He took a deep breath of the warm afternoon air, lit another cigarette and then continued his story, without looking into my eyes.

'I remembered everything as if it were yesterday: how I met Anne, how it'd been good at first, but that then she'd started cheating on me, about how I'd found out she was having an affair with that damn college professor, about the way she made a fool of me, and then what had happened that morning, the talk with Wieder, my arrest, my hard time in the hospital.

'I studied the labels of the pills Wieder had prescribed me, then I went to a chemist's and asked the guy there whether they were for amnesia. He told me they were for flu and indigestion. The guy I'd thought of as my pal and benefactor for years was in fact just a guardian frightened that one day I'd remember what had really happened. He'd kept me close by so that he could keep an eye on me, na'mean? Man, I felt like my head was exploding . . .

'For a few days I didn't even leave the house, and when Wieder came over, I told him I had a headache and just wanted to sleep. I almost felt sorry that I'd gotten over the fucking amnesia.'

'Did Wieder sense anything?'

'Don't think so. He had his mind on his own business. I was just a piece of old furniture to him. In fact, I think I'd become invisible to him, I guess. He wasn't scared any more that I might say or do something. He wanted to go to Europe.'

'And then you killed him.'

298

'I'd always thought of doing it, after I got my memory back, but I didn't want to go to jail or the nuthouse. That day I'd forgotten my toolbox at his house. I'd fixed the downstairs toilet earlier and we'd eaten lunch together. I had a job early the next morning, near where I lived, and I decided to go to Wieder's to get the toolbox. Before I rang the bell, I went round the house to the backyard and saw that the lights in the living room were on. He was sitting at the table with that student, Flynn.'

'Did you see that guy I told you about, Frank Spoel?'

'No, but from what you told me, I was probably just one step from bumping into him. I came back around the front of the house, unlocked the door and saw the toolbox by the coat rack; Wieder had probably found it in the bathroom and then left it there for me. I took it and left. He didn't even realise I'd been there. They were both talking in the living room.

'On the way home I said to myself, If anything happens, that guy will be the prime suspect. He's head over heels in love with that girl the old man is after, so that would be the motive.

'I went to the bar at around eleven, just so I could be seen there, as an alibi. I chatted to the owner, who knew me. He was getting ready to close. I knew that he never wore a watch and he didn't have a clock on the wall. Before I left, I said, 'Hey, Sid, it's midnight. I'd better get going.' When he testified, he said it was midnight, never remembering it was me who told him, na'mean?

'I still didn't know what I was going to do. It

was like in a dream — I don't know how to describe it. I wasn't sure the student had left; the weather was still bad, and I thought that maybe Wieder would invite him to stay overnight. I had a leather sap, which I'd found a few months earlier in the glove box of a car I'd been repairing. Don't know whether you've ever handled one, but it's a damn good weapon.'

'I had one back in the 1970s.'

'Well, I went there, quietly unlocked the front door and went in. The lights were still on in the room, and when I walked in I saw him lying on the floor, blood everywhere. He looked real bad: his face was smashed, all swollen and bruised. The windows were wide open. I closed them and turned all the lights out. I'd brought a flashlight with me.'

He turned towards me.

'I was sure Flynn had done it. I thought they must have had an argument after I left, and got into a fight. When you beat up a guy that bad it means you're prepared to risk killing him, doesn't it? One heavy punch blow, and *pow!* The end!

'I didn't know what the hell to do. It was one thing to hit the guy who'd made a fool of me and pretended to be my friend after he'd fucked my wife and put me in the crazy house, only to get me out of there so that he could be my jailer, but it was another thing to hit a guy lying on the floor, more dead than alive.

'You know, I think I'd have split and left him there, or I'd have called an ambulance, who knows . . . But just then, as I was leaning over him, with the flashlight lit beside me, he opened

300

his eyes and looked up at me from the floor. And I saw his eyes, and I remembered how I'd followed him that evening when Anne went into the hotel room, how I climbed the stairs and put my ear to the door, like a moron. As if I didn't already know what was going on inside, I had to go and listen to him screwing her. I remembered that bitch, who used to laugh at me and call me impotent, after I'd rescued her from a life on the street.

'And that was that, man. I took out the blackjack and hit him once, hard.

'I locked the door, I tossed the blackjack into the lake and went home. Before I went to sleep, I thought of Wieder lying there, dead, covered in blood, and I have to tell you, I felt good. I didn't feel at all sorry about what I'd done, or rather about finishing what some other guy had started. I went back to the house in the morning, and the rest you know. I didn't find out that Flynn wasn't the guy who beat him up until you came here a few days ago. Anyway, until that reporter came here, I hadn't even thought about it too much. For me the whole thing was dead and buried. And that's everything, man.'

'Wieder died two hours later, at least that's what the medical examiner said. You could have saved him if you'd called an ambulance.'

'I know what they said, but I'm still sure he died on the spot. Anyway, it doesn't matter any more.'

'Before leaving the house, had you opened the drawers and scattered some papers on the floor, trying to suggest a robbery?'

'No, man, I just left.'

'You sure?'

'Yes, I'm damn sure.'

I wondered for a couple of moments if I should push forward.

'You know, Derek, I've been thinking . . . You never found out who killed your wife that night . . . '

'That's right, I never found out.'

'And that didn't bother you?'

'Maybe it did. So what?'

'The love of your life was lying on the floor in a pool of blood, and the first thing you did was to call her lover and ask him to save your ass. You called 911 eight minutes *after* your conversation with Wieder. Quite odd, don't you think? Just curious: the professor really believed you? Did you discuss with him, face to face, about the murder?'

He took his pack of cigarettes out of his pocket and saw that it was empty. 'I've got another one in the workshop somewhere,' he said, pointing to the glass porch.

'I hope you're not thinking of doing anything stupid,' I said and he looked at me in surprise.

'Oh, you mean . . . ' he said and started to laugh. 'Don't you think we're too old to be playing cowboys? There are no guns around here, don't worry. I've never held a gun in my life.'

As he went into the workshop, I put my right hand in my pocket and slowly released the safety with my thumb. Then I cocked it and kept it gripped in my hand. I'd been a cop for more than forty years, but I'd never had to shoot anybody.

Through the grimy glass, I saw him rummaging around on the workbench, which was scattered with all kinds of objects. Then he bent down and rummaged inside a box. He came back a few moments later holding a pack of Camels between the thumb and index finger of his right hand.

'See? You can take your hand out of your pocket. You've got a gun in there, haven't you?'

'Yes, I do.'

He lit a cigarette, put the pack in his pocket and gave me a questioning look.

'Now what? I hope you realise that I wouldn't repeat all this to a cop. I mean a real one.'

'I know you wouldn't.'

'But you think I killed Anne, don't you?'

'Yes, I think you killed her. At the time, the detectives searched her past, looking for potential leads. I read the report. She wasn't a hooker, Derek. Before meeting you she worked as a barmaid in Atlantic City for about two years, in a place called Ruby's Cafe. She was described by everybody as a nice young lady, decent and intelligent. Probably everything was in your mind — I mean the bad guys asking you for money, her troubled past, screwing around with lots of men and laughing at you behind your back. It wasn't real, man, you made that all up. I'm not even sure that she was involved in a love affair with the professor. Maybe she'd just asked him for help. When you recovered your memory, you also got your nightmares back, didn't you?'

He looked me straight in the eye, running the tip of his tongue slowly over his lower lip.

'I think you'd better get going, man. It's not

303

my damn business what you believe or not. I have to finish packing.'

'It's time to play ball, Derek, right?'

He pointed the index finger of his left hand at me, curling his thumb to make the shape of a pistol.

'You were real smart with that, I mean it.'

He showed me to the front door.

'Derek, when did Leonora go to Louisiana?'

'About two weeks ago. Why do you ask?'

'No reason. Take care.'

I felt his eyes on my back all the way to the corner, where I turned, getting out of his sight. Derek didn't seem to know that things were done without wires nowadays. All it takes is a special pencil in the breast pocket of your jacket.

A couple of minutes later, as I was pulling out of Witherspoon Street in my car, I could hear the police sirens. Somewhere in a document about Simmons, I remembered, it was claimed that his dad had moved to another state years ago and disappeared. I wondered whether anybody had checked that story out at the time. He'd told me that Wieder had hypnotised him at one point. Had the professor found out what his patient was truly capable of? How the hell could he have given the keys of his house to a creep like that? Or was he certain that his amnesia was irreversible and that Simmons would permanently remain a bomb without a detonator? But the detonator was there all the time.

On the way to the airport, I remembered the title of Flynn's book and the maze of distorting mirrors you used to find at carnivals when I was a kid — everything you saw when you went inside was both true and false at the same time.

It was getting dark when I merged onto the turnpike. I started to think about seeing Diana again and what would come of it in the end. I was as nervous as if I were going on my first date. I remembered the gun — I took it out of my pocket, engaged the safety and hid it in the glove box. In the end, I'd finished my life as a cop without having to use a gun on anyone, and I said to myself that it was a good thing it'd turned out like that.

I knew that I'd forget all about that case, just like I'd forget the other stories that made up my life, stories probably neither better nor worse than anybody else's. I thought that if I had to choose just one of my memories, a story that I'd remember to the very end, a memory that Mr A would never be able to take away from me, then I'd like to remember this calm, quiet, hopeful ride on my way to the airport, when I knew I was going to see Diana again, and maybe she'd decide to stay.

I saw her coming through the exit and noticed she was only carrying one small bag, the kind of hand luggage you take on a very short trip. I waved at her and she waved back. A couple of seconds later we met by a bookstand and I kissed her on the cheek. The colour of her hair was different, she wore a new perfume and a coat I'd never seen before, but the way she smiled at me was the same as ever.

'Is that all you've brought?' I asked her, taking her bag.

'I've hired a van to bring my other things out next week. I'm going to stay for a while, so you'd better tell that young lady of yours to hit the road, and fast.'

'Are you talking about Minnie Mouse? She left me, Dee. I think she's still in love with that guy Mickey.'

We walked to the parking lot holding hands, got into the car and left the airport. She told me about our son and his wife and our granddaughter. And listening to her voice as I drove, I felt all my memories of the crime story that had been obsessing me for the past few months peeling away one after another, fluttering out of sight down the highway, like the pages of an old manuscript carried away by the wind.

Epilogue

Derek's story caused enough of a splash for the ripples to reach all the way to a small town in Alabama. Danna Olsen called me a few days later, while I was on my way to Los Angeles to meet a TV producer. I also had a meeting with John Keller, who'd recently moved to the West Coast and rented a house in Orange County, California.

'Hello, Peter,' she said, 'I'm Danna Olsen. Remember me?'

I told her I did and we exchanged a few words before she got to the point.

'I lied to you back then, Peter. I knew where the rest of the manuscript was, I'd read it before Richard's death, but I didn't want to give it to you or anybody else. I was angry. Reading it, I realised how much Richard had loved that woman, Laura Baines. Even if he seemed angry at her, there was no doubt in my mind that he died loving her. It wasn't honest for him to do that. I felt like an old horse that he kept around just because he didn't know what else to do. I'd taken care of him and put up with all his eccentricities, and believe me, there were a lot of them. He'd used up the last months of his life writing that book, while I was right there beside him. I felt betrayed.'

I was somewhere on Rosewood Avenue, in West Hollywood, in front of the restaurant where

I was supposed to meet the guy.

'Ms Olsen,' I said, 'given the recent circumstances, I mean the arrest of Simmons, I don't think that — '

'I'm not calling you with a business proposition,' she said, making things clear from the outset. 'I expected that the manuscript would no longer be of much interest to you as an agent. But all the same, Richard's last wish was that his manuscript be published. Apart from the story with Baines, you know how much he wanted to be a writer and I think he'd have been overjoyed if you'd accepted his project. Unfortunately he didn't live to see it. But I now realise that it'd be a good thing to send it to you all the same.'

I didn't know what to say. It was clear that I wasn't going to be dealing with a true crime story, as the premise, Flynn's entire theory, had just been blow apart by the latest events, which proved that the author's imagination had embellished on real events. John Keller had had a long phone conversation with Roy Freeman, the retired detective who'd become a media star — 'EX-DETECTIVE SOLVES TWENTY-EIGHT-YEAR-OLD MURDER MYSTERY' — and had temporarily moved to his ex-wife's house in Seattle to get away from reporters. John had sent me an email in which he explained briefly that there was no mystery left to the story at all.

But I couldn't say this to her, because she knew it all too well.

'It would be great if I could take a look at it,' I said, waving at the producer, who was walking toward the restaurant, his face almost entirely hidden by a pair of immense green sunglasses that made him look like a giant cricket. 'You still have my email address, don't you? I'll be back home tomorrow, and I'll find the time to read it.'

The producer spotted me, but he didn't bother to lengthen his stride or wave back. He looked calm, indifferent, an attitude meant to underline his importance.

Ms Olsen assured me that she had my email address and that she'd send me the manuscript straight away.

'The last few weeks were hard on him, Peter, and I think that it shows in the final chapters of the manuscript. There are things in there which . . . But anyway, you'll see what it's all about.'

★   ★   ★

That evening I met John Keller, who picked me up outside my hotel. He was tanned and had a two-week beard, which suited him.

We had dinner together at a Japanese restaurant called Sugarfish on West 7th Street, which John told me was the latest trendy spot and where he'd booked us a table. The waiters kept coming every five minutes, bringing us different dishes, none of whose contents I was able to identify.

'How about that!' he exclaimed when I told him about my conversation with Danna Olsen. 'Think about it! If she'd given you the manuscript at the time, you wouldn't have got me hooked on the story, I wouldn't have looked up Freeman, and he wouldn't have dug up those old files. And we probably would never have found out the truth about the murder.'

'On the other hand, I'd have a book to sell,' I said.

'A book that wouldn't have been true.'

'Who'd have cared about that? Do you know something? Richard Flynn was unlucky right up to the end. Even after his death, he missed out on his chance to publish a book.'

'That's one way of looking at it,' he said, raising his small cup of sake. 'To Richard Flynn, the unlucky guy.'

We toasted to the memory of Flynn, and then he enthusiastically told me about his new life and how happy he was to be working in television. The pilot of the series he'd been roped into co-writing had a good rating, so he was looking forward to breezing through at least another season. I felt happy for him.

★   ★   ★

I haven't read the manuscript yet. I found it in my inbox after I got back to New York. I printed out all 248 pages, in 12-point Times New Roman, double-spaced, and put them in a file on top of my desk. I've been keeping it there, like those monks in the Middle Ages used to keep human skulls as a reminder that life is short and transient, and after death the judgement comes.

Most likely Richard Flynn had been wrong to the very end. Laura Baines had probably stolen the professor's manuscript and left him to die on the floor, but she hadn't been his mistress.

310

Derek Simmons had been mistaken when he'd thought that Richard Flynn had fled through the glass door after beating Wieder. Joseph Wieder had been wrong about Laura Baines and Richard Flynn having a relationship. They'd all been wrong and had seen nothing but their own obsessions through the windows they'd tried to gaze through, which in fact turned out to have been mirrors all along.

A great French writer once said that re-membrance of things past is not necessarily the remembrance of things as they were. I guess he was right.

Acknowledgements

I'd like to express my gratitude to everybody who helped me with this book.

My literary agent, Marilia Savvides of Peters, Fraser + Dunlop, not only fished my story out of the slush pile in no time, but also helped me to polish the manuscript once again, doing a great job. Thanks for everything, Marilia.

Francesca Pathak of Century and Megan Reid of Emily Bestler Books edited the text, a process that couldn't have gone more smoothly or more pleasantly. Working with them was a privilege. I'm also very grateful to the wonderful teams at Penguin Random House UK and Simon & Schuster US. Francesca and Megan, I also thank you for all your wise suggestions — they enriched the manuscript and made it shine.

Rachel Mills, Alexandra Cliff and Rebecca Wearmouth sold the book all over the world within the space of just a couple of weeks — and what an unforgettable feast that period was for all of us! Thanks, ladies.

My good friend Alistair Ian Blyth helped me set sail on the stormy waters of the English language without drowning myself, and it was no easy task. Thanks, man.

I've kept the most important person till last: my wife, Mihaela, to whom this book is dedicated, in fact. If it hadn't been for her trust in me, I'd probably have abandoned literature a long time ago. She's always reminded me who I am and to which realm I truly belong.

And my final thanks go to you, the reader, who picked this book from among so many others. Nowadays, as Cicero said, children no longer obey their parents and everyone is writing a book.

Other titles published by Ulverscroft:

THE DROWNING CHILD

Alex Barclay

When Special Agent Ren Bryce is called to Tate, Oregon to investigate the disappearance of twelve-year-old Caleb Veir, she finds a town already in mourning. Two other young boys have died recently, but in very different circumstances. As Ren digs deeper, she discovers that all is not as it seems in the Veir household — and that while Tate may be a small town, it guards some very big secrets. Can Ren uncover the truth before more children are harmed?

NIGHT SCHOOL

Lee Child

It's just a voice plucked from the air: 'The American wants a hundred million dollars.' For what? Who from? It's 1996, and the Soviets are long gone. But now there's a new enemy. In an apartment in Hamburg, a group of smartly dressed young Saudis is planning something big . . . Jack Reacher is fresh off a secret mission and a big win. The army pats him on the back and gives him a medal. And then they send him back to school. It's a school with only three students: Reacher, an FBI agent, and a CIA analyst. Their assignment: to find that American. And what he's selling. And to whom. There is mortal danger ahead, amid signs of a world gone mad . . .

THE RIVER AT NIGHT

Erica Ferencik

Win Allen doesn't want an adventure. After a miserable divorce and the death of her beloved brother, she just wants to spend some time with her three best friends, far away from her soul-crushing job. But athletic, energetic Pia has other plans. Plans for an adrenaline-raising, breath-taking, white-water rafting trip in the Maine wilderness. Five thousand square miles of remote countryside. Just mountains, rivers and fresh air. No phone signal. No people. No help . . .

TATTLETALE

Sarah J. Naughton

One day changes Jody's life forever. She has shut herself down, haunted by her memories and unable to trust anyone. And then she meets Abe, the perfect stranger next door, and suddenly life seems full of possibilities and hope . . . One day changes Mags's life forever, too. After years of estrangement from her family, she receives a shocking phone call. Her brother Abe is in hospital, and no one knows what happened to him. She meets his fiancee Jody, and gradually pieces together the ruins of the life she left behind. But the pieces don't quite seem to fit . . .